High Risks

High Risks

Adrian "Ox" Mendez

www.urbanbooks.net

Urban Books, LLC
300 Farmingdale Road, N.Y.-Route 109
Farmingdale, NY 11735

To the extent that the image or images on the cover of this book depict a person or persons, such person or persons are merely models, and are not intended to portray any character or characters featured in the book.

ISBN 13: 978-1-64556-583-3

First Trade Paperback Printing June 2024
Printed in the United States of America

10 9 8 7 6 5 4 3 2 1

This is a work of fiction. Any references or similarities to actual events, real people, living or dead, or to real locales are intended to give the novel a sense of reality. Any similarity in other names, characters, places, and incidents is entirely coincidental.

Distributed by Kensington Publishing Corp.
Submit Orders to:
Customer Service
400 Hahn Road
Westminster, MD 21157-4627
Phone: 1-800-733-3000
Fax: 1-800-659-2436

High Risks

by

Adrian "Ox" Mendez

Chapter 1

"It's a fuckin' shame that it had to come to this, bruh, and I kind of liked you too. Thought you had certain swag to you that every nigga should have. Now, look at us, sitting here going through this over a couple of dollars that can be made back before it was even missed. Damn, my nigga, I thought you were smarter than this." Standing in the middle of the room with a few of his work associates, Blacka spoke, looking across at Troy, who sat strapped to a table, barely coherent about what was being said to him at this point.

It had been over two hours of nonstop torture since Blacka and his men entered the Brooklyn residence without invitation. Blacka never usually visited the homes of anyone who worked for him. He expected that his employees would come to him if anything important was to be discussed. For some reason, Troy either didn't grasp that concept, or he was attempting to pull a fast one on Blacka by not paying him the few dollars he owed for the product he so happily accepted and reaped the rewards of. Now, with two of his top henchmen, his brother-in-law, and one of his truck drivers, Blacka had to come and make a statement in front of his other close workers to let them know he would not tolerate this sort of insubordination.

"Damn, Blacka, I don't see how this nigga is still even alive through all this shit. There ain't really anything left to do to his ass. At this point, I don't even think he can feel anything else with all the pain that he has been through," said Malachi. He talked with his hand covering his mouth so that he wouldn't vomit at the sight of Troy laid across a table. He was badly battered and faintly gasped for air. The moans from his mouth were totally inaudible due to the temporary loss of movement in his mouth. All of his teeth had been viciously extracted with a pair of pliers, one by one, at the hands of one of the two silent Jamaican barbarians who seemed to enjoy every moment of slowly mutilating this man in all forms of sadistic ways.

"Yo, my nigga, all I can tell you is that I got some real fuckin' professionals on my team, and I expect everyone to act accordingly at all times. See, this is why I fucks with my niggas right here 'cause when they do some shit to a mothafucka, they do that shit to perfection. You would swear these niggas were doctors or some shit," he said, pleased with the means of retribution that Reef and his partner concocted. Blacka spoke happily as he gripped Reef's hand in the form of a handshake.

Picking up the empty syringe that lay on the table amongst the rest of the materials that the Jamaican duo had laid across a small table that was next to the victim, Blacka asked, "Yo, I ain't gonna ask where you got this shit from, but what is this shit y'all gave him, and how did y'all even know about some shit like this?"

"When you love wha' you dom, mi friend, you have fi learn how fi do it so that everyone else can love it too. Since we know that you did wan' fi talk to the bwoy an' find out 'bout your money, we just inject him with a 'ting called Tetrodotoxin. This way, he can hear wha' you ah say, but him can't feel wha' we ah do to him. Only 'ting him heart might bust 'cause him still can see wha' we ah do to him, so him ah go panic himself to death." With a chuckle, Reef explained the poisonous toxin that his partner, Dummy, administered to their victim that blocked their victim's nerves, causing muscle paralysis and leaving him completely paralyzed.

"Yo, I'm surprised that he even made it this long. Look at that shit, man. That nigga better thank God that he can't feel that shit . . . fuck." Squirming at the sight of what Dummy was doing to Troy at the present moment, Dwight fought back the urge to vomit once again. The mute man was taking a scalpel and making two long surgical incisions in the form of a cross on Troy's abdominal area.

"Naw, man, this ah nothin' fi we friend right here. It ah go take a lot more than this fi make my bwoy crack. Him is still with us. Him just ah close him eyes fi ah little while. Hold on an' me can fix it so that him can keep him eyes open." The strong Jamaican accent came from the deadly yet calm man with a head full of dreadlocks that hung way past his shoulders as he motioned toward Troy as he lay on the table. Pulling a wooden handle ratchet knife with three silver stars along the side, Reef grabbed hold of Troy's closed eyelid using his eyelashes as a grip and used the sharp blade of his knife to slice it off his face.

The terror that ran through Troy's mind was easily translated through the rapid motions of the pupils of his eyes as he helplessly watched as his once business associates slowly mutilated him, limb by limb.

Using the palm of his hand to slap the side of Troy's face lightly, the diabolical man turned to Dwight and said, "I told you that him did have some life left inna him. Dummy gwan finish teach the bwoy him lesson."

Heeding what his partner said, the silent of the two men walked over to the table to retrieve the portable oxygen concentrator that he needed to make sure that Troy didn't make a premature exit before he was done with literally showing him what he was made of. Placing the mask over his victim's face and activating the machine, Troy was given a fraction of relief from the oxygen as he lay struggling to breathe due to muscle paralysis in his lungs.

"Why help him breathe if y'all plan on killin' him anyway? That shit don't make no sense to me, just making us have to stay here longer than we have to be because these niggas are on some Hannibal Lector shit. Let's wrap this shit up before these crazy niggas start cooking this mothafucka or some wild shit like that." Malachi protested the prolonged torture, not knowing how much longer his stomach could withstand what his eyes were witnessing. Walking toward the window to get a breath of fresh air to calm his stomach, he shook his head, thinking that maybe Blacka was going too far.

Ignoring Malachi's complaints of him taking too long, Dummy grabbed the pair of thick canvas working gloves on the edge of the table and pulled them on his oversized hands. Looking into his victim's face with cold, brown eyes, Dummy grinned at the thought of what he had planned for Troy. Using the fingertips of the coarse gloves, Dummy pulled back on the four corners at the intersection of the cut that he had previously made across Troy's stomach, opening him up and exposing the insides of his entire lower abdomen.

"Before we go any further, I just wanna know one thing, bruh," Blacka said as he stepped forward, grabbed Troy by the chin, and lifted his head up toward his. "What made you think that it would be okay to take my shit and just walk away with it like I'm just a pushover or something? What burns me the most is that I treat y'all niggas better than I treat my own family, and this is what I got to go through over a couple of funky-ass dollars."

"Bruh, you know that the safe in the room is open, and it got a good twenty grand in there that this nigga ain't gonna need no mo . . ." Approaching the table, Malachi's words came to an abrupt halt when he focused on what Dummy was doing to Troy. Without warning, he felt the muscles of his own stomach violently contract as his head lunged forward while vomit immediately projected out of his mouth onto the floor.

"There you go, talking about that safe again. I done told you that it ain't even about the money no more. It's all about the principle of the situation. Obviously, you ain't got the stomach for shit like this, so maybe you need to go and start filling out job applications online or some shit 'cause I ain't got time or tolerance for weak niggas around me. That's the reason why this shit right here had to go to the next level, to make sure that we eliminate all weak links before shit really get out of hand." Disgusted with his brother-in-law's display of weakness, Blacka chastised as he extinguished the half-smoked Newport cigarette that he held on the pupil of Troy's exposed eyeball.

Standing to the immediate left of Blacka, Dummy stood impatiently waiting to continue with what he was doing. Curious to see what was next, Blacka stepped to the side to allow his silent assassin to continue what he was about to do to his insubordinate associate. Like an artist painting a portrait, Dummy stepped back, briefly examined his human canvas, stretched his hand out to Reef, and motioned for him to pass him something.

"Hey, bwoy, how come you nuh have your own tools fi de job? Why you always wan' fi dirty up my things? Yo, make sure next time you bring your own tings or learn fi use your fingernail an' cut open tings," Reef complained. Although questioning and arguing in protest, he retracted the blade from the wooden handle again and handed it over to his partner.

Kneeling in front of Troy with the knife in his hand, Dummy paused momentarily as though he just remembered something needed to carry on with his procedure. Even though the thrill of the kill mostly came from listening to the last words that escaped from his victims' mouths as he did whatever cruel acts he chose to perform, he was more than sure that for what he was about to do, the sounds might be unbearable even for him.

An exhausted look of panic and terror overwhelmed Troy as his one good eye squinted, following every movement of Dummy's hand. The oxygen mask that was still strapped to his face began to fog as Troy's breathing started to escalate in panic as he lay helpless, watching as Dummy stood over him like a mad scientist with a brand-new guinea pig.

"Ah wha' you ah wait pon, my yout'? You must really feel like we nuh have nothing better fi do than stand up here and watch you take play with the bwoy like a fat cat with one little mouse. Hurry up and done the bwoy so me can go get sumthin' fi eat 'cause me hungry to bloodclaat." As anxious as everyone else in the room, Reef tried to provoke Dummy into hurrying up and getting to the grand finale so that he could go and satisfy the hunger that was building up in his stomach.

Paying no attention to the remarks made by his comrade in crime, Dummy took the point of the knife, poked it into Troy's chest, and began to carve a pattern. Like a child trying their best to color between the lines of his favorite coloring book, Dummy cocked his head to the side with one eye closed as he maneuvered the blade up and down Troy's chest, making an occasional loop and turn. The panic in Troy's eyes as they rolled back in his head was as though he actually felt the sting of the flesh on his chest separate under the sharp blade. It seemed like forever to even the onlookers in the room who watched as the man mutilated the battered man's flesh with what turned out to be some form of sacrificial graffiti. Standing up and stepping back to examine his work, Dummy reached down and dragged the coarse glove across the open wound to wipe away most of the blood that flowed from the fresh cuts.

Chapter 2

"Bwoy, mi never know you could even spell. Mi proud of you, mi friend." Joking, Reef took a pull off the blunt he had in his hand as he also examined the work of his partner. The word "Judas" was carved across Troy's chest in crooked, bloody letters made out of the various incisions that Dummy made.

"Mothafuckin' genius, that's what it is. I'm mad at myself for not thinking of that shit first. Bring this shit back to the biblical days of the Old Testament. An eye for an eye and all that good shit some of you niggas must have forgot about. Nigga, you just became a modern-day martyr for the cause of righteousness amongst hustlers. We might name a hustler's commandment after situations like this: Thou shalt not do stupid shit and expect to get away with it," Blacka said while talking to Troy and the rest of the men who were in the room at the same time.

With head cocked to the side and a smirk on his face, Dummy shook his head in a motion of saying that this was nowhere close to being over. Then he reached his hand into Troy's open abdomen, grabbed hold of a one-inch piece of fleshy, coiled-up organ, and began to pull while taking two steps backward slowly. Uncoiling what was Troy's small intestine to the entire length of twenty-three feet, Dummy grinned and turned to Reef.

"You is like a big fuckin' kid. Didn't me tell you that me hungry and you fi hurry up so me can go eat? Now, stop show off fi Blacka and finish wha' you ah do. You say you wan’ fi use the thing that you make me buy, so gwan and use it.” Holding a puff of marijuana smoke in his lungs, Reef spoke, fighting the urge to cough from the exotic weed that he smoked while enjoying Dummy’s performance.

Exposing a smile with a wink of his eye, Dummy waved his hand a few times to motion for his friend to keep his mouth shut and get ready to enjoy the special treatment he put together when he first heard of the visit they planned to see Troy. With medieval torture being a fascination of the Jamaican-born sociopath, he tended to exercise his fetishes on his victims. Today was Troy’s turn to try out the effects hydrofluoric acid had on human flesh.

Reaching down to the floor where his duffel bag was, Dummy emptied its contents on the floor, exposing a five-pound poly bottle of the highly corrosive acid. By how Dummy cautiously handled the blue polytetrafluoroethylene container, you could fathom precisely how dangerous the contents were. Excited to see the end results of what he had in store for Troy, he grabbed the bottle, held it up in front of Troy’s face, and silently taunted him with it.

“Do we even wanna know what is in that shit right there? That shit ain’t nuclear radiation or some wild shit like that, is it?” Holding his hand over his mouth with his eyes squinted from the sight of Troy laid out on the table with his organs hanging out of him, the voice of Dwight came from the window so that he wouldn’t throw up all over the floor like Malachi did.

“That, my friend, is hydrofluoric acid. Even though it is one of the weakest acids known to mankind, it is still good enough to make any problem just melt away in a matter of seconds." Taking another pull from the exotic weed wrapped in a chocolate Dutch Master, Reef explained the contents of the container to the curious bystander.

Placing the container on the table, Dummy began to exercise caution as he cracked the seal on top of the container. Covering his mouth and nose, the Jamaican man lifted the container over Troy's head and tipped it so that a single drop landed on his forehead. Immediately, the powerful solution began to slowly eat a hole about a quarter of an inch in diameter through the skin, exposing the bone of Troy's skull.

"This shit is the perfect way to change somebody's mind, literally. This shit just gets better and better. Pour that shit all over that nigga's face, and even his mama can't recognize his ass when this shit is all over with. I hope the rest of you niggas are paying attention to this shit right here. Just remember that this ain't no fuckin' circus, so I don't expect to be surrounded by a bunch of clowns. I need thorough niggas on this team, or you will be dealt with accordingly," Blacka warned, addressing the other men in the room.

"You know that we all are down for you, bruh. Ain't no way that you gonna even have to worry about no shit like that from the rest of us," Malachi said as he continually wiped the corners of his mouth for the remainder of the bile that he recently projected.

"That's the same thing that this nigga told me last week, and yet, we are here over a couple of fuckin' dollars." With a glare in his eye, Blacka stared at Malachi, immediately retorting his statement.

"Ah wha' you ah wait for, bwoy? You hear wha' the man say. Dump the thing pon the bwoy an' get him mind right," Reef said from behind a cloud of smoke.

As requested, Dummy reached down, pulled the oxygen mask from over Troy's face, and tossed it on the floor. Once again, tipping the blue bottle over Troy's head, Dummy slowly poured the corrosive liquid over Troy's face as though he were pouring a very thin pancake batter over a hot skillet. Being careful not to use all of the acid, Dummy placed the remainder of the container back on the floor and securely put the lid on top of it. Holding his hand over his nose to ensure that he did not inhale the toxic fumes from the acid, he stood over Troy and watched as the solution dissolved into his flesh and began to eat away at his entire face. A mist of blue smoke rose in the air as the sound similar to thinly sliced bacon being sizzled on a grill whispered in the room while Troy's chest began to heave up and down rapidly.

"Look like my bwoy heart about to bust out ah him chest. Guess him wasn't so tough after all. Me wonder which ah go happen first. If him have a heart attack or him face finish eat away. Anybody wanna make a bet on which happen first?" Reef asked, turning to Blacka as though he expected a response

"I ain't fuckin' wit' you and your crazy-ass bets, bruh. Y'all niggas know a little too much about this shit for me to put money up against y'all." Realizing that Reef was not being rhetorical, Blacka dismissed the idea with a chuckle of placing a wager on Troy's already doomed fate. Looking down at Troy's chest, he could see that it was rising up and down at a much-slower rate until it finally came to a stop.

"See wha' me say? Me tell you that him heart naw go make it through that boss. Looks like fi we work done here, and me can finally go and full me belly wit' sum food," Reef stated, realizing that their sacrificial lamb had finally died due to heart failure. He was ready to go and eat.

"Yes, please, let's get the fuck out of here before this nigga really starts to stink up the place. He already smell like he done shitted on himself, but I don't see how that's possible with all his fuckin' guts sittin' on the floor over there. Thanks for the show, guys, but next time, I will just let one of y'all tell me what happened instead of watching it for myself," Malachi said, glad to be through with this whole horrific ordeal.

"Y'all have got to be some of the most squeamish niggas I know. You ready to go now just 'cause you see a little blood and guts hanging out. I'ma start walking around with some pacifiers to stop you niggas from crying all the damn time." Although he was ready to go before the fumes from the acid made their way into his lungs, Blacka jokingly chastised Malachi for wanting to leave in such haste. He was pleased that he made his point for all his immediate employees to witness and know that he was about getting results and not inadequate excuses.

"So, y'all just gonna leave this nigga like this in here?" Dwight asked as everyone prepared to leave the house.

"What you want us to do . . . dig a hole in the desert and bury this mothafucka? We gonna let this nigga lie here and feed the rats for a few days and see what's left of him by the time someone does find his ass. Right now, we got to get you ready for your out-of-town trip next week to pick up that shit from our people out there in Arizona. This shit has to go without any problems, or we might find ourselves living this day all over again, and we damn sure don't want that." Putting his arm across Dwight's neck and lightly patting his shoulder, Blacka subliminally reminded his driver that his operation would not tolerate mistakes.

"I got you, boss. Ain't no reason to worry about nothin' with me at all. As long as they straight on their end, everything gonna go smooth as usual. You already know that I'm on point all the time," Dwight said as he cocked his head to the side and looked up at Blacka, who stood about half a foot taller than him.

"That's what I wanna hear, my nigga . . . That's what I wanna hear 'cause we can't afford to be losing money due to stupid shit, especially when I got to pay my niggas right here for their services. I'm sure that you don't wanna be the reason why these niggas can't get paid." Blacka spoke while pointing to Dummy and Reef as they gathered their tools and placed them inside the duffel bag.

"Yo, Blacka, you never did say how much money this mothafucka owed you in the first place. I know you said that shit don't matter, but I just gotta know. How much was it?" Malachi asked as he walked behind Blacka and prepared to exit.

Taking his arm from around Dwight's shoulder, Blacka turned around and said, "Like I said, it's all about principle. Not only was he dodging me for a few funky-ass dollars, but the nigga was walkin' around like I couldn't do shit about it. If I let one nigga take a penny and get away with it, soon, every nigga out there is gonna come around and leave me one penniless mothafucka. I can' have that shit. Matter of fact, go an' get that cash from out of the safe in the other room, and we'll call that his fee for having me go through all of this shit for seven hundred and fifty fuckin' dollars."

Malachi's mouth hung open as Blacka turned around and walked away. He couldn't believe that he just witnessed a man being gutted open, mutilated, and his face melted away by acid over $750. He understood that Blacka had a point to prove, but this was a little too extreme for these circumstances. Turning to go to the other room to retrieve the $20,000 in Troy's safe, he realized that working for Blacka, he had more to fear from him than he did from the police or other hustlers in the streets.

Walking past the Jamaicans as they checked to ensure they did not leave anything behind, Malachi concluded that he should walk a straight line and handle his responsibilities until a change of command was made.

Chapter 3

"I know what I said, but I'm waiting on one of my drivers to drop off a load before I can go anywhere, Kanisha. I don't know what you're getting so excited about. I said that I was gonna come and help him move it as soon as I'm done with this." Driving through the East New York area of Brooklyn in his darkly tinted 2012 Audi A8, Blacka spoke to his sister Kanisha through his Bluetooth. He reassured her that he would be at her house to help her husband move their mother's antique china cabinet that their father had just refinished from the basement into the living room area where it belonged. He was finding it hard to concentrate on the road and his sister's nagging while enjoying the company of his passenger, whose head was buried in his lap.

"You been saying that since we moved in here. Had you guys done it then, I wouldn't have to be in y'all's ear every day about the same shit. It's a shame that between the two of you so-called men, neither one of you has any idea how to keep a woman satisfied without either spending money or pulling down your pants." Kanisha spoke loud enough into the phone so that her husband, Malachi, could hear what she was saying about him and her brother from the other room, where he cowered from her ranting.

"I don't see why you won't just let me hire some guys to come and move that shit. I can get them out there probably way before I even finish doin' what I'm doing, and you can find something else to do besides think of reasons to curse me out," he said, glancing down at the blond-streaked hair that rose up and down in his lap. Blacka could feel the ball of Safiya's tongue ring circling the head of his dick just before she took his whole member into her mouth. Never did he think that she would be so anxious to please him when he picked her up for the first time since meeting her at the photo shoot party. After a quick bite to eat, she made it clear that since their brief conversation at the event, her mouth had been craving more than just food.

"You know damn well that I don't want nobody in this house until I get it all together. It's bad enough that I had to deal with the contractors working on the steps out front for the last two days. The last thing I need right now is some pack of Mexicans coming over and banging up shit against the walls, scratching up shit," she said. She quickly dismissed her brother's idea of hiring someone to come and move the cabinet. Kanisha knew her brother was probably running the streets with one of the many women he randomly picked up. What she couldn't understand was that with all the women that Blacka slept around with, he constantly sat around worrying about what his alleged girlfriend, Angela, was doing with her time.

"Yo, 'Nisha, why you gotta be difficult all the time? What you think I'ma do? Grab a couple of crackheads off the corner? I'm talking about professionals that get paid to do shit like that every day so that people like me can do whatever it is that they get paid to do. Shit!"

Pulling up into the parking lot of the hotel, Blacka found a spot right next to Safiya's red 2002 Honda Civic that she had parked there earlier when Blacka insisted that they ride together in his car to the restaurant. Since it was almost time for his shipment from out of town to arrive, Blacka decided that he would much rather deal with the treatment that Safiya was delivering while working every muscle in her throat than the nagging voice of his sister. So, to keep peace with his sister, he decided to do what would bring peace to everyone around . . . lie.

"You mean to tell me that you would rather pay someone to carry something from downstairs to upstairs instead of doing it yourself? You know that Daddy and his friend brought it downstairs, so it ain't like it's impossible. You're just being fuckin' lazy as hell. Believe me, if I could have done it myself, I wouldn't be askin' y'all 'cause it would have been done already." Getting frustrated with her brother and husband procrastinating, Kanisha exhausted herself by asking until she literally felt short of breath, but she didn't want to cause a panic with either her brother or husband, so she just silently paced herself with deep, relaxed breaths.

"All right, 'Nisha, I'm gonna call Dwight and see where he is to see how long I have before he gets here. If I got time, I will come now. If he's almost here, I will just go and open the spot up so he can get in to unload the truck. Either way, I'm gonna be there tonight, so you can finally get off my back." Realizing that this was the only way to bring the conversation to a peaceful conclusion, Blacka decided that the best thing to do was to agree with Kanisha so that he could give his date the attention that she was working so hard to get.

Not sure if Safiya was even aware that they were back at the hotel, Blacka sat back with the phone to his head, trying his best to maintain the conversation with his sister while fighting the urge to discharge a load of semen down Safiya's throat. With the seat of his pants wet from the saliva that ran from Safiya's mouth down the shaft of his dick to his balls, Blacka was more than ready to take her to the room and put her flexibility to the test.

"I'll believe that shit when I see it. I've been hearing that shit since we got here, but I'm gonna see what happens tonight. I promise that if you make me sit here waiting on you, and you don't show up, me and you are gonna fight like animals in the wild, and I ain't even playing with you." Although she knew that her brother always had her best interests in mind, she knew he was fully capable of lying to women to get out of a situation. Before she let him get off the phone, she added, "If I have to call you one more time and remind you to come and get this shit done, you better believe that when you *do* show up around here, I'm gonna deal with you like a nigga who stole from me, so make the right choice."

"A'ight, 'Nisha, I got you, so just chill. I'll be there as soon as I get the word from Dwight. You ain't gotta call and remind me neither, so you can put your gun back on safety and relax. I'll talk to you later." He dragged his words as he felt the back of Safiya's throat tighten around the head of his dick. Blacka unwrapped his hand from her hair long enough to press the button on the side of his Bluetooth to end the call. Then reaching across to the passenger seat, Blacka lifted the back of Safiya's shirt and began to run his hands up her bare back, causing her to arch her ass in the air as she attempted to go deeper while making herself gag.

"You ready . . . to go inside . . . or . . . do you wanna . . . stay in this car . . . all night?"

Bringing her head up and down to say a few words at a time, Safiya spoke with her eyes locked on the swollen tip of Blacka's dick that was saturated with her saliva. Everything about him turned her on, from his smooth chocolate skin to his relaxed, monotone voice. The fact that he obviously could afford the finer things in life by the looks of his car and clothes was definitely a plus. Amazingly enough, Safiya found that the more she pleased him, the more she felt her clitoris throb as though she were on the verge of an orgasm herself.

"Hell yeah, I'm ready to go inside."

Dealing with my sister and her crazy shit, I damn sure need to go inside and get some shit off my mind the right way.

Reluctantly pulling up the zipper on his jeans and turning off the ignition to the car, Blacka spoke before leaning over to the glove compartment to retrieve the box of Magnum condoms that he purchased earlier that day. Watching Safiya straighten up her hair in the mirror on the passenger visor, he was tempted to pull his penis back out to start fucking her right then and there, but the car's limited space was nowhere close to the amount of space that he wanted to have her stretched out in. Besides, he still had about two hours to kill before Dwight pulled into town to drop off his cargo at the warehouse just across the street from the hotel. Being a man who plays life by strategy and not chance, Blacka was sure that he was close to where his priority was, even when he divulged in pleasure. He had no plans to spend the whole night romancing this girl since he did indeed have a bona fide girl that outshined all the other women who broke their necks trying to get close enough to him to be able to call him by his government name. Although Angela was where his heart would lead him, his dick, on the other hand, would lead him toward sexual freaks like Safiya so that he could do all the nasty, disrespectful things that he didn't think Angela would go for.

Entering the hotel from one of the side entrances, Blacka walked directly behind Safiya and watched the rhythm of her ass as she walked in the four-inch platform heels that she wore that increased her height to five foot nine. Even in tight-fitting jeans, her fierce walk made her behind resemble two midgets in a plastic bag fighting over a piece of candy, and she knew it. The thought of having her bent over in front of him with his dick buried balls deep inside of her gave Blacka an erection that was visible from the outside of his loose-fitting jeans.

Once they got to the outside of room 219, Blacka had the room card key already in his hand, ready to enter and begin the joyride that he planned to have on her. With Safiya's hand grabbing his penis through his pants and leading him through the door of the room, Blacka slapped the left cheek of her ass and pushed her down on the queen-size bed with no intention of wasting any time with meaningless conversation.

"Ooo . . . If you think you gonna take out your frustration with your sister on my cookies, then you are so right, papi," Safiya said. She lay on her back and seductively bit down on her bottom lip, welcoming Blacka to have his way with her.

Being a firm believer that actions speak louder than words in the bedroom, Blacka stood looking down at Safiya on the bed and began removing his clothes. He said, "Baby girl, the last thing on my mind right now is my sister, so why don't you take off them clothes, and we'll do all the talking afterward?"

Staring back into Blacka's hypnotic, brown-eyed gaze, Safiya pulled her shirt over her head before realizing it. Her pussy throbbed as though it had a heartbeat of its own. The sight of his sculptured shape made her imagination run wild with fantasies of what pleasurable damage he could do to her. She was excited to find out whether his strong demeanor was compatible with his sexual performance.

Looking down to see him unbuckle the Gucci belt around his waist, Safiya unconsciously held her breath in anticipation as she began to undo the button on her jeans. Propping up on her knees to maneuver the pants off her waist and over her ass, Safiya reached forward and grabbed hold of Blacka's dick and pulled it toward her open mouth. Cooperating with her unspoken request, Blacka pulled the band of his boxers down and stepped out of them and his pants with two steps. Then he moved closer to Safiya's awaiting mouth.

Rotating her neck and her right hand in sync, Safiya took his dick into her mouth slow and as deep as she could go, releasing a slurping sound followed by an occasional gag. His breathing deep through clenched teeth, emitting a low hissing sound, motivated her to intensify her performance. She leaned back and spit straight across his fully erect eleven-inch shaft. Then she used both hands to stroke Blacka while running her tongue across the base of his scrotum.

Feeling his knees buckle under the pressure of the sexy Cuban mouth, Blacka decided that it was time that he took control of the situation to remind her that he was the only one who was going to make anyone squeal in that room. Using his left hand, he brought Safiya's head in toward his pelvis, forcing a little more than half of his penis down her unsuspecting throat. Safiya was turned on by the fact that even though he was choking her by the way her cheeks bulged as saliva spewed from the sides of her mouth and her eyes teared up, he was applying more pressure than she could handle. But Safiya didn't run away from the challenge. His right hand reached across her back and began to assist in pulling her pants down from her waist. The slight struggle with the tight jeans over her ass didn't hinder Safiya's oral performance as she kept moving her head back and forth as she hoisted her behind in the air to help Blacka in his struggle.

Finally releasing her forty-four-inch hips from the bondage of her pants, Blacka firmly slapped her left ass cheek and gripped it at the same time, spreading her open toward the window of the room. Moans of excitement escaped from Safiya's mouth as he ran his hand down the center of her ass toward her wet spot, inserting his middle and ring fingers knuckle deep inside her slippery, pink hole. Leaning forward with his pinky and index finger spread like bullhorns, Blacka rapidly moved his wrists back and forth, causing his two inserted fingers to rub against the little round nub located about one to two inches back from her vaginal opening, making Safiya cream all over his hand.

Trapped between Blacka's pelvis and his hand, Safiya squeezed her eyes closed in ecstasy as he provoked her G-spot, making her come. She was exhausted and amazed that within a few minutes, he was able to pinpoint her pleasure spot as though he had been studying her for years. She released his dick from her mouth and began to kiss around his pelvis.

Listening to the heavy breathing coming from Safiya, along with the thick, white liquid on his two fingers that made them resemble a freshly glazed donut, Blacka could tell that she had reached her climax, giving him a sense of control.

The air-conditioning that was keeping the room cool suddenly began to carry a smell toward his face that wasn't pleasing. A rancid smell seemed to be getting stronger and stronger. Having an idea of where the scent originated, Blacka held his right hand two inches away from his face and breathed in. His suspicion was correct. The smell was coming from Safiya. Growing up with his mother and sister, Blacka witnessed his mother strictly enforce the importance of good hygiene on his sister. He felt that any woman who didn't follow those guidelines shouldn't be worth his time.

"Hold on, shorty . . . Give me a second . . . I gotta run to the car and get something," he said, stepping away from

Safiya. Blacka spoke while putting his foot back into his pants and boxers that lay together on the floor.

"Huh? What you need out of the car right now, babe? I got everything you need right here," she said, turning over on her back, seductively whispering as she spread her legs, rubbing her fingers through the thick, curly bush of pubic hair, squeezing her swollen clitoris between two fingers.

"I got to get my phone just in case my peoples need me to give them directions when they get here." He spoke a lie off the top of his head. Blacka fought the urge to tell Safiya that her pussy smelled like an old septic tank that needed to be flushed out with a pressure washer and disinfectant. Throwing his shirt over his shoulder so that he could hurry up and get away from the smell that lingered in the air before it clung to his clothes, Blacka moved toward the door, ignoring her request for him not to leave. Ironically, the sound of Damien Marley's hit song "Welcome To Jamrock" erupted from his cellphone in his back pocket.

"Ain't that your phone ringing now?" Safiya asked, sitting up on the bed, confused about why he was rushing to go to his car.

"Yeah . . . Yeah, it is. I thought it was in the car all this time 'cause . . ." Lost for words, Blacka pulled the phone from his back pocket and stared at it as though he had never seen it before.

"Is there something wrong, baby? Don't you want *this*?" Using her left hand to squeeze her right nipple, Safiya lay back on the bed, inserted two fingers on her right hand inside of herself, and then placed them in her mouth. The look on her face when she tasted her own vaginal secretion resembled a baby being spoon-fed something with a strong, bitter aftertaste.

"Yeah, shorty . . . You really need to get a handle on what you got going on down there. That shit ain't sexy, ma. That shit so bad that you can't even stand it, so you know something gotta be wrong. I'm gonna go and take care of that shit at my sister's house. You can stay here and use the shower if you want to. Just remember that checkout is at eleven."

He exited the room, shaking his head in disappointment. Blacka looked back at his phone to return the call that he just missed. Just by the ringtone, he already knew who was calling him, and, as usual, they were punctual with the call. Walking down the hotel corridor toward the exit, Blacka cued his phone to return the call to see what news his Jamaican henchmen had for him.

Chapter 4

"Ah wha' gwan, my lawd? Just call ya phone an' mi never get an answer. Start fi think you nuh have time fi de poor people again." Answering his phone promptly on the second ring, Reef spoke with a strong island accent.

"My bad, bruh, I was just making my escape from some bullshit that I was caught up in. What's good, though? Did y'all get over to homeboy and find out what's up with my shit?" Now walking across the parking lot toward his car, Blacka looked down at his hand, hoping the hand sanitizer in his glove compartment would help disinfect Safiya's skunklike pheromone. The evening he planned had taken a drastic change, but hopefully, Reef had some good news regarding the debt that he and his partner went to collect out in Far Rockaway Queens from Roshan.

"Ya, mon. Everything good with my bwoy. Him did get lock up by the police the other day, and them have him inside ah wait fi de judge, but him left the money with the baby mother an' tell her fi give it to you if you did stop by 'cause him phone inna him car." Reef informed Blacka that Roshan was arrested earlier that week but left the money he owed to him with his baby mother so that she could pay off his debt, and Reef's news proved Roshan's loyalty to his commitments. The $12,000 debt wasn't what really concerned Blacka. It was the fact that he had not heard from Roshan in a few days when he was supposed to have met up with him that Monday morning with the money.

"See, that's why I fucks with Roshan. Most niggas would have got a speeding ticket and made up an excuse why I couldn't get my money on time, and this nigga is sitting in jail and still made sure that I got what was mine. That's the type of niggas that I need to keep around to make sure that shit continues to run smoothly. Find out from his girl what she needs to get him out. If it's a lawyer or bail, tell her to hold onto the cash, handle whatever he needs, and consider whatever money that's left over as a bonus."

"You is a regular Santa Claus, mi friend. The real poor people's governor. Me an' Dummy still right outside of the house, so we ah go give her back the money so she can stop cry an' deal with getting my bwoy out." Knowing the kind of man his boss was, Reef knew that once he heard about the situation, he would do whatever he could to help. That's one of the reasons why he had such a high respect for Blacka. Like a good general, Blacka always made sure that his soldiers' needs were accommodated so that they would be willing to lay down their lives for him when the time came to engage in battle.

"Just don't let that shit get around. Next thing you know, I'll be handing out more money in the hood than the NAACP. When y'all get back, I got something for you just for going out there to check on things for me." Squeezing the bottle of Purell hand sanitizer on his hand, Blacka vigorously rubbed his hands together, trying to get rid of the smell before it got into the interior of his car.

"We ah go grab a little sumthin' fi eat, 'round ah Nagasaki up inna Hempstead, an' then we can link up with you later unless it's sumthin' you need us fi deal wit' right now," Reef said. He dug in his pocket to pull out the envelope filled with hundred-dollar bills to hand back to Roshan's teary-eyed baby mother. Reef suggested that he and Dummy meet up with Blacka later in the evening so they could go to their favorite Jamaican restaurant located not too far away on Long Island.

"Naw, chief, that's straight. I'm gonna go by the house and take care of some shit for my sister before she ends up hiring y'all to come knock on my door. When y'all reach back on this side, just hit me up, and we'll take it from there," Blacka said. He started the ignition to the car as he waved his hand in front of his face to see if the sanitizer had any positive effect on the foul aroma Safiya left behind. Since he still had time to kill before Dwight's arrival, he decided that the best thing to do was go by Kanisha's place and take care of the china cabinet that she insisted on moving immediately. Disappointed in what a catastrophe his planned escapade was, Blacka was pleased to know that the night wouldn't be a total loss once he received confirmation that his shipment was safely delivered.

With surprisingly light traffic on Linden Boulevard, Blacka was able to reach the Flatbush section in remarkable time, giving him the confidence that he should be done and back to the warehouse in time to make sure that everything went as smoothly as it should.

Pulling up on the block that he grew up on, Blacka saw a lot of familiar faces of friends of his parents and some of their children who still stayed in the neighborhood. Luckily, there was an open parking spot not too far from the front of his sister's house, so he didn't have to waste time circling, looking for a place to park his car. The sudden vibration on his phone let him know that he had an incoming text from Angela that read, "See you in the morning," with a happy face icon attached. Not a fan of sitting down and relaying messages back and forth with his thumbs, Blacka cued his phone to call Angela so that he could hear her voice when his phone unexpectedly started to ring with Dwight's name appearing on the caller ID. Like an anxious child with a cast on his hand trying to open a present, Blacka fumbled with the phone while maneuvering the steering wheel to park the car.

"Yo, Black . . . Black . . . You there? Just wanted to let you know that I'm pullin' into town now, and I should be at the spot about nine thirty," Dwight said, speaking into the phone on the table in front of him. He let his employer know what time he would be meeting up with him to drop off his delivery.

"What happened to eight o'clock . . .? How the fuck all of a sudden the shit is nine thirty? I know I damn sure ain't say nine thirty, so tell me wha' the fuck is so important that I got to wait. 'Cause you should already know by now that I can't stand sitting around waitin' on some nigga, especially when he got shit that belongs to me. So you need to get on your job or find yourself without one." Sitting in the driver's seat parked in front of his sister's home, Blacka spoke through the Bluetooth in his right ear as he looked down at his gun-metal steel, rose-gold-trimmed Armani watch in frustration. It was now after seven thirty, and the last thing he wanted to hear was that he had to wait any longer to take care of his business.

"Some asshole on the Delaware Memorial Bridge caught a flat, and instead of everybody minding their fuckin' business, they wanted to stop and stare at this nigga while he talked to himself on the side of the road. You know the last thing you got to worry about with me is running off with your shit, bruh. Hell, you treat me too good for me to do some dumb shit like that." Knowing that he was much later than expected, Dwight gave his reason for his delay, hoping Blacka believed him. Although his nerves were on end, he tried maintaining his composure so Blacka wouldn't think there was a reason to worry.

Sitting in the metal chair, he leaned over to the phone and continued, "I'm mad that by the time I get there, all of the good spots to get food from will be either closed or serving whatever bullshit that they got left over in the kitchen."

"So why is you waitin' until now to tell me? You could have called me and told me this about half an hour ago instead of having me sitting here waiting like some kind of puppet." Although he wasn't going to go back to the storage unit until he got the phone call from Dwight saying he had arrived, Blacka spoke, giving Dwight the impression that he was already at their rendezvous point awaiting his arrival.

"My bad, boss man. I really ain't want to bother you until I knew what was going on. I didn't think that you would be already there waiting on me this time, or else I would have at least called and told you that I was gonna be late." With sweat starting to flow down from the top of his bald head, Dwight wanted to end the call, but due to his present situation, he was left without control over his phone.

"All right, then, nigga, you say nine thirty, so that's when I expect to see your ass comin' around that corner with my shit. Get your shit together, bruh, 'cause trust me, it will be much less of a headache if I just get someone who knows how to get shit done on time. You starting to act like you brand new to this, and I really ain't got time to be holdin' no nigga hand while trying to make this bread."

Opening the door to his car and exiting onto the sidewalk, Blacka's half-an-hour window to help out sister Kanisha was unexpectedly extended by an hour and a half, giving him more time than he wanted to help her and her husband Malachi move things around. Making what he hoped to be the final arrangement with Dwight, he hung up the phone and made his way to the front door of the home.

Inspecting the front steps and the automated wheelchair lift that he had just paid the contractors to install in the home, Blacka was pleased that they completed the job on time and was done to perfection as promised. It had been only two weeks since his sister moved back into the home after the untimely death of their parents. Since this was the house they grew up in, Kanisha couldn't bring herself to get rid of it.

Recently being confined to a wheelchair due to complete kidney failure caused by her diabetes, Kanisha needed assistance to get in and out of the home. Blacka made sure that all of her needs were fully accommodated. Just so that he didn't add to her worries, Blacka made it his business to hide his illegal actions from Kanisha. As far as she knew, all of the money he made came from the small trucking company in which he invested his part of the insurance money from his parents' accident. Even though he felt ridiculous by the extent that he had to go to keep up the charade of being a law-abiding, taxpaying citizen, he knew it was well worth him not taking the risks of breaking the little bit of spirit that his older sister was holding on to. He had often come close to telling her what he was doing, but the thought of the long, worrisome speech always brought him back to his original plan of secrecy. As long as his circle did their job and kept their mouths shut, he had no worries about her finding out. Hell, at this point, operations were running so smoothly that it was hard to imagine that even the police would find out what he was up to.

Blacka found himself smiling, thinking back to when he used to search between the cushions of the raggedy couch that was in the basement, trying to find enough change to buy a Philly Blunt so that he could roll up a five-dollar bag of weed that, most of the time, he and two other friends had to chip in on. Now, years later, he was on the steps of the very same house all grown up, commander in chief of a flawless trafficking operation with soldiers that would lay down the lives of their firstborn babies before they betrayed his trust.

"Hello . . . hello . . . yo, Blacka . . . yo . . ." Leaning forward toward the phone that lay on the table in front of him, Dwight spoke in vain, hoping that Blacka hadn't yet hung up the phone, but when the home screen on his phone appeared on display, he knew that the call had been disconnected. Hanging his head down and shaking it, he felt as though his breath was being sucked out of him slowly as he watched the hand from across the table pick up the phone and begin to speak.

"So, that's all you got for us? Some guy on the phone talking about how late you are? That shit is not gonna fly with us just like that, my friend. We need something a lot more than some monkey yelling at you on the phone to let you just walk out of here. Do you know with the amount of shit that was in the back of that truck, you probably will never get a chance to touch another woman again? I don't know about you, but I love pussy too much to let some other motherfucker stop me from getting it. So, what the fuck is it gonna be? Do I get one of those pretty orange jumpsuits, and I can take you to where you can meet your next boyfriends, or are you gonna do this so we all get out of here and go home and get some pussy?" With his knuckles pressed down on the steel table in the center of the small room, Lead Investigator Braxton continued the minor interrogation that had been going on for less than an hour but progressed a lot faster than he anticipated.

Sitting on a steel chair with one hand cuffed to the arm, Dwight was a nervous wreck thinking about the trouble that he was in with both the police and Blacka at the same time. Everything was going so well and according to plan . . . until he got to the end of the New Jersey Turnpike, and all of the lanes closed except for one. Unknowingly following the flow of traffic into the awaiting arms of two state troopers who were also accompanied by an unmarked black van carrying a K-9 unit, Dwight felt as though they were watching every step that he made from the moment the arrangements were made for him even to pick up the shipment. He was approached as if the truck were completely transparent and the contents were visible for everyone to see. Without using the K-9 dogs, the police went directly to where the contraband was stashed within the furniture that was aboard the vehicle. As soon as they discovered what it was that they were looking for, they immediately handcuffed him and escorted him to a substation that was located at the toll plaza, where they had been interrogating him ever since. When he first attempted to tell the police that he was just a driver hired to make a delivery and was totally oblivious to what was stashed within the cargo, the investigator laughed and began to tell him the names of the people involved in the whole transaction. One name they did mention that they seemed to focus on more than anything else was Richard Nelson, otherwise known as King Blacka.

"I'm saying, though, man . . . Ain't no wins in this shit for me, man, at all, so y'all might as well do whatever it is that you gonna do. Shit . . . I'll be much safer in jail than just baptizing my damn self in fire by doing some shit that's gonna guarantee my death," Dwight said, looking up at the inspector. Dwight spoke with his eyes glazed over in despair, thinking of the situation that he was caught up in. He had witnessed firsthand what Blacka's henchmen were capable of when one of the guys who worked for him out in Brownsville decided to skip out without paying a few dollars. To this day, he could still hear the screams of terror as the two sadistic Jamaicans stripped him naked and carved the word "Judas" in his chest with a sharp wooden-handled knife that one of them always kept. Then they proceeded to do more unthinkable things to the poor man. There was no way that he would voluntarily go up against that just to keep himself out of jail for maybe a couple of months since it was the first major offense on his record. In his mind, the possession charge wouldn't get him more time than he could handle.

"All right, my friend, you wanna go to jail? Cool. Just know that you ain't who we want, but we'll give you a place to sit and think about how stupid you are for the next ten to twenty years. Some of you motherfuckers really need to rethink that whole no-snitchin' bullshit 'cause while you're locked up eating a cock sandwich, that same asshole that you are protecting will probably be balls deep in your mom, not giving your stupid ass a second thought."

With his knuckles turning red from pressing his fist down on the table, Braxton spoke while staring into Dwight's eyes, knowing that he would break and cooperate at any point. The truth was that although he could prosecute Dwight for the truckload of narcotics, he would much rather get the head of operations that he was sure was directly responsible for the death of Troy Mandel. Braxton could read Dwight's eyes and clearly see that he was not built to spend more than a few hours in a jail cell, much less close to a decade. He planned to make Dwight stay in police custody. At the same time, they would run him through the system so that he could attach the necessary strings to ensure that his newfound puppet's moves corresponded with assisting in the apprehension of this self-proclaimed King Blacka.

Chapter 5

"Bredren . . . Mi nah go let you kill me off wit' de cigarette ting . . . Move from round side ah me before man box down yu' pussyclot!" Reef's impatience caused him to lash out at the guy who was innocently standing there enjoying a Newport. Although the man wasn't small in size or even timid by nature, the tone of the irritated Jamaican, along with the rubber grip handle that peeked out from under his shirt, was enough for him not only to walk away without a quarrel but also to extinguish his cigarette immediately.

"Dis man must tink sey man ah cartoon. Ah nuh tree thirty the man seh fi reach an' now ah wha' time? Quarta pass bumboclot four . . . Ah joke ting dis!"

Patience was usually Reef's strong point among the duo, but one thing that triggered his nerves was tardiness. Waiting on the Brooklyn corner made him feel vulnerable to anything, whether it be a bullet or an informer out to do a good deed for monetary gain. Although he had nothing but love for the ghetto neighborhood that seemed like a concrete version of home, he was well aware that in the concrete jungle, the thin line between love and hate was a barrier that many were willing to cross for the price of nothing.

Today was supposed to be a quick meet and greet to discover what happened during his short stay in jail. There was a major question mark about how he was released so quickly without suffering severe consequences.

Naturally, Blacka had certain suspicions, so he needed to send his special tactic force to assess the situation to see if Dwight was a problem that needed to be eradicated. Dwight had them standing impatiently, waiting for his late arrival.

"Sorry for being late, y'all. I had to take Sandra to pick up the kids from school and drop them off so I could have the car to meet up with y'all." Even before the 2006 Nissan Altima could come to a complete stop, Dwight shouted his explanation out the open window, knowing that being late was not accepted by either of the men.

"Nuh bother with the fuckery inna mi ear 'bout pickney 'affe reach home from school after dem ah no fi you pickney dem. Ah works man de pon, make Sandra walk her foot or learn fi ride de bus!" Grabbing the handle to the rear passenger door, Dummy couldn't help but smile as Reef preached down to Dwight for not having his priorities straight. What was funnier to him was that Dwight would always be running back and forth, catering to this woman and her five children whom he had only known for six months, while his own child gets no attention at all. To top it off, Sandra was now six months pregnant, and Dwight was convinced that he was about to be a daddy.

"Y'all need to stop making those kind of jokes all the time. It's not like she control me or nothing. She's just pregnant and needs me." Dwight felt a slight relief when he saw smiles on their faces as they entered the car. He ignored the ridicule of helping care for kids that weren't his, and he prepared himself to tell the two men what news he had to bring.

"Mister Dummy . . . What's good, my friend?" With a nod of respect, Dwight addressed the silent man as he entered the vehicle from the rear. The idea of having the deadly dread right behind him put chills up his spine.

"Come make we move from 'round yah, so drive up the road an' talk de business. Mi nuh wan' sit inna dis duty car all day wit' no long argument." Kicking a half-eaten bag of Cheetos with an empty Snapple bottle rolling back and forth under the passenger seat, Reef pointed forward, instructing Dwight to drive down Nostrand Avenue.

Driving down the block, Dwight constantly looked in the rearview mirror, not for any cars approaching from the rear but in fear of what may erupt from the backseat at any point. He was well aware of Dummy's credentials of being a walking nightmare. If there was indeed a Freddy Krueger, Dwight was sure that even he checked under his bed before he went to sleep to ensure the mute monster wasn't lurking. With Dwight's recent apprehension by the law and quick, unexplainable release, he was unsure what to expect from the dangerous duo he had heard so many terrifying stories about.

"The detectives were really on my ass, but they couldn't really fuck with me 'cause I told them over and over that I didn't know what was loaded in the back since I'm just a driver. The motherfu—" Dwight began, only to be interrupted.

"You mean to tell me sey that dem let you go 'cause you tell them you never know what did inna de back ah de truck? Mi never hear no fuckery like dat before inna mi life. Mi never hear nobody talk dem way out ah de jailhouse when dem already inside. Something nuh sound right wit' dat story, boss, an' me wanna know wha' really happened before we get mad in this li'l car." Reef's outburst caused the nervous driver's heart to jump. Instinctively, he looked in the rearview mirror only to be greeted by the sinister stare of Dummy.

"I'm tellin' you it was crazy to me too, but I wasn't gonna sit there and ask them why they letting me out. I just got my shit together and hauled ass out of there before they changed their minds." Dwight spoke as he looked forward at the road with both hands gripping the steering wheel, fearing the possible reaction to his words. Holding his breath, hoping that his words were convincing to the two men who obviously had suspicions of what he said to the police, Dwight nearly failed to stop for the red light at the intersection. As pedestrians passed by with angry faces from being fresh off of a congested Flatbush Avenue-bound number two train, Dwight's mind raced to find the right words to deliver the news.

The callous grip on the left side of his neck that came from the backseat made his body go into a state of temporary shock. A flash of heat surged through his body as though the devil himself was touching him, and his eyes caught the reflection from the rearview mirror of the silent assassin's face directly over his right shoulder. Without saying a word, Dummy's facial expression proved more effective than a face-to-face chastising from an aggressive army drill sergeant. Frozen at the intersection, Dwight's mental prayers of disappearing went unanswered as his neck began to cramp under the pressure of the backseat passenger's intensifying grip.

"Bwoy, if you nuh stop gwan like you can't talk me, ah go make sure you can't talk fi true," Reef warned. Revealing the blue steel .38-caliber snub-nosed Taurus M85, Reef suggested that Dwight should hurry up and gather his words before their patience was utterly depleted.

"That's it, man. I swear nothing else happened. I am still shocked 'cause I thought I was a goner for sure. Y'all should know by now that I wouldn't say nothing about nothing to the police or anybody else. Look how long I've been holdin' down my job without any problems. Y'all know me, man." Dwight's trembling voice of protest was just a hope that his closer-than-average acquaintance with these two notorious killers was enough to keep him alive long enough to park his car at least.

"Then you done know seh we nuh ramp fi kill off a bwoy no matter if a friend or fi mi daddy."

Dwight's eyes were now focused on the right thumb on Reef's hand as it guided back the hammer of the pistol. The sound of the barrel revolving caused his eyes to widen while his bottom lip slowly lowered so his mouth hung open in disbelief.

"That's why I wouldn't do nothing to fuck around with any of y'all. I would rather do twenty years on my head than tell them anything that would cross Blacka. Y'all gotta believe me, man. I put that on everything I love." The sounds of car horns from impatient motorists behind him indicated that the traffic signal had changed from red to green, but until instructed to do otherwise, he could not find the nerve to take his foot off the brake pedal to proceed forward.

"So let me get dis story straight an' you tell me if it make sense to you. You get pull over by the police wit' a truckload ah drugs, an' you get fi walk out the door 'cause you tell them dat you never know that it was inna de back. An' we supposed to believe dat is all that happened jus' 'cause you say so?" The snarl on Reef's face was not as intimidating as the pressure under his rib cage from the nozzle of the short but very powerful hand cannon.

Not sure what he should say next, Dwight continued to sit in a state of suspended animation. Knowing the type of men his passengers were, he didn't think his chances of leaving the driver's seat alive were in his favor. Provoking the men, who, until minutes ago, he considered himself fortunate to be friends with, was not his intention at all. Whatever it was that he had to say to get out of the target site of the West Indian sociopath, he was more than willing to oblige—twice, if necessary. The sounds of irritated motorists at the Brooklyn intersection alerted Reef to his surroundings. It brought his thoughts of perforating Dwight’s lung at a close range to a more rational thought.

“Hear this. Make we go park up an’ sit down an’ reason ’cause me wan’ hear ah wah this story one more time. Maybe you can remember a little bit more so we can make sense out ah dis ting.” Dwight silently sighed in relief as Reef tucked away the gun, and Dummy released his clutch on his neck and sat back in his seat.

Chapter 6

Driving without knowing his destination made Dwight feel uneasy about how the rest of his day would go. There was now a strong possibility that his loved ones would be notified to come and identify his body in whatever remains that these diabolical men may leave behind. Realizing that his lie was transparent, he felt overwhelmed with shame and fear for his life. Now, he wished he had kept his mouth shut and suffered the consequences like his first mind told him to do. Since he was already past that point, the only thing left for him to do was to try to get it over with and obtain the incriminating evidence that Blacka was indeed head of the whole illegal operation the police requested. And then to get as far away as possible before it was linked back to him. It all sounded so simple when Braxton made the proposition for his freedom. Now that he was staring in the face of his inevitable death, he wished that he could go back in time and do things a completely different way.

"Bust a left turn when you reach up ah Clarendon and come offa' dis road. Too much traffic down ya so," said Reef. He noticed a Crown Victoria in the side mirror that had been riding a few cars behind them for a while. Reef wanted to see if it was just a coincidence or if his instinct of being followed was correct. Without even voicing aloud his feelings of being stalked, his counterpart, Dummy, was looking over his shoulder inconspicuously as though he had the same suspicion.

As Dwight turned at the next intersection, he felt a slight relief that, for whatever reason, Reef's attention wasn't focused on reprimanding him for things that were beyond his fault. He was concerned about what the Jamaican's complex was rooted in. Whatever it was, it had Reef studying the side mirror of the Nissan as though he were performing oral surgery on himself. Curious about what it was that had the undivided attention of his disgruntled passenger, Dwight used the advantage of the rearview mirror to see exactly what was behind them. Within ten seconds of him turning, a white, four-door sedan made a left and followed the same path that he was on. Following Reef's navigation via finger-pointing, he made the first left onto East Thirty-First Street . . . only to see that the white car made the same maneuver.

"De bwoy dem ah ride behind us, ah wha' de pussyclot dem ah itch up under we tail for?" Reef kissed his teeth while his eyes trained on the mirror, watching the vehicle as it appeared to follow him. Instinctively, his fingers found their way back to the rubber grip handle of the snub-nosed revolver that, at this point, seemed destined to be put to immediate use. In the backseat, his partner was once again on the same mental wavelength as the sound of a black .50-caliber Desert Eagle registering a hollow-tip bullet in its chamber broke the uncomfortable silence in the car.

"They look like they are following us every turn we make. It could be from when I blocked up traffic back on Nostrand. Even if they stop us, all they can do is ask for my license and registration, and I have all of that right here, so we're good. Just make sure they don't see nothing to give them a reason to ask us to get out of the car." Dwight wasn't a die-hard gangster and was not willing to engage in a shoot-out with the New York Police Department, especially since he was the only one in the car without a gun. He tried to reassure Reef and Dummy not to take any hasty actions that could get them locked up, shot, or even killed. If everything went as well as he explained, they should be on their way within ten minutes with nothing to worry about. It was just another random stop that was an everyday thing in the Brooklyn neighborhood.

"Bredren, mi nuh deh pon no long argument with' no Babylon bwoy. If mi feel sey dem ah go draw down pon me, mi ah go draw down pon dem first, but mi ah go gwan cool an' let you deal wit' de case an' see how dis ting ah go run," Reef expressed. He did not appreciate the unwarranted harassment that most people within the urban community have grown to accept and decided against violent retaliation. He let Dwight handle the situation like a model, law-abiding citizen. Back in his native island of Jamaica, police stopped citizens on the road for two reasons: to arrest them or to kill them. There was no reasoning with them and walking away with a mere slap on the wrists. So, naturally, his first reaction was to hold court in the street with a pending sentence of death. His decision to adapt to his current environment by not immediately engaging in a small war with the approaching officers even shocked his partner.

Still driving down the street, Reef and Dwight inconspicuously watched the movements of the white vehicle that followed their course in the mirror. The occupants were barely visible through its front windshield due to the dark tint on the glass that was a trademark for all government-issued vehicles. With a spotlight right above the driver's side mirror, there was no doubt that these were not just average motorists cruising through the streets.

Dwight already pointed out the fact that there was no scent of marijuana in the car, so the only thing that the situation could possibly turn into was a routine traffic stop, which could lead to a big inconvenience since there were weapons in the vehicle. Since coming to the United States, the two Jamaican men had made it their primary objective to stay clear of the law since they were on temporary visas under false names, which, at this present time, had expired over a year ago. If the situation got to the point that the police did take things one step further by asking to search them or the vehicle, the last thing that the men wanted was to be detained for possession of an illegal firearm, so the only option to avoid that was to stash the weapons in the car itself. Untucking the revolver from beneath his belt buckle, Reef inconspicuously slid it between his seat and the driver's seat until it was beneath the seat. Observing his partner's actions, Dummy used his foot to conceal his gun under the same seat.

"Y'all could've just kept them tucked away where you had them. Ain't no reason for y'all to put both of them under my seat. I told you, all they gonna do is run my license, and then they have to let us go when it comes back straight." Dwight's words to ease the nerves of his passengers were said in vain as they continued to remove all paraphernalia from their pockets to conceal within the vehicle. With the strict penalties of New York City's gun laws to worry about, Dwight was not very comfortable with the idea of the two men stashing the weapons under his car seat. Who's to know what previous crimes those guns were involved in, and Dwight did not want to be the one to be held responsible for them. Unfortunately for him, his suggestion was responded to only by a serious peripheral glare from Reef's eyes. Those eyes had the piercing effect of a slow-moving hollow-point bullet coming straight at his head.

"Well, if everyting is all right, den everyting is all right." The words came from Reef's mouth with a calm tone as he leaned comfortably back in the passenger seat with his eyes now inconspicuously looking through the side mirror. "You know wha'? At dis corner turn left."

"Right here at this corner? You sure you wanna turn that way, man?" Confused at Reef's directions, Dwight was hesitant to turn in that direction because that was the block of the sixty-seventh precinct. Driving in front of the police station with an unmarked police car following behind them did not seem like the smartest option for them in this situation, but the looks he got from his passengers were as though they were sure that things would not transpire into a problem.

"When you get pon de next corner, you ah go let Dummy out at the store, and him ah go buy one calling card, and the two ah we ah go wait inna de car." While using his chin as a pointer, Reef indicated to the driver that he should park at the store at the intersection of Snyder and Nostrand Avenue and wait for his partner to return to the car.

Dwight was as confused as ever at this point. A calling card was the last thing that should have been considered a priority now, with the police following their every turn. Why the hell that seemed to be a good plan was far from Dwight's imagination, yet he found himself following the directions that he was being given. In reality, he would rather face the consequences of the law than of his passengers. Just as he began to pull into an available parking space, the unmarked car turned on its flashing lights, revealing that it was indeed what the three men had suspected.

In a state of panic, Dwight was tempted to mash his foot on the accelerator to get away from the police, but he had already boxed himself in behind the car that he pulled up to, so that would only result in him causing an unnecessary wreck. What surprised him were the calm expressions of his passengers, who seemed not to be alarmed at all that they were being pulled over in a car that was carrying two illegal firearms, and God only knew what else was stashed in other areas of the vehicle.

"Fuck!" The word seemed to push its way out of Dwight's mouth as he glanced in the rearview mirror to see the police lights flashing. His fears had come to life, and his heart felt as though it had dropped as he witnessed the doors of the government vehicle open up with two men stepping out.

Dressed in casual attire of jeans and T-shirts with the bulge of a bulletproof vest, the men approached the car slowly, each one with their right hand placed on their hips, clutching the grips of a 9 mm Glock 17. Dangling around their necks was a silver-beaded chain with a gold shield that read "City of New York Police Detective," which intimidated Dwight much more than the guns that they seemed anxious to put to use. Anxiety began to take control of Dwight's pulse. However, mentally, he was trying to keep his composure so that he would not give the approaching officers reason to prolong their already unwelcome encounter.

During the short distance it took for the two men to reach the side doors of the Nissan, the nervous driver used the few moments to build a relationship with God so that he could somehow be spared of the consequences that might await him. The knock on the driver's window indicated it was time to put all his fears aside and try to remain calm. Rolling down the window, Dwight plastered an attempt at the innocent look of a law-abiding citizen in a routine traffic stop.

"License and registration," the militant tone came from outside the window. With one hand still gripping his sidearm, the officer extended his left hand out toward Dwight for the documents that were being requested.

The other officer stared at the faces of the two passengers who seemed to be at ease during the situation.

"Can I ask why you stopped us, Officer?" Dwight inquired nervously, retrieving the registration from the glove box.

"Do yourself a big favor and let me ask the questions, and *maybe* you can be on your way. But for the record, your middle brake light is out," the officer replied with an annoyed tone.

The last thing Dwight wanted was to provoke anything with the police, especially with all of the illegal contraband that was sitting under his seat. Taking the advice, he handed the paperwork and his license over to the cop. He quickly glanced up to see the face to match the voice of authority, and his eyes locked with the officer's, and he saw a familiar glare. Dwight quickly broke the stare and guided his attention toward the steering wheel like an extremely bashful boy caught looking at a girl he admired. In the back of his mind, he wished on every star in the universe to grant him a pair of ruby slippers to click together so that he could be in a safer place.

Still standing there without paying attention to the papers in his hand, the officer leaned down toward the car window and began scanning the vehicle's interior. He looked at the faces of the passengers as though he were taking mental pictures of those faces and began to speak. "If you gentlemen plan on continuing to drive through my city, I expect that you get that brake light fixed." With those words, he handed Dwight back his documents and signaled his partner with a nod that it was time for them to leave. They walked toward their car.

Inconspicuously, Dwight watched the car in the rearview mirror slightly reverse and pull away just as fast as it came on the scene. The pounding in his chest slowed down, and his breathing was back to normal. He evaded a situation that could have been much worse than he was ready to handle. A grin of victory covered his face from ear to ear as though he were looking at a winning lottery ticket. He turned to his immediate right to tell Reef that he had everything under control, and there was no reason to be concerned with the two officers who evidently had nothing better to do than patrol the area for broken brake lights. However, he was met by an evil glare accompanied by a yellow-toothed smile.

"Bredren, ah wha' kind of thing that?" The question came out of Reef's mouth without movement of his lips. The look on his face was more concerned about why the police let Dwight ride off without so much as looking at his license. His gut told him that something was not right. The police seemed more interested in studying his and Dummy's faces than anything else. In his mind, he felt this brief run-in with the law was not just coincidental. And whenever he felt he was right, he was right—even if he was wrong. His mind was made up that Dwight was an informant working for the police.

As Dwight pivoted his head toward Dummy in the backseat, he was met with the same strange glare that sent a cold chill washing throughout his body. With no words spoken by the silent demon, even a blind man could read the message streaming through his eyes. Yet, Dwight maintained the same simple grin on his unsuspecting face.

"So, y'all still gonna get the calling card from inna the store?" Nervous about what to say or do, Dwight managed to push the words out of his mouth, feeling the tension in the car rise to temperatures hotter than he could handle.

Feeling the sudden urge to exit a vehicle that somehow miraculously became a waste of time for the police to interrogate further, Reef reached under Dwight's seat to retrieve his gun as Dummy did the same from the rear. While gathering their belongings, the two men used their eyes to scan the vehicle's interior to see if anything looked suspicious but came up with nothing. Still, the feeling surged through them.

"We ah go an' get the card and link up wit' you later so we can talk. Take care of Sandra an' her children, mi friend."

Dwight immediately detected Reef's subliminal threat toward Sandra and her kids. He never paid any attention to his personal life to say anything like that. At least, that's what Dwight thought.

"Just 'member you did say you swear pon everything you love, mi friend. So everything you love jus' might be inna trouble."

"A . . . All right then, y'all. I will c . . . call you later on a . . . and we can link up t . . . then." Dwight found himself stuttering his words out of sheer nervousness. Watching his passengers exit his car, Dwight felt as though he had just escaped the clutches of the Grim Reaper himself. The pressure he had to endure for that short encounter was more than his nervous heart could take. The term "caught between a rock and a hard place" was hardly a description of his situation. He was more like caught between a volcano and hell—one will kill you in an agonizing death, and one will torture you to a point where death is your best option. Driving off slowly, feeling as though his world was closing in, he wondered to himself, *Why the fuck those stupid-ass cops have to show up and fuck up everything? Now, I got these animals plotting on Sandra an' her kids*. He had to come up with something—and come up with it quickly. Time may not be on his side because the two Jamaicans didn't have a reputation for hesitating at getting at their prey.

Chapter 7

"Now, if it was me, you would be having a fit right now. When you want to go somewhere, I always got to hurry up and get ready, but when I want to go see a movie, you wanna sit on the computer instead of getting ready. You can at least act like you came to town to spend some time with me, Blacka, and whatever is on that computer should be able to wait." Sitting on the edge of the bed, Angela slipped her foot into the new high heel shoes she had bought earlier that day when Blacka had sent her shopping. She was growing impatient watching him invest his time with the computer rather than getting dressed for the movie that she made him promise to take her to.

"I'm ready when you are, girl. All I have to do is put on my clothes, and we out of here. It ain't like I got to get all dolled up like you do. We're just going to a movie, not the high school prom." Still drawn to the seventeen-inch screen, Blacka's eyes were staring at the screen, but his mind was wandering to the major loss that he had just suffered at the hands of the police and even more baffled about how his driver was miraculously released without so much as a bond posted.

It had been almost a month since he was last in town, and it probably would have been longer if it weren't for the delinquency of one of his people, who stayed only a few hours away in Georgia. He planned to make moves with the shipment loaded in the back of the truck with some of his people he had set up on the South Side of Atlanta. However, all that went up in smoke, so his trip was now strictly for pleasure, if that was even possible with all that was on his mind. Since he was there and spending money faster than he could breathe air on everything that made Angela smile in the store, he might as well make the ride down to Orlando and check on operations that he had going on in the Pine Hills area. For now, he had to try to enjoy himself at least a little since he was with the girl he had been in love with since high school.

"What the hell is so important that you can't even look to see what I got on? I bought all this shit just so that you would like it, and you probably busy fuckin' with one of your sorry bitches. Tell me why I shouldn't just grab that shit and sling it out the window?" Carrying on with her usual drama that she thought was cute, Angela playfully grabbed over Blacka's shoulder toward his laptop.

"First of all, I done told you over and over again to stop calling them hoes 'bitches.' They deserve at least that much respect. Second, you better not touch this computer because whatever I got to spend on a new one will mean that you will have to go without a few pairs of shoes, and I know you don't want that," Blacka joked as he playfully deflected Angela's troublesome hands away from the electronic device.

Thrilled to have the man back in her life who would provide her with every material desire for whatever time his business allowed him to, Angela threw herself across his back as she continued playing with him. The smile on her face only appeared when he was in her life. Even at a younger age, Richard proved to be different from the other guys who grew up in her neighborhood. While most guys were only interested in getting their dicks wet and playing sports, Richard was more low-key.

Unlike the rest, he spent most of his time with his family at the fabric store they owned in the Brownsville section of Brooklyn. It wasn't until after their death that he turned toward criminal activity, but that didn't change his calm demeanor. His main concerns weren't flashy cars and jewelry. It was for the well-being of his sister, who was battling against diabetes.

"Well? You still ain't say nothing about my nails or my outfit." Extending her hands toward Blacka's face, Angela waited for his approval of her appearance.

"You know you look nice, girl. Why are you trippin'? Lemme guess. You just want some attention from big poppa, huh? OK . . . Stand back and model that shit for me." Realizing that Angela's persistence would not allow him to continue on the computer, Blacka closed the laptop and placed it to the side to let her know that she now had his undivided attention. He reached over to the ashtray on the nightstand, grabbed the half-smoked blunt of Pineapple Express, and pulled his lighter out of his pocket.

"Oh . . . You want a show now . . . You must think a bitch can't work these heels or something. I'm gonna show your ass who the *real* American Top Model is. I'll put them skinny bitches to shame, and you better recognize." Happy to oblige with his wishes, Angela stepped back away from the bed and placed one hand on her hip and the other on the back of her head like a model on a photo shoot. With her mouth pouted, she began a runway strut from the foot of the bed toward the bathroom door, dramatically swinging her hips from side to side.

For the first time, Blacka paid attention to what Angela was wearing, and he was pleased with what his eyes focused on. Angela's red gathered V-neck BCBG dress clung to her shape in the best way possible. Caught in a state of suspended animation, Blacka sat up on the edge of the bed with the unlit blunt hanging from his mouth while holding the lighter inches away from his face.

Standing in the doorway that separated the bathroom from the bedroom, gripping the frame with her back turned toward her man, Angela looked over her shoulder down to her forty-two-inch behind that seemed more pronounced from the five-inch heel of the Prada python skin stiletto pumps. Knowing she had him caught in a trance, Angela slowly rotated her waist to the beat of a song in her head while running her tongue across the Victoria's Secret sparkling lip gloss that coated her top lip. "Sexy" was a lazy man's way of describing her appearance in that outfit. Angela was showstopping gorgeous from her head to her freshly pedicured toenails.

"So, what do you think, Big Poppa? Do you like it, or do you fuckin' *love* it?" Confident in her appearance, Angela rhetorically asked while tracing her hands across her voluptuous frame.

"What I'm thinking is that it's a damn shame that I probably spent a house note on a dress that I'm about to tear right off of that sexy ass," Blacka said while standing up from the bed and approaching Angela.

"Oh no, nigga . . . We goin' to the movies before you get to touch a strap on this dress. You ain't gonna have me stuck in this house watching TV while you lay here snoring," Angela teased, pushing her eager boyfriend away. "Besides, the dress wasn't expensive at all. It was the shoes that cost $1,200."

"Twelve hundred for a pair of shoes, Angie? Can you click them shits together and get to Kansas? What happened to the last pair of shoes you spent two grand for?" Blacka asked, knowing that he was in a losing argument. He has been spoiling his girl ever since he was capable of doing so. To him, she was worth every dime that he could ever hope to accumulate in the streets. At this point, his asking how much she spent was just a comical routine.

"Those shoes were blue, and as your eyes can see, this dress is red . . . or are you color blind like the rest of the dogs?" Angela's sassy response was followed by sticking her tongue out at Blacka.

"So, I guess that ain't have no blue dresses, huh? Girl, you is a trip. You're the only woman I know who will dress to kill just to go to the movies. You would think that you were going to the Grammy's or something, lookin' like your booty done swallowed Beyoncé whole," Blacka said while still trying to reach for Angela, only to get his hands once again slapped away.

"I can take it back to the store if you want, and I'll make sure I also take back this too," Angela said, holding a small pink-on-pink-striped Victoria's Secret shopping bag. "But that would mess up my plans for us later after the movie. So, why don't you play nice, get dressed, and don't spoil my night, and I will make yours into something special."

Deciding to give in to the request of his determined girlfriend, Blacka headed to the bags Angela brought back from the store for him to see what they contained. Inside the bag was a tan True Religion shirt, a blue pair of True Religion jeans with the horseshoe logo embroiled on the back pockets, and a matching hat. A shoe box in another bag contained a pair of size fourteen brown leather and canvas high-top rubber sole shoes that matched the outfit perfectly. Pleased with her selection, Blacka began to pop the tags off the clothes when his phone rang. It was the sound of Damien Marley's "Welcome to Jamrock" ringtone, which let him know that it was the call he was waiting for.

"Yo, what's good, my nigga . . . Everything straight? . . . Y'all talk to him? . . . Cool, I'll see y'all up top in about two days. Tell Malachi I said to go ahead and tell them boys in Philly that they can get what they need in the morning once I get in contact with Zulu in Bushwick to get it together . . . All right, my nigga . . . Peace." He depressed the button on the side of his Bluetooth, concluding the call, satisfied that his associates had taken care of the little matter in New York and were on their way to Georgia to retrieve a debt owed to him. Now, he could truly relax his mind and enjoy the time he was going to spend with Angela, who was doing everything to get his full attention.

"That ain't the same Malachi that's married to Kanisha, is it? I didn't know that you fucked with your sister's husband. I didn't think that Kanisha would have that shit at all," Angela stated, proving that she was listening to his brief conversation.

"She don't know shit about it. It's funny as hell, though, because he plays the role so well by getting up in the morning and acting like he still going to work. As far as she knows, he's in charge of dispatching the trucks and taking shipping orders. Hell, I even make paychecks for his ass so that she don't find out that he's hustlin' again."

"What you mean 'again'? I thought he was the Goody Two-Shoes type who went to work and paid taxes. Boy, I tell you, y'all niggas . . . It's fucked up how niggas can lie their asses off and get away with it for a little while, but when y'all slip and get caught, y'all start crying like Keith Sweat," Angela said while shaking her head at how Malachi was deceiving his wife. "You better make sure that's all he's lying to her about, and he ain't bringing no shit home to her."

"First of all, who is 'y'all'? I ain't got nothing to do with what he telling her about how he getting his money from. I ain't tell that mothafucka to lose his job. The only reason I put him in is 'cause he's with my sister. And he already know that his worst mistake will be to bring home some bullshit to Kanisha 'cause I'll make him scream in pain until he shit on himself if even one teardrop falls from her eyes," Blacka responded. Then he took off his white wife beater, preparing to go into the shower.

"Y'all both need to come clean and tell that woman what y'all out there doing before she finds out on her own and busts both of y'all asses," Angela said, standing in the doorway watching Blacka getting undressed. She discreetly admired his tattooed brown skin complemented by a muscular physique. Feeling the slight tinglin' of excitement generating between her legs, she found herself fighting the urge to get undressed to join him in the shower. Her anticipation of his arrival started only moments after his last departure three weeks ago. The distance between them secretly drove her mad, but she never made it visible to him.

"Listen, all I know is that he lost his job and asked me for help. I ain't gonna just give a grown-ass man money, so I gave him a little position that he really ain't got to be out there like that but is still makin' some paper," Blacka said stepping out of the Polo pajama pants and heading into the shower.

"Just remember that the next movie starts in an hour and a half, so don't spend all day in the shower. With traffic, it should take us about forty-five minutes to get to City Walk," Angela said, grabbing the remote for the television. She sat down on the edge of the bed, encouraging Blacka to make haste and get out of the shower so they could start their evening at the movies.

Chapter 8

After a few minutes of scanning through the guide channel of her Dish Network system and finding nothing that captured her interest, Angela spotted her Yorkshire terrier running into the room at top speed. It had been six months since Blacka brought the tiny dog home to her as a birthday gift. At the time, the puppy was so small that Blacka walked in with him concealed within one of his Polo shoe boxes. It wasn't until Angela saw the lid of the box move after Blacka put it down that she realized that inside was the same puppy she had fallen in love with at the pet store when they went out for lunch earlier that day. Immediately, the puppy claimed the shoe box aa his private territory and was never seen too far from it, which gave her the idea to name the dog Polo.

"You better slow your little ass down before you run into something, and I'll have to beat your ass right in front of your daddy," Angela yelled at Polo as he came barreling around the corner with his little legs barely able to manage the turn from the entrance to the bedroom toward the bathroom door where the dog was heading at top speed.

"What? I know you ain't out there rushing me. I just got up in this mothafucka five minutes ago. We gonna get there on time, so just chill and let a nigga wash his ass properly. If I start smelling like old hot dog water, you gonna be trying to act like you don't know nobody," Blacka said, sticking his hand out of the shower with soap running down his face. He spoke, assuming that Angela was talking to him rather than the dog. "Get your ass out of here . . . get from around here . . . I ain't playing with you, Polo . . . I'm gonna fuck you . . . Angie, come and get this crazy dog before I grab his ass and drown him."

"Polo, get your ass out here and stop all that damn barking. I don't know what the hell done got into you, but you better calm your ass down." Angela yelled at the dog that continued to bark at Blacka as he stood in the shower. Polo was usually a quiet dog that rarely barked, even when he needed to go outside to handle his business, but for some reason, the dog relentlessly tried to get the man's attention in the shower. "I don't know why he's acting like that. I guess he must be showing off or something, but he usually would have shut up by now. I know his ass ain't hungry, and we just came back inside from his walk and shit stop, so there really ain't no reason for him to be acting crazy like that."

That very moment, the sound of the doorbell, accompanied by a heavy repetitious knock at the front door, boomed throughout the town house, causing the couple to pause briefly at the unexpected disturbance.

"U.S. Marshals. Open up the door. We have a search warrant!" With those words, the wooden front door splintered off its hinges as a group of men flooded the home with guns drawn from their holsters. Within moments, over a dozen men dressed in black fatigue suits accompanied by a bulletproof vest with the initials DEA printed across the chest in big yellow letters swarmed the house.

Six of the dozen immediately rushed upstairs, where they encountered Angela standing at the top of the stairs. They forced her to lie flat on her stomach while they proceeded through the rest of the house. Polo's barking stopped as he cowered under the bed as the stampede of strangers infiltrated the home.

"What the fuck y'all got going on? How the hell y'all just rush up in here like we did some shit? Y'all damn sure ain't got to be havin' her all laid out on the ground like she's some kind of animal," Blacka yelled. Dragged to the ground naked and wet, he complained as three agents struggled to restrain him. He was more concerned with the well-being of Angela than he was with the fact he was on the ground with the knee of one of the agents depressed in the side of his neck.

"Richard Anthony Nelson, you are under arrest for the trafficking and distribution of narcotics. You have the right to remain silent. You have the right to an attorney. If you cannot afford an attorney, one shall be appointed to you . . ." Once the agents finally placed the handcuffs on Blacka, one of them read him his rights as the other presented the physical copy of the warrant by tossing it on the ground next to where his face lay.

"Yeah, get me my lawyer so he can see how the fuck y'all got me here with my dick out and your bitch ass sitting on my back. Y'all think y'all can just handle anybody just any kind of way because of a badge around your necks." Blacka spoke freely, threatening them with actions from his lawyer, knowing that Angela's house was the safest place for the police to search without finding anything incriminating.

"Keep running your fuckin' suck muscle punk, and I'll shove an eight ball up your ass and let the K-9 tear that shit out of there," the agent pushing his knee harder into the side of Blacka's neck, spoke while applying pressure.

"What are y'all doin' in my house? What's goin' on, Blacka? Why are y'all hurting him? He didn't do nothing," Angela questioned as she was being escorted to the middle of the bedroom floor with her hands bonded behind her back.

"Just be easy, baby. They ain't hurtin' nobody over here. Bunch of bitches with guns happy to get a chance to put their hands on a man. Fuck-ass fagot won't even let a nigga put on some pants or nothing. He probably gonna go home later on an' put on his sister's dress and finger himself in the booty while sitting in the closet." Even with his face pressed into the carpet of the bedroom floor, Blacka continued to provoke the agent verbally.

"How about we play a game called suicide by cop, where you run your mouth until I feel like I've heard enough to pump a hot shot in your fuckin' skull while your girlfriend prays that I don't shove the hot nozzle of this nigger tamer in her rusty cunt and pump off three more rounds? Or you can shut the fuck up now, and I might let you live long enough to be somebody's girlfriend for the next twenty years," another agent said, who stood above Blacka with the sight of the weapon trained on his head. His black-gloved index finger was ready inside of the trigger guard of the 9 mm Heckler & Koch MP5SD3.

"Baby, please . . . Just let them do what they got to do and get out of here, please." With her face full of tears, Angela hysterically pleaded with Blacka to stop provoking the agents who were obviously eager to bring harm to him and whoever else proved to be insubordinate.

"Yeah, baby boy, listen to the pretty little lady and behave yourself before we have your face matching that sexy red dress that she has on. Hey, Agent Blue, you think maybe we have to strip search this one over here? I would hate to think that she could be hiding something up in that sweet spot of hers. The warrant does say that we have to completely search and seize *everything* on the premises." With lustful eyes, that agent slowly moved toward Angela while he still had the infrared laser sight mounted under the nozzle of the suppressed assault weapon dancing across Blacka's face.

The third step that the agent took toward Angela proved to be a bad choice as Polo lunged from under the bed and sank his teeth into his Achilles tendon. The unexpected attack from the little dog not only brought incredible pain to the agent, but it also caused his reflexes to jolt his index finger across the trigger, firing off a three-round burst in the immediate direction of Blacka and the other agent who sat on Blacka's back restraining him. Luckily for Blacka, two of the rounds missed him only by inches, penetrating the floor by his head, while the third ripped through the boot of the agent on his back and entered his foot, causing him to dismount Blacka while screaming in pain.

"Son of a bitch . . . Blue . . . Blue . . . Are you all right? Are you hit?" Shaking Polo off his leg, the agent turned and asked his comrade the obvious.

"You blew his left foot off . . . He ain't got no choice but to be all right now," Blacka comically responded while laughing at the blundering agent's accidental shooting. "Y'all probably gonna try to blame that shit on me, but that shit was funny enough that I just may take that charge on the house."

"It's time that I told you little punk ass good night before I end up bringing you down to the station in three separate plastic bags," the agent said, fed up with Blacka's antics and pissed at the fact that the Yorkshire terrier bit him. He delivered a swift kick to Blacka's temple, rendering him unconscious.

"Why are y'all doin' this to him? Just please search the house and let us be. I promise you that there is nothing here, and we didn't do anything wrong," Angela pleaded, now alone to defend herself against the infiltrating agents. She hoped they were ready to go through the procedure of searching the home at this point. She was more than positive that her house did not harbor any illegal materials, so whatever they were looking for, they were not going to find at all.

"Found it." The voice that came from the other room announced the discovery of whatever it was that they came to find. Walking into the room holding a cellphone that Blacka had left in the house over two months ago, the agent smiled as though he had found the cure for cancer.

Chapter 9

"Hello . . . Hello . . . Hello?" Frustrated with the silence on the other end of the phone, Kanisha found herself about to hang up on the anonymous caller, who seemed to refuse to acknowledge her greeting on the phone. It was the third time in the last five minutes that she had received the now harassing calls without hearing a peep from whosoever was calling. Since the call was coming in on her house phone that she barely remembered the number, she could only assume that it was just some telemarketing service that may have acquired her phone number by random selection.

"This is Global-Tel with a call from . . . Pick up the phone, Nisha . . . calling from an . . ." The computer-generated voice on the other end went unheard as Kanisha pressed the button on the cordless phone, prematurely ending the call while kissing her teeth, annoyed at the constant disturbance from her favorite reality show.

"Suga', who was that on the phone got you suckin' your teeth like you ready to tell somebody about they momma's fat, hairy ass?" her husband joked as he walked into the bedroom from out of the shower.

"Probably one of your girlfriends trying to signal you to come on over, so you better hurry your ass up. Maybe now I can watch my show in peace. Just make sure that she washes her ass and put enough money in your pocket for both of us. Let them bitches know that if they wanna play that, they got to pay what they weigh," Kanisha replied while cradling the phone base so that it would charge. Whoever wants to play phone games now will have the voicemail to deal with.

"Now, my hoes ain't did nothing for you to be calling them bitches. That is just very rude, and you need to apologize," Malachi continued to joke as he put on his Ralph Lauren flannel pajama pants, preparing to crawl up into the bed with his wife. "And what are you watching now, *The Real Housewives of Neptune*?"

"Look, Mr. Funny Man, as you can see, I'm trying to watch my show, so your little comedy act will have to wait for another hour and a half when it's over."

Malachi glanced at the screen to see what had his wife hypnotized and glued to the television with such attentiveness, only to see that it was frozen in a frame because his wife had paused the program so as not to miss a moment while briefly entertaining his antics.

"Two hours for one show . . . That a lot of time minding other people's business, ain't it? I thought these things were only an hour long." Malachi continued to speak while grabbing a pillow on the bed, ignoring Kanisha's request to be left alone.

"They are one hour . . . This is last week's episode, where she asks Bernard about the money that he claimed to have loaned her husband, and after it goes off, this week's episode comes on for an hour. So if you wanna chat, you're better off going on Facebook or something 'cause I ain't with it right now." Joking seriously, Kanisha readied the remote so that she could continue to watch as NeNe chastised Bernard.

Once again, the high-pitch digital pulse of the telephone broke through the air, alerting an incoming call. Malachi saw the look of disgust on his wife's face as she threw her head back in frustration. It cued him that he should answer the phone and deal with whoever it was that continuously called the house. The display on the caller ID read Global Tel Communications. The phone number had an area code of 407. The only thing vaguely familiar about the incoming number was that it was from the Orlando area, the same area code as Kanisha's brother's cellular phone.

"Hello!" With authority, Malachi amplified his voice through the phone receiver.

"This is Global Tel Communications with a collect call from . . . Nisha, pick up the phone . . . an inmate at an Orlando correctional facility. To hear the rates for this call, press nine; to accept, press five." Cued by the loud response from the called party, the computer-generated voice immediately kicked in, accompanied by a familiar voice.

Recognizing the voice of Blacka asking for Kanisha to pick up the phone, Malachi pressed the number five on the telephone keypad to accept the call.

"Hello . . ." Malachi once again spoke into the mouthpiece of the phone, anticipating a response.

"Goddamn, y'all got me calling y'all back-to-back n' shit while y'all playing games on the phone. This is like the fifth time that I called and somebody picked up the phone and then hung up. I mean, how hard is it to push a fuckin' button and accept the call?" Blacka immediately voiced his complaint about having to call repeatedly.

"We didn't know that was you calling all that time. For some reason, Kanisha didn't hear nothing on the other end of the phone, so she hung up. Yo . . . What the fuck happened, son? How you get locked up? You all right?" After briefly explaining the miscommunication with the telephone, Malachi began to shower Blacka with questions about his current situation.

"Man, let me tell you what bullshit they trying to say I'm in. They trying to run me in for some cocaine-trafficking shit that I ain't had nothing to do with. That nigga Dwight got caught with some shit in the rig that I let him use and gonna tell the boys that I'm the one that he runnin' the shit for. I swear to God if I ever see that moth-afucka . . ." Knowing that the phones in thc jails were monitored, Blacka explained what happened while deliberately exempting himself from guilt, although he was, without a doubt, involved to the fullest degree.

"Get the fuck out of here. That nigga was using the trucks for that when he said he was just going to be doing some commercial deliveries to make some cash to buy his own rig. I remember when you looked out for him, gave him the keys, and said he could use it as long as he maintained it. That's fucked up when you look out for people and they shit on you the first chance that they get." Continuing the charade for confidentiality, Malachi responded, assisting in pledging Blacka's innocence.

"That's why it doesn't pay to help niggas out these days. I damn sure won't be nobody's meal ticket no more. Anyway, they got Angie and me jammed up in here. I need for y'all to post her bail immediately so that she can get out of here. My baby ain't built for this shit," Blacka explained on the phone, knowing that Angie's only option for money was him, and he wasn't about to let her down no matter what.

"What about your bail? You want us to post that too, right?" Malachi asked while grabbing a pen off the dresser in preparation to write down the necessary information to post the bail immediately as requested.

"These niggas is talking about I got to wait for a federal bail hearing in the morning, but they shouldn't have any reason to hold any serious shit on Angie. Just get her out of here so she can do what she can do from the outside." Blacka already knew that they planned on dragging him through the system until either he cracked or they had concrete evidence to send him to prison. With Angie out on the street to make sure that he got the top-of-the-line lawyer to deal with his case, he should be able to fight the case that was pending against him. Besides that, the thought of her having to spend one night in jail because of his actions did not sit well with him at all.

Kanisha sat up on the bed at full attention, her ears hanging on to every word Malachi said, trying to piece together what he was saying. It was evident that somebody was calling from jail, but mentioning the truck gave her the strong feeling that her brother was somehow involved. She watched Malachi's every move keenly and continued to listen to his conversation with the strong urge to interrupt to inquire who he was talking to on the phone.

"Is Nisha there? She probably gonna flip the fuck out when she finds out about this shit here," Blacka said, dreading that the answer would be yes. The last thing he needed was for his sister to start playing the mother role and chastising him for getting into trouble.

"Yes, sir, she is sitting right here with her antennas way up in the air, trying to see what the hell I'm talking about, so I'm just gonna put her on the phone, and you can tell her everything that she is about to start asking me." Malachi handed off the phone to his wife, not wanting to be the middle man in that conversation. He knew that his wife was a drama queen that would make a speeding ticket seem like the end of the world, so he was sure that she would be damn near hysterical when she found out what her baby brother was going through.

"Hello . . . Richard . . . Where are you? What's going on? Why are you in jail?" Kanisha immediately shot a bunch of questions at her brother, forcing him to reenact the explanation he had previously given Malachi.

"Everything is going to be all right. You know you don't got to worry about me. Once they do their investigations, I should be getting out of here since I ain't have nothing to do with that shit that Dwight said I did. Y'all just make sure that Angie gets out of here ASAP and get me a lawyer that's on point. I can't have one of these public pretenders get me stuck with a life sentence." Blacka continued to pacify his sister so that she would not worry herself to a point where it affected her health. He didn't want her blood pressure to rise and possibly trigger something with her severe diabetic state.

"What I don't understand is if they caught this guy with a truckload of whatever it is that they caught him with, why are they holding *you* accountable for his actions?" Kanisha was confused about how her brother was tied into someone else's wrongdoings.

"You have one minute remaining on this call." The computer-generated voice interrupted the conversation, informing both parties that the call would be terminated in another sixty seconds.

"Listen, don't worry about me. Just get Angie out of here, and I can get any lawyer to prove I had nothing to do with this. They will have no choice but to let me go. Let me speak to Malachi real quick before this shit disconnects." Knowing that the call would soon end, Blacka once again tried to ease his sister's nerves by telling her that things would work out for the best. He wished that things were indeed that simple. He knew he could be held accountable for everything the Feds were bringing down on him with no problem. To cover his tracks, he would have to have a set of hands on the outside to make sure things get done. It was time that he fully deputized his brother-in-law until he could get a grip on the situation he was facing.

"I'm glad that you can take this shit so lightly. It must be nice not to have a care in the world when you are locked up in some white man's prison. I hope you have a good time in there while we stay out here and worry about whether somebody tries to rape you or something." Kanisha could only assume the worst could happen to her brother while he was in that jail without her there to protect him. In her eyes, he would always be the little boy hiding under the bed while she was on the phone with her friends. Little did she know that her baby brother was feared and respected by all major hustlers from the Poconos, New York, to Apple Valley, California.

"What you need to do is stop watching all of those bullshit television shows and get back to reality. There ain't no way that somebody is gonna hold me down and take my ass, so you can get that sick shit out of your head, okay? Tell Malachi that I am going to call him right back to find out about that lawyer that he said that he could get a hold of for me while you get on your phone and find out what the deal is with Angie . . ." The phone call came to an abrupt end as the time had expired. Blacka was relieved that he could make arrangements for Angela to be bailed out so that she wouldn't have to spend more time than necessary inside the jail. Now, it was time to put the words in Malachi's ear about what he needed to do.

Chapter 10

Using his index finger to hold down the receiver of the phone that hung on the wall of the inmate intake area, Blacka took a moment to think about what his next move would be. Truthfully, the Feds did have him dead to the wrong, but he was not willing to just sit back and accept the consequences of his actions. Since he was in this situation because of someone running their mouth, his best move would be to make sure that they wouldn't speak about him or anything else, for that matter. Although it would be easy to put the word out to just simply kill Dwight for his insubordination, that would leave the chance that the Feds would try to tie him to that murder and leave him back at square one. He was definitely going to have to play this like chess instead of checkers. Releasing the receiver on the phone, Blacka once again dialed the number to his sister's house to give Malachi the simple instruction that would launch a shot of retaliation in a war someone started who obviously didn't know any better. After two rings, he could hear that someone had already answered and was being given the instructions via the automated system.

"Yo, it's me, bruh. Kanisha told me you was about to call back, so I took the phone downstairs while she found out about Angela. She said something about a lawyer, but I thought you said that you were gonna have your girl do that when she gets out," Malachi spoke into the phone while walking down the stairs of the two-story home, making sure to be out of earshot of his wife, knowing that Blacka wanted to talk about more than just a lawyer.

"Yeah, Angie can take care of all that when she gets out. That will be no problem at all, but right now, I need you to do something else for me," Blacka said, getting straight to the point. "Call up Isis and tell her that I got locked up down here in Orlando, and I want her to come and see me ASAP. I need for her to do some things for me."

"Don't she stay out in North Carolina? What if she say that she can't make it out to see you?" Malachi asked, wondering why Blacka would have to see Isis when he had to deal with the snitch in his camp.

Holding the phone two inches away from his face, Blacka shook his head, closed his eyes, gritted his teeth together in frustration, and spoke in a low growl. "I didn't tell you to *ask* her. I told you to *tell* her to come and see me."

"All right, bruh. I'm gonna call her right now and let her know what you said. I got you." Hearing the tone of Blacka's voice, Malachi immediately felt it to be in everybody's best interest to just do as Blacka requested.

"Once she gets here and we sit down and talk, we should have this whole thing figured out. But in the meantime, I need you to collect all the money I got scattered out there before people spend beyond my means, you feel me?" Blacka would not let his absence from the street allow his income to come to a crashing halt while he sat in jail.

"So, what are you gonna do now, bruh? This nigga done told on you and put you in a jam. That shit can't just sit like that," he said, looking up the stairway to make sure that his wife was still preoccupied upstairs and not listening in to his conversation. Malachi wanted to see where Blacka's head was at.

"First of all, the nigga didn't tell on me because I ain't do shit for anybody to tell. What happened is the punk-ass coward got caught doing some bullshit, and he's trying to use me as a scapegoat, but that shit ain't gonna fly. Once I get the right lawyer on my team, these country mothafuckas are gonna have to let me up out of here." Once again annoyed at Malachi's reckless talking, Blacka spoke, declaring his innocence to all accusations.

Catching his mistake, Malachi finally took into consideration what Blacka was going through and what the possible consequences could be. It had only been a couple of months since he was affiliated with his business, but in the little bit of time that he was a part of the organization, he counted more money than he had earned with his previous job that he held for seven years. It was just getting to the point where he had caught up on all the household debts he and Kanisha had accumulated over the years. Now, he was ready to splurge a little bit. With Blacka in prison, the lifestyle that he was just getting accustomed to would come to an immediate halt. And unless, by some miracle, Chase Bank decided to rehire the 2,000 employees who were laid off due to downsizing, he was about to be without an income to take care of his family. After sitting back and watching the habit of millions of Americans paying for things he struggled daily to afford, Malachi wasn't excited about rejoining society as a mere working-class citizen.

"You right, bruh. You know that I know that you ain't have nothing to do with whatever that nigga had going on, and soon, they'll have proof of that. Just keep a cool head, and shit will fall into place. I'm gonna call Isis and make sure she get down to you. We damn sure don't need you locked up for some bullshit you ain't got nothing to do with," Malachi said, trying to make up for his previous flaw. Malachi once again added his subliminal testimony of his brother-in-law's innocence. Taking a deep breath and a brief mental contemplation of the consequences of asking an already frustrated Blacka any questions, he conjured up the nerve to ask, "So, I guess somebody has to tell everybody that they are on vacation until we get this shit settled, or do you got somebody to keep shit in motion while you are away?"

"Listen, bruh. Right now, the only thing I can concentrate on is how I'm gonna get these people off my back. Everything else is just gonna have to wait. I spent my time feeding that motherfucka and his family, and in a blink of an eye, he turns his ass up at me and shits all over my face." Blacka spoke while noticing a deputy sheriff approaching the holding cell with keys in his hand.

"I feel what you saying, bruh, but you can't let one monkey stop the show. We got a business to run and our families to feed. What it boils down to is that it is always gonna be family first, so that's what we got to live by. I ain't been sleeping for the last couple of months, so I know what to do and how to make sure it gets done. All you got to do is say the word, and I will handle everything that needs to be done with no problems. You already know that with me, loyalty is not just a word. It's a lifestyle." Malachi put forth his speech of persuasion, hoping his brother-in-law would reconsider shutting down all operations while he was away.

"Nelson!" The wiry-framed sheriff barked surprisingly louder than expected from such a small man. "Richard Nelson, you have one minute to get ready for transport to the interview room."

Using a hand gesture, Blacka acknowledged the deputy's order. He prepared to end the call with his brother-in-law. "I'm gonna hold you to those words, and for my sister's sake, I hope you live up to them. These people are calling for me to go to some interview shit.

Probably gonna shine some bright light in my eye or some shit to get me to confess like them clowns on that show *The Next 48*."

"Let them do what they want. The truth will always stay the same. You ain't have nothing to do with that shit, and that's all to it. Tell them mothafuckas to pull out the waterboard and cow prod because they just wasting their fuckin' time," Malachi lightly joked.

"I don't know about inviting these boys to put a cow prod to my nuts, especially since Polo had done bit a chunk out of one of them, making him shoot the other dick in the foot," Blacka said while laughing for the first time.

"What?" Malachi said in shock.

"Let me get off this jack and see what they talking about. Just do what I asked and do what you said you would. Tomorrow, Reef and his boy is supposed to be dropping off something for me. Tell them to keep that, and there is more to come for some shit that I want them to handle. I will holla at y'all probably tonight or tomorrow. And tell Nisha not to worry about nothin'." Placing the handset on the receiver of the phone, Blacka approached the cell door in preparation to be shackled up for transport.

Disconnecting his end of the line with a push of a button, a grin of satisfaction engulfed Malachi's face. The thought of having the whole operation under his control, even for a short period, should drastically change his financial situation, which could only be much better than his current situation. Using the connects already in motion, it would only be a matter of time before he gained the same respect that his brother-in-law had. Only he would be sure to be much more cautious about who he lets in on the operations. However, his fantasy of becoming an overnight kingpin paused when his wife's voice from the top of the stairs called him back to reality.

"Babe, is Richard still on the phone?" Kanisha inquired.

"He just hung up the phone because he was about to go to some interview room for questioning or something. He said not to worry yourself to death about him and just find out what the bail will be for Angela and post it as soon as possible," he said, walking up the stairway.

"He ain't got to worry about Angie because I just called the jail, and they said that they never processed her, and when I called her on her cellphone, she picked up on the second ring," Kanisha spoke while staring at her husband straight in his eyes as though she was searching for something as he ascended the stairway.

"That's good. Now he can at least have that off his mind while he fights these bullshit charges that they're trying to press on him." He noticed his wife's curious stare, so Malachi slowed his pace as he could only wonder what was on her mind.

"Bullshit, Malachi? Angie wonders if there is more to this than what we know. And tell me something. Were you ever gonna tell me that you got fired, or were you gonna keep up the story about you leaving to help Richard out with his so-called business?"

Chapter 11

Stuck at the window of the small room, Dwight studied every car that passed down the narrow street. He was so paranoid that he wouldn't let his guard down long enough to shower. Since he got the news from Braxton that Blacka had been arrested by federal agents a few days ago, Dwight's nerves had been on fire in anticipation of some form of retaliation from the two men that he feared more than God himself.

It was apparent to Sandra that something was wrong with him and that something or someone had him scared of his own shadow. She found his behavior extremely bizarre and was starting to worry about whatever had his mind bending in every direction at once. At first, by how he would grab his phone to make discreet calls at the same time every night, she automatically thought that he was involved with another woman and was ready to confront him about it. Her suspicions of his infidelity were so strong that she was about tell him to pack his things and go let that other woman pick up after him and clean his dirty drawers . . . until she accidentally walked in the room and caught the butt end of one of those late-night phone calls. Then she definitely knew it wasn't a woman who had his attention. It was something far more serious. Often, she spotted him sitting by that same window, mumbling incoherently while banging his forehead with the palm of his hand. It all started the same day that he came home ranting about her being the reason that he was late to some important meeting that he had for that day.

"Dwight . . . Food is ready for you whenever you want to eat, babes," Sandra said, holding the plate of curry chicken with white rice. She nervously spoke loud enough for Dwight to hear, only to get the same silence that had been making her nervous in her own home. It had been two days since she noticed that he wasn't eating anything. His diet now consisted of Newports, weed, and Dr. Pepper, which did not add to his already small frame.

"Babe, you have to eat something or at least talk to me and let me know what's going on. Whatever it is, it can't be that serious," she said, trying to break the barrier of silence that Dwight had constructed between them. She attempted to get him to open up and say something, whether it be what was bothering him or even if he told her to shut her mouth and mind her own business. She just wanted some form of communication. By the look on his face as he slowly turned in her direction, exposing only his profile, she could tell that something she said may have just been the key to opening him up.

"Not that serious . . ."

Although she witnessed his mouth move, the low voice that came from within was barely recognizable to her. It was the voice of a broken spirit, not the aggressive, smooth-talking man who would make her feel safe knowing that he had the confidence of a lion in its natural habitat. Dwight spoke as though he was on the verge of tears, and the glimmer in his watery eyes made it look like he had been crying.

"Talk to me, baby. It's been days now, and you haven't so much as said hello. The kids are scared to even come near you." That was truly how she felt about herself, but she used the children to attempt to touch a sensitive side of him in order for him to confide in her. Never being one to pressure him or any other man to speak his mind, Sandra was trying a new tactic.

"Better if they didn't even know me right about now. 'Cause of me, they may never make it to school in the mornin'." The words flew out of his mouth before he could think about them. Even in his state of a near-anxiety attack, he was aware that he said something that would alarm Sandra.

"Something wrong with the car, babes? Is that what's bothering you? We can take a bus if that's what's got you worried." Naïve to what Dwight was subliminally trying to say, Sandra assumed that they would not be able to attend school the next day because of car trouble.

For a moment, Dwight thought to himself that he should just allow her to be left in the dark about the whole situation, but since their days were numbered, he would let her know exactly what was going on. Maybe she could pack up the kids and head somewhere out of harm's way, but he was aware of the lengths that Reef and Dummy would go to just to get to their targets, so he was convinced that running would only delay the inevitable.

"There's nothing wrong with the car, munchkin. I wish it was something that was simple enough to fix." Using his pet name for Sandra, he extended his hand toward her to embrace her as he broke the news. He figured this would help calm her down when she broke out into the hysterical crying he expected.

Sandra approached him slowly, still holding the plate of food in her hand. Her mind was thinking of what it could be that he had to tell her. This was a side of Dwight that she was unfamiliar with, and she did not like it at all. This timid man who sat before her was making her uncomfortable, and she could no longer give him the title of the man of the house. But her feelings for who he truly was and what he would do for her and her children, without any remorse, was more than enough for her to help him overcome his troubles. She would stand at his side like a real woman would for the man she loved. Taking his hand with hers, she looked into his watery eyes and prepared to tell him that whatever he was going through, he didn’t have to go through it alone. But before she could speak words of her affection, Dwight continued.

“Reef and Dummy are vexed with me, and they said they are gonna do something to you and the kids—” Before he could finish his statement, he felt the hot West Indian cuisine, immediately followed by the impact of the stoneware plate that Sandra violently drove into the center of his face, knocking him backward off the wooden table chair that he was posted in.

` “Ah wha’ you ah talk about, Dwight? What the fuck you mean by that?” In an excited rant, Sandra’s emotions jumped from concern about what was troubling the man in her life to being frantic over the welfare of her precious children. She was finished with tiptoeing around Dwight’s bruised ego. She would do whatever it took to discover what was happening and how it concerned her children.

Although he got what he well deserved, Dwight did not anticipate that that would be her reaction. Looking up from the ground, wiping the Indian spice from out of his face, he saw rage in her eyes as she hoisted her foot off the ground with intentions to stomp in his face. Quickly maneuvering out of the way of her wooden-heeled sandal, he found himself trapped against the wall of the window where he had been stationed for the last few days. The kicks he felt delivered to his back weren’t as hard as they were repetitive. Sandra used the side of the window frame as leverage as she made a strong effort to kick an explanation out of him. Her anger was well warranted since he sat there for the past few days with knowledge of potential danger to her and the children, and all this coward could do was sit in the corner and cry.

"Listen to me, baby girl. It's not my fault, at least not all of it. The police fucked up everything by showing their face at the wrong time. I tried to save my ass, and they jumped the gun. Now, they know what the deal is . . . and I know they do." He lay in a fetal position, trying to protect his vital areas from the kicks Sandra continuously delivered. He tried to explain the situation. For her to fully understand, he knew he would have to tell her everything, even the parts he was ashamed of. She would definitely look at him differently when she found out exactly what he had gotten himself involved in.

With her leg exhausted from expressing her anger on Dwight's spine, Sandra paused momentarily to hear the words that this coward had to say. She was well aware of who the men were through the stories that Dwight would tell her. Most of them sounded like urban legends of carnage that would be used as scary campfire stories. The thought that these monsters had bad intentions for her and her children made the hairs on her neck stand on end with a combination of fear and anger. She feared them, but her rage was projected at Dwight for bringing this chaos into her life. Tears welled up in her eyes as her leg slowed. She needed answers to questions that she didn't even know how to ask, but somehow, she was going to have to rectify this, even if it meant that she delivered Dwight's dead body to their front door.

"Tell me, Dwight, why are those sick friends of yours coming to do us some harm when we have nothing to do with whatever you are involved in? Hell, we don't even get any kind of real money from you for the bills around here," Sandra chastised as she made a last attempt to kick him in the back of his head that he did his best to keep it well-guarded.

“They’ve got me in a bind, and it’s too fuckin’ late for me to get out of it . . . I should have told them no from the start, but now, it’s over . . .” Dwight gasped out the incoherent words barely audible enough for Sandra to comprehend. His thoughts rushed through his mind so rapidly that it didn’t leave room for the pain in his back to be a factor. Sitting up, using the wall to brace himself, he placed the palms of his hands on his face, masking his eyes so that the tears that were about to fall wouldn’t be visible.

The sight of him in this weakened state only angered Sandra further. She had no more time to pacify his emotions, especially if the life of her children was at risk. After a slight pause, her eyes traveled across the room toward the cabinet above the refrigerator. She charged toward the cabinet and swung it open. A chill of satisfaction surged through her body as her fingertips found what she was searching for.

She gripped the polymer handle of the Glock 27 that Dwight kept in the kitchen for protection. She quickly pulled back the steel slide with aggression. She was very familiar with handling a gun since Dwight ensured she could protect herself whenever he was not at home. She was raised in the streets of Brooklyn. Her choice of men had always been hustlers who ended up in jail or dead, so she was far from naïve toward the art of urban combat. By the weight of the firearm, she was aware that it was fully loaded with hollow-tip bullets designed to explode on impact. She was fully prepared to perforate Dwight from head to toe if he did not man up and bring resolution to this deadly situation. The sound of the metal slide registering the .40-caliber hollow tip in the chamber had drawn Dwight’s attention as she maneuvered her way toward him.

“This is the last time I will ask you, and then you can speak your piece to God himself.” With the barrel of the gun resting on the bridge of Dwight's nose, Sandra made it crystal clear that she was no longer tolerating his behavior.

Sitting there, feeling the cold metal pressed against his face, Dwight could feel his eyes crossing as he looked at the angry woman standing before him. The thought of provoking her to pull the trigger to end his misery crossed his mind but was immediately removed by one fact. He was a coward. The thought of getting shot was not something that he was ready for at all. It was time to come clean and let her know exactly what put him in the predicament that he was in . . . a predicament that was guaranteed to make her look at him differently and probably kill him regardless. He was ashamed of what he had become, all at the cost of keeping himself out of trouble. Had he taken responsibility for his actions and accepted the charge of trafficking narcotics instead of making a deal with the detectives at the precinct, he would never have been in this jam. Now, he was one of the lowest forms of life in the urban community . . . he was a confidential informant whose identity was no longer confidential.

Using the gun's muzzle as his focus point, Dwight began to explain how his travel home on the Brooklyn-Queens Expressway turned into the worst night of his hustling career. After being detained in what seemed to be a routine traffic stop where the police searched his vehicle once they found out what was in the rear of the truck he was driving, Dwight regretted the one mistake that he made. Instead of going straight to Brooklyn like he was supposed to, he used the extra time that he felt that he had to stop and get an ounce of Grand Daddy Purple from his Puerto Rican connect Pito out in Newark, New Jersey, only to find himself in a police holding cell. After hours of sitting in the one-window room without anything but his thoughts, the door swung open for the entrance of two detectives. These weren't the same men who pulled him over, but they knew who he was.

It turned out that his trips out of town to different states and back had not gone unnoticed by the city's narcotic task unit, as they had been watching him for quite some time. They noticed his truck making various trips transporting narcotics from a location in Queens to multiple points throughout Brooklyn. One evening, he led them right to the home of Richard Nelson, who was suspected to be the possible leader of the operation.

It had been only a few weeks since the brutal sacrificial-like killing that took place in Brownsville of a known drug dealer, and Dwight's truck being spotted entering the scene of the crime only hours before made him a great place to start questioning. It wasn't too long after the interrogation Dwight broke down. He involuntarily spurted out that although he was not involved in the killing, he did hear a rumor about a man named Blacka, who was said to have been responsible for hiring two men to execute the murder.

He felt as though his back was against the wall as the police threatened to use the surveillance footage to tie him in with the murder if he did not cooperate in apprehending Blacka. The police offered him exemption from all charges if he provided substantial proof that Richard Nelson was indeed head of operations and was responsible for the heinous killing of Troy Mandel. It didn't take any time for Dwight to agree to entrap Blacka into admitting his crime while recording him with the surveillance equipment that would be installed in the interior of his vehicle. At the time, it appeared to be a quick solution to get him out of a bind. Besides selling weed to these men, he had no personal ties to them, so why should he put their freedom in front of his own?

With the gun now lowered to her side, Sandra stood before him with her mouth wide open as she absorbed the drama-filled story that she was being told. The look on her face transformed from rage to confusion as she watched as every syllable fell out of Dwight's mouth. The palm of her hand started to sweat around the polymer grip of the pistol as she subconsciously tightened her fingers around it. She wanted to ask so many questions but didn't know where to start, so she said the first thing that came to mind: "Why?"

"What else could I do, Sandra? They were threatening me with the murder charges and the dope charges. If I didn't agree to something, it was gonna be my ass on the line, but I didn't think it would come to this." Dwight looked up through teary eyes. His heart felt a brief relief that his ears heard the sound of her voice rather than the sound of a gunshot, which meant there was time to negotiate out of his immediate demise. Feeling ashamed of his behavior and realizing that the gun was no longer pointed at him, Dwight sat up straight in an attempt to regain his composure. It was time that he buckled up and took action to protect his loved ones. Suddenly, an idea surged through his mind that could possibly assist in keeping everyone safe. He would ask the detectives to place his family under protective custody until they apprehended Reef and Dummy.

"What are you doing?" Sandra asked, raising the gun from her side. She spoke in a dangerously soft voice as she watched Dwight reaching into his pockets. The man she was living with was obviously a stranger to her at this point, seeing that so much was going on in his life that she was utterly in the dark about. The fact that he never confided in her with any of this was something that really bothered her and made her trust level in him decrease incredibly low. She took all precautions with Dwight as though he were a hostile, captured criminal.

"Just getting my phone, babe. I'm going to call the police and tell them that I need you guys in protective custody until I can take care of everything. Put down the gun, baby girl, and let me do this before it's too late." He paused with his palms facing Sandra in a form of surrender. Dwight tried to soothe the angry woman while letting her know he had a solution for their problem, but it had to be initiated immediately.

"What makes you think they can do that, Dwight? You think those police give a fuck about you or me and the kids? They just want you to do their job for them at whatever risk that it may cost you or your family, you fuckin' fool!" Projecting her anger through her voice, Sandra's hands began to shake in front of Dwight's face as though she had Parkinson's disease. She was angry and scared, not knowing who to trust. She was on the verge of an anxiety attack. She slid her finger into the trigger guard of the pistol and contemplated blowing this man's head clean off of his body.

"That's the only choice we have right now, baby. Without the cops, what can we do but sit here and be scared, waiting to get killed? You heard about how they found that mothafucka Troy. Do you think these niggas play games? It's time to get some kind of protection."

Speaking up for the first time, Dwight put his fears aside and explained to Sandra that although their options were limited, it was time to exercise them. Ignoring the weapon in his face, he got his phone out of his pocket and began dialing the number for the investigator's department. Within moments, an operator answered.

"Homicide Department, how may I direct your call?" the nasal voice on the other end of the phone answered.

"May I speak to Investigator Braxton, please," Dwight replied. "Yes, I will hold."

Sandra stood across from him attentively, once again watching his lips as they moved as though she were hearing impaired. Convinced that Dwight was wasting her time, she was thinking of an alternate route of getting out of harm's way, even if it meant packing up and leaving the state tonight. She was already familiar with Georgia from when she lived with her baby father, Adrian, in Arbor Glen Apartments on Godby Road in College Park in 2000. Watching Dwight stand there holding the phone, waiting to speak with whoever he called was driving her insane. She found herself pacing while glancing out the same window that Dwight had been stationed at for the last few days in the same paranoid fashion.

Chapter 12

"Homicide . . . Special Investigator Braxton speaking . . ." the deep voice answered the phone after a two-minute wait.

"Yeah, Braxton, this is Dwight. Aye, man, these dudes are threatening my girl, and I need y'all to get her and her kids into some kind of protective location before these niggas do something crazy." Speaking loudly without yelling, Dwight asserted himself to show Sandra he was putting a strong foot forward to get results.

"Who is this . . . Dwight? Not the same Dwight that has been dickin' me around and has yet to provide anything helpful in this situation. The same Dwight that doesn't answer my calls or return my messages about coming in to make a recorded statement? Had me starting to think I was calling some bitch begging for some pussy. I know that's not the voice of someone who is delinquent on his side of the deal, calling me with demands that I take care of your girlfriend. Do you have anything to bring to the table, or should we just come pick you up now and run you in on this murder charge and get an easy conviction? The footage of you entering the residence a few hours before the body was discovered is enough evidence for even a jury full of blind Baptist preachers to see that you're guilty." Showing his authority, Braxton boomed into the phone to remind Dwight precisely who was in charge and in the position to make any demands.

Not concerned with his girlfriend's welfare, Braxton turned a deaf ear to his request. Being a fifteen-year veteran with the unit, Braxton has encountered countless informants, and all of them were the same. They were cowards who would rather see someone else receive consequences that they were terrified to accept for themselves most of the time. It didn't take much for someone to give up information on an acquaintance. Although informants have served as a valuable tool in solving many crimes, Braxton was disgusted that these individuals exercised no honor or loyalty in their lives.

"Listen, I told you the same day that you guys pulled me over for no good reason and almost got me killed. I can't make no promises to you until y'all can do something to protect me. I gave y'all the recording of what they was talking about inside the car. That should be enough to show that I'm trying to work with y'all, but y'all gotta work with me some." Dwight quickly defended himself, reminding the investigator that he had given him an audio recording of their conversation inside the Nissan. He emphasized how bitter he was that Braxton and his partner, Stephens, pulled him over on a bogus traffic stop, causing the suspicion of the deadly Jamaicans.

"And I told you there wasn't nothing on there that I can use. Besides that goddamn jungle talk, the only thing I could hear was your teeth chattering like a wet monkey left in the cold." Not satisfied with the contents of the recording, Braxton still pressured Dwight to get something that could hold some weight in the courtroom to guarantee a conviction. If he got these guys, he wanted to make sure he could hold them.

"What you mean that wasn't any good? We spoke about what happened in the house and how somebody might have saw them." Now holding the phone directly in front of his mouth, Dwight didn't understand why they couldn't go off what was on the tape.

"No. We have *you* talking on the tape about the crime scene, and we hear only one other voice that didn't say anything implicating that he was involved in any crimes. Hell, the other guy in the car didn't say anything at all." Braxton nonchalantly spoke into the phone with no compassion toward anything that Dwight was saying.

"How many times do I have to tell you that he don't talk 'cause he *can't* talk, so how is he going to say something? What do you want me to do—get him to write you a fuckin' note?" Now angered, Dwight shouted back into the phone as he noticed Sandra pause from her pacing with a strange look on her face. She darted across the room toward the closet and grabbed two suitcases tucked in the back corner.

"Listen, when you have something that we can use, bring it in, and in the meantime, I don't wanna hear no damn crying from you about you needing a fuckin' babysitter. Either that or turn yourself in for the trafficking and murder charges, and this case will be closed. The choice is yours." Hanging up the phone, Braxton used a scare tactic to ensure that Dwight would do as he agreed upon and bring him something to close this case that he honestly had no leads for.

Frustrated, Dwight held on to the dead phone line. He watched Sandra stuffing her children's belongings into the suitcases. She looked determined as she scanned the area for all the necessities that would fit in the bags. Where she could be going was a mystery to him, and he dared not ask.

She no longer clutched the handgun next to the bags and was more focused on getting out of there. She no longer had any questions to ask or any further things to discuss because it was evident from the conversation Dwight just had with the police that her safety was not something that he or the police could guarantee. She hurried up and packed what she needed to pick up the kids and be on the road to safety, far away from Dwight's chaos within minutes. There was no turning back at all as far as she was concerned. This son of a bitch jeopardized her life just so that he could stay out of a jail cell, and that was not the type of man that she could continue to lie in a bed with.

"What did you expect, dumbass? A black limousine to pull up front and take us off to a secret location in the mountains somewhere while you play superhero and catch the bad guys? Did you *really* think those police care about what happens to you or me?" Without pausing to gather her belongings, Sandra mocked Dwight's plan of getting assistance from the police. The thought of them lifting a finger to help her and her kids sounded ridiculous to her from the very start.

"I had to give it a try. It was the best thing I could come up with that could benefit us right now," he said. He reached into the same closet to retrieve a duffel bag to accommodate his belongings as he prepared to follow Sandra's lead and get as far away from here as possible. They could go somewhere far, start a new life, and leave all this foolishness behind.

"Benefit *us?* Let me tell you what would benefit *us* right now. What would benefit *us* is that there will be no more *us!* I am getting away from you and your shit right fuckin' now. Don't follow me, don't look for me, just stay the fuck away from me and my kids with that crazy shit! When you gamble on somebody's life, make sure it's your own and leave mine out of the equation!" Taking a moment from packing, Sandra made it abundantly clear that she wanted nothing to do with whatever Dwight had planned for the future because they were through. She regretted the day that she allowed his small-time, hustling ass into her life.

"Where you going to go, baby girl? I can't just let you go out there and defend yourself if they catch up with you." Stunned at her decision to leave, Dwight made a plea for her to reconsider, although deep down, he knew he had no right to ask her to stay by his side.

"Catch up with me? You better hope they don't catch up with me because the first thing I'm going to do is tell them exactly where they can find your ass. Shit, I'll drive them to your mama's house and tell them to tear that bitch apart just for giving birth to a worthless piece of shit like you!"

Zipping up the first bag, Sandra continued to badger Dwight to let him know that there was no alliance between them, and she was closing this chapter in her life without any plans of ever reopening. She was ready to negotiate Dwight's whole family with her predators just to show how much she despised him.

Her words brought a brief moment of rage within Dwight, causing him to rush across the room to physically confront this woman who made a threat that he took seriously. There was one thing that he was overly sensitive about, and that was his mother. As a single mom, she raised Dwight while attending college and working her ass off to make sure that he had all that he needed. Knowing that Sandra and his mother never really got along because of the number of children she had for a woman who had never been married, he didn't put it past her to do such a horrible thing. Regardless of whether she meant it, the fact that she referred to his mother as "that bitch" was not something he was going to tolerate, especially from someone who was walking out the door to go her separate way.

All the frustration that he was going through with the police and living in fear of his own shadow because of the men he betrayed came to a boil. Balling his fist back in the air like an Aztec warrior in battle, he lunged forward, intending to knock Sandra's head off her shoulders. However, it took less than a second for him to realize that mistake might end up being his last. Snatching the gun up from next to the bag, Sandra aimed and fired three shots, one piercing Dwight through the bicep of his right arm. Standing there with one hand holding the smoking gun, Sandra didn't so much as blink or show any sign of remorse as the Aztec warrior screamed in agony while clutching his arm that was bleeding profusely.

"You really think I am about to let a weak little man put his hands on me? Your bitch ass was just balled up in the corner scared of the boogeyman, but you got the strength to come and hit a woman?" Talking between her teeth and snarled lips, Sandra aimed Dwight as he scurried to take cover behind the wall that divided the living room and the hallway leading to the bedroom. Training her right eye on the sight of the pistol, she fired two rounds that penetrated the wall only inches from Dwight's head. Although he wasn't visible, she could hear him bumping into the walls trying to find refuge in the bedroom.

"Stop playing, woman! You shot me in the arm!" From behind the bedroom door, Dwight grunted through the pain that was surging through his arm. He was losing blood rapidly and felt trapped and helpless.

With the only alternate way of leaving the apartment being the window, Dwight stumbled over toward it to execute his escape. He opened the window to the second-floor Brooklyn apartment, stuck his leg onto the fire escape, and ducked down through the window. Closing the window to secure all barriers that were between him and Sandra, who was firing three more shots through the bedroom door, he prepared to descend the iron ladder that led to the street. The pain in his arm was hindering his movements more than he had expected, so getting down the ladder wasn't going to be as easy as he had anticipated, but his options were very limited. Either deal with the bullet in his arm and get the hell out of there or stay and catch a bullet in his skull from an angry woman. Grabbing the side of the iron rail with his left hand, he looked down at the street and nearly lost his balance, almost falling below to the asphalt.

A car was there that hadn't been there very long. He was positive because it was the same car he was gazing out of the window, hoping *not* to see. The black and grey two-toned 1993 Mercury Grand Marquis with a chrome finish sat idling directly across the street from Dwight's bedroom window with dancehall tunes from the early nineties sounding from the speakers. It was them . . . the two men who knew that he planned on betraying them and vowed to bring harm to his family for his act of insubordination. They sat in the vehicle with their eyes locked on Dwight from the moment he had stepped out of the window.

Dwight's heart stopped as he saw the tinted window of the car slowly roll down. Time seemed to freeze as a hand extended from the vehicle with the index finger pointing in Dwight's direction. In a hypnotic state, Dwight's eyes follow the direction the finger was pointed, leading him to the window that he just used to escape a violently escalating domestic situation. In the window, he saw the hostile woman struggling to lift the window. It had gotten off track when he slammed it closed. Feeling as though he were caught between the devil and hell, he closed his eyes, silently pleading with God to provide him with some form of miracle to get him out of the trial and tribulation that he was currently in.

"Get the fuck back in here, big man! A minute ago, you was big and bad, ready to whip my ass, remember?" Finally forcing the window open, Sandra stuck her head out, waving the gun back and forth. The steel slide was retracted since the weapon had expended all eight rounds. Although she was out of ammunition, her adrenaline had her pumped up enough to fight this man fist to fist right there on the fire escape, if necessary.

"We ah go let you and wifey sort out your little problems, and we will check you later, bredren." The sound of an approaching police siren accompanied the voice that yelled from the dark car across the street. Evidently, someone must have reported the sound of multiple gunshots being fired. The Mercury then casually pulled out of the parking spot and proceeded down the block at the exact moment when three police cars came screeching to a halt below the fire escape that Dwight was using as a refuge.

Chapter 13

He sat in front of the two-way video monitor, awaiting the start of his noncontact visit from the person he could only hope could help him in his present situation. It has been over a week since he spoke to anyone outside of the correctional facility he was residing in for an undetermined time. Blacka used that time of solitude to conjure up a plan of revenge against the coward who betrayed him—a plan whose only flaw was that he would not be able to see it delivered firsthand.

Waiting for the blank video screen to come to life to reveal the identity of his visitor, Blacka used the dull reflection from the monitor to groom himself. No matter the situation, he felt that the appearance of a man was a definition of his character. The tangerine-orange polyester, state-issued jumpsuit, and white T-shirt were far from the designer clothing he had grown accustomed to caressing his skin. Even the soap issued to the inmates seemed to dry his skin to a point where only a hefty amount of lotion could be used to conceal his dry, leathery skin. Just then, the screen illuminated, revealing his visitor, who turned out to be the very person that he needed to initiate his retaliation against his enemy. Without hesitation, he picked up the handset cradled next to the video monitor.

"You look like you getting ready for an interview with Barbara Walters or somebody the way you getting your swag together. I hope you ain't disappointed that it's just little ol' me," the voice of his longtime friend, Isis, came through the receiver of the phone while the half-a-second delay on the video screen made it appear that her lips were still moving, although she was through talking. Even the glitches in the video setup couldn't mask the beautiful facial features of the tall, bronze-skinned goddess whose complexion was accented by the fiery-red, shoulder-length locks that only added excitement to the already-stunning woman.

"I prefer to see your face more than anything else right now, besides freedom, of course, but you know that ain't coming no time soon. What's good with you, baby girl? I'm glad that you made it down here so quickly." With a debonair grin, Blacka spoke to his friend, who had proven more reliable than anyone he knew. No matter what time of the day or how long of a distance to travel, Isis always made it her priority to do whatever was necessary to assist him when needed.

"Your brother called me on the phone, gave me your message, and then called me every two hours since. Kept asking if I left yet and how long it would take me to get here. I started to fuck with him and said that I was gonna drive because I was scared of flying, and that man damn near had a heart attack talking about 'Blacka said this' and 'Blacka said that.' Why you got that man under pressure like that?" With her index finger, Isis played with a single lock of her hair while speaking into the phone handset.

"Shit, that man wanna act like a boss, so he gotta be able to do boss shit. If he can't do something as simple as delivering a message, then I really ain't got no use for his ass. You should have told his ass to pay for your ticket and hotel just to see if he had the heart to tell you no." Laughing at the expense of his ambitious brother-in-law, Blacka could share a genuine laugh with a true friend.

"You already know that I had to try him just to see where his head was at," Isis said while silently admiring her longtime friend. Even on a computer screen wearing a raggedy orange jumpsuit, Blacka still had a certain animal magnetism to him that built the foundation of her unspoken fantasies. "Not only did he pay for the ticket, but I got a chance to let the locks blow in the wind in the convertible Mustang that he so gladly paid the rental fee for. Messing with your ass, I probably would have had to get on the Greyhound. You better take notes from that boy and learn a little something."

"I damn sure ain't about to sign up for any class that he's teaching. Only thing that I can learn from him is that a sucker is born every day. Besides, any fool can spend money that they have, but is he willing to ride you up Utica Avenue on the handlebars of his bike just so you could get home before your moms did?" Rekindling an old childhood memory that he and Isis shared, Blacka looked directly at the camera at the top of the monitor to ensure that she saw his full facial expression snarled the left side of his lip in a sarcastic manner.

"How long you plan on playing that old card, boy? That shit was years ago, and you always leave out the part about you having to stop eight times 'cause that hill was killing you," she said, laughing at the memory of a younger Blacka struggling up the hill with his skinny arms trembling under the pressure of balancing her on the handlebars.

"See, you got the story all fucked up . . . I stopped nine times, and it was only because the chain kept coming off of the bike. You already know that a nigga got that natural Zulu strength. I could have ran up that hill with you on my shoulders with a full cup of water and not have spilled a drop," Blacka said, flexing his arm in view of the camera. He contested Isis's much more realistic version of the story. "Besides, you had your damn hair all in my face, stopping me from seeing the road ahead of me."

"Boy, you really need to stop that shit. You was half a block away from catching a damn heart attack," Isis replied, using laughter to conceal her hidden desire for Blacka's strong chocolate frame. She wiped the tears that filled up her hazel eyes. Since her adolescent days of attending public school, she had a silent crush that only grew stronger as they both matured. Never did she openly reveal how she felt for him while watching him grow closer to a woman that she never thought met up to the standards that she hoped he had for himself. "Now, I know that you ain't have me come down here to talk about what we were doing when we were kids. Tell me what the fuck is really going on."

"One of the drivers got caught with a load of shit in one of the trucks that we contract out, and the bitch nigga gone and told the boys that I was running shit up and down the East Coast. Now, they are trying to connect me to some other shit that may be nationwide. So, now they got me chained down in here while the mothafucka that is supposed to be in here is running the streets while they make me out to be some kind of kingpin." Blacka began to tell Isis everything that he knew so far. She already knew the ins and outs of Blacka's operations, so she knew he was indeed the person who authorized the shipment in that truck and was fully aware of its contents. But she also realized that for the sake of his possibly upcoming trial, he shouldn't speak recklessly where any monitoring ears could interpret an admission of guilt to the crimes that he was trying to be proven innocent of. Reading his facial expression on the video monitor, she could decipher what he was really trying to say without using words that may incriminate him further than the testimony of the insubordinate employee who turned him in.

Continuing to tell of his apprehension, Blacka stared directly into the camera's lens to guarantee that Isis had full view of his face so she could fully comprehend his words. The more he spoke of the situation, the more his rage built up within him to the point where he found himself gripping the receiver of the phone with such intensity that every vein in his right arm appeared above his skin's surface. He spoke of how, with his assistance, Dwight could stop the bank from foreclosing on their home since they could no longer afford the mortgage on their fixed income. He told of the product that he gave to his younger brothers in Georgia that was guaranteed to bring back a profit of over $200,000, and he has only received ten thousand, along with a promise to have the rest delivered as soon as possible.

He went on for a few minutes about how he handed Dwight $8,000 in cash so that he could buy a car for his pregnant girlfriend and the five kids that didn't belong to him just so that she didn't have to drag them on the bus to go to school every morning and that he did expect to be repaid. The one thing he emphasized with everyone within his circle was loyalty. To him, it was much more than a word. It was a lifestyle, a lifestyle that Dwight was evidently not a part of, and for that act of treason, he was ready to strip away all that he had done for him in the worst way.

"You mean to tell me that you shelled out eight grand to some broad that you ain't even fuckin' just so that she don't got to take the bus? Let me find out that you is just as bad as your brother with trickin' on random bitches. What the fuck are y'all Brooklyn niggas turning into? So what the bitch is pregnant and got five other kids to tote around. She got six other mothafuckas that can take turns putting her ass in a cab every day." Looking into the camera, Isis chastised Blacka for what, in her opinion, was classified as ignorant generosity on his behalf.

"This ain't the time for you to focus on that shit. I need you to look at the big picture and make shit happen. I need you to tell the boys that I need them to do a little cleanup work to make sure that, by the time my trial comes around, Dwight will have no choice but to tell the truth. But I need him there to tell these people that he was only trying to save his own ass when he told them that I was involved in any of this shit." By mentioning the two men he referred to as the boys, Isis could tell that Blacka wanted extreme action taken toward Dwight, but she couldn't figure out exactly how when Blacka requested that he still be around to tell the truth to clear his name.

"I'm sure I can get the boys to talk to him, but what do you think they can say to Dwight to make him come to the trial and testify that you are innocent? Maybe they should talk to his family to convince him to do the right thing," she suggested. That way, instead of Dwight receiving a visit from the Jamaican goons, it would be more effective if they dealt with his family and forced him to testify on behalf of Blacka when the time came.

"I like that idea, baby girl. That shit right there is exactly what needs to happen so that nigga know that shit is serious." Satisfied with Isis's suggestion on how to deal with Dwight, Blacka smirked while balancing the phone receiver between his shoulder and ear as he rocked back and forth in the chair, rubbing his hands together.

"You know it's going to be awhile before your trial even comes around, baby. Are you sure that's all you need for me to do for you while you in here? You have a long ride ahead of you," she added. Without hesitation, Isis brought the reality to Blacka that if he was planning on remaining in state custody until the day of his trial, he could be there for a considerable length of time. She wanted to assure him that he could always count on her to do whatever was within her means to ensure he didn't suffer more than necessary.

"I do need you to do something else for me that I don't really trust anybody else to do . . ." Blacka said.

"I got you, baby. What is it?"

"I want you to check up on Angie for me and tell her that I'm sorry that they ran up in her shit like that to come and get me. Tell her that I ain't mean for her to get caught up in any of this shit and to come down and see me when she get a chance. I also need you to check up on Theresa and make sure that she got everything so that her and Crystal is all right. Crystal's birthday is next week, and I was supposed to be doing something big for her, but it looks like those plans are cancelled now," Blacka said, getting mad at the thought that he was going to miss his daughter's sweet sixteen birthday party because of Dwight's treacherous acts.

"That's right. Baby girl is all grown up now. Don't even worry about it 'cause you know Auntie Isis is about to take her shopping for all the shit that you would say no to," Isis said with a humorous tone, attempting to bring light to the situation that obviously was stressing her friend out.

Isis was more than willing to check up on Blacka's daughter, whom she considered to be more like a niece than just a daughter of a friend, but she was not too excited about delivering any messages to Angela. In her opinion, Angela was not worth the time and effort Blacka invested in her over the years. She was attractive, but in Isis's opinion, her spirit was stained with an ugly smudge of jealousy and hatred. She has never made any effort to get better acquainted with Blacka's daughter just because she was conceived when she and Blacka were in a relationship. And because of that, she spends more time shopping with Blacka's money than trying to encourage him to do better things like spending time with Crystal. For the sake of her friendship with Blacka, Isis was going to do the tasks that he requested without protest just to get a chance to see this bitch face-to-face so that there would be no mistake about the vibe that she has for her.

"I can't believe that she is all grown up already, and I ain't gonna be out there with my gun making sure none of them li'l muthafuckas in the neighborhood get it fucked up and try to push up on her the wrong way," Blacka with his head in his hand. He attempted to mask the tears forming in his eyes, thinking of the times he would be missing in his little girl's life. His relationship with Theresa already prohibited him from spending the time he really wanted to spend with Crystal to the point where he missed the first four years of her life just because of his relationship with Angela.

"You act like this is your funeral or something, baby. This shit ain't even started, much less over with. Don't forget that you got a team out here that will do whatever it takes to make sure that you get back out on these streets like the boss that you are," Isis said, offering words of support, which was the only thing that she had left at this point. Seeing Blacka at a vulnerable point was a very rare sight, and strangely, it made him more attractive to her. Just to know that a man could face the hardships of street hustling on an everyday basis without so much as blinking an eye but will come to tears at the thought of not being able to witness the maturity of his child was a sexy sight that more men should be willing to display.

The screen on the monitor flashed blue three times to indicate that the visitation period was about to be concluded after the remaining three minutes. Aware that their time was ending, Isis quickly thought of what else she should know before she left to go back to North Carolina. At this point, she knew that she was to contact

Reef and Dummy to let them know how Blacka wanted to handle things, check up on Crystal to take her shopping for her birthday, and give the message to the trifling bitch that should have been right here supporting her man. Looking at Blacka's face on the monitor, she could see the feeling of defeat settling in him, and she could not bear to see him in that state of mind.

"Listen, hurry up and get your ass out of here and take care of that so that we can get back to doing what we do best, baby girl," he said, faking a moment of cheer as he addressed Isis. He smiled his best fraudulent smile, although he knew she was well aware of his mental dilemma. "Make sure you don't get her none of that hoochie mama shit that you be rockin'. My baby girl ain't trying to pick up some old nigga with gold teeth and a set of van keys in his pocket."

"Boy, you know you ain't got no good goddamn sense," Isis said, laughing into the phone. She wiped the single tear that formed in the corner of her eye and continued. "You know damn well that I'm one of the classiest bitches that you ever met in your life, and if there was a nigga with a van, she would just have to fight me for him, especially if that shit is carpeted with a fridge and a couch in it."

"All right, mama, I got to get out of here and get back to the land of paradise. You take care of yourself and be good out there," Blacka replied, saying goodbye to his longtime friend. He couldn't help but crack a genuine smile at Isis's dramatic hand motions as she spoke. Her sassy attitude made her always hold a special place in his life that most people looking in from the outside would never understand. She was one of the few women he genuinely loved without actually loving her.

Chapter 14

"All right, baby boy, just make sure you keep your head up and don't sit in there worrying about shit that you know we got under control out here. Just sit back and get your little jailhouse workout on and make sure that they don't catch your cute ass dropping the soap in the shower. We don't want nobody to get them cookies." Trying to uplift Blacka with laughter spoken into the phone, revealing the smile that had many men fall in love instantly. In her heart, she wished that the boundary of the video monitor wasn't separating them so that she could wrap her arms around his neck to embrace him. Taking less than a second to ponder that thought, she reminded herself to give Blacka the good news about her son, Genesis, just making the starting lineup on his school's basketball team. However, before she could utter another word, the monitor's screen went black, bringing the visit to what seemed to be a premature conclusion.

Getting up from the chair and preparing to leave the building, she saw a young girl to her left sitting and crying while staring at the blank video screen. Feeling the pain of the distraught woman, she walked over in an attempt to comfort her.

"Don't worry, mama. They can't hold him forever. Everything is going to be all right," Isis said while placing a hand on the young woman's shoulder. She offered words of condolence to the woman who she felt needed to have some support . . . only to be incredibly surprised by what she voluntarily walked up on.

"Get your fuckin' hands off of me, bitch. You don't know me or what the fuck I'm going through. For all I know, you are probably that bitch that got his head all fucked up about me and won't even accept my mothafuckin' visits." In a surprisingly harsh voice, the distraught stranger pushed Isis's hand off her shoulder and began to scream random false accusations.

Since the stranger was in an obviously lousy mood, Isis didn't take offense to the defensive attack of the visitor, who still sat there wiping the tears from her eyes. As the person spun around, exposing more than just the profile of her face, more of her features were exposed, revealing her true identity and causing Isis to stifle a laugh.

"You right. It ain't none of my business, and I should have just stayed out of it. I'm so sorry for bothering you." Isis spoke politely toward the apparently emotional stranger. Then she turned around to walk and leave and avoid laughing in the visitor's face.

"Oh, this shit is funny to you, huh, bitch? I hope you still think it's funny when I fuck your ass up in here 'cause I don't give a fuck. I swear to God that I'll snatch them fake-ass eyes out of your head and drag you around by your hair in this mothafucka, so just try me, bitch. You think you can just take some shit from me, and I'm gonna sit back and just swallow that shit, bitch? Hell naw, bitch. I ride for mine!" Dramatically throwing the chair back and standing up, the visitor began yelling, creating a scene in front of everyone in the visitation area, including the correction officers on duty.

"First of all, my nigga, you got the game fucked up in more ways than just one. I damn sure ain't fuckin' with no nigga that would stick his dick in you, so you really need to calm the fuck down before somebody end up getting more than just they feelings hurt up in here." Without fully turning around to face the hostile visitor, Isis spoke through her teeth, not appreciating the unwanted attention that she was now getting from the entire room.

"Hurt? Bitch, only one that's gonna get hurt up in here is your amazon ass. Don't think that anybody up in here is scared of you. You can ask that nigga about me. I ain't the average bitch. I go hard in the mothafuckin' paint all day. Matter of fact, we ain't even got to talk no more, bitch. It's what the fuck ever!" Escalating the situation and putting on a show for everyone, the visitor spoke, then hastily charged toward Isis with her arms extended.

Using the expression on the person who stood facing her expression as a mirror, Isis was aware of the threat that was approaching from behind her and turned around and reacted quickly. Sidestepping the wild attack, Isis threw her forearm forward, making direct contact with her attacker's face, followed by a kick to the groin, bringing the mindless attack to an end.

"Who the fuck you think you runnin' up on, bitch-ass nigga? You think I got time to be playing games with your punk ass? I done told your ass already that I ain't got nothing to do with you and your fagot-ass man, but you act like you can't hear. Now, look at you." Standing over the visitor, who now lay on the ground in the fetal position clutching his testicles, Isis began to scream.

The room filled with laughter as bystanders witnessed what most initially thought was a young woman in distress get knocked down with two strategically placed hits. However, laid out on the ground with the red and blue striped sundress that still displayed a tag from Target hiked up between his thighs, the cross-dressed man screamed in agony. With blood profusely flowing from both his nose and top lip, the would-be assailant grunted through clenched teeth that were coated with his own blood, hoping that there were no more blows to come. The last thing Isis wanted to do was to become a spectacle for a room full of strangers, but in this case, she was defending herself against someone who unjustly attempted to do her harm. At least, that's what she thought, so she reacted accordingly. Mad that she had to step out of her usual character of conducting herself like a lady, Isis unballed her fists and picked up the Coach bag that she threw to the floor in the heat of battle, noticing two of the correction officers approaching rapidly.

"What the fuck is this shit? You tell me you two don't have enough sense to wait until after you leave a jailhouse to start a fight?" The Caucasian officer with the low buzz cut spoke loudly and militantly as he pushed past the crowd to the center of the attraction. It wasn't until he got close to the situation that he realized what was taking place, and instantly, the short, stocky man busted out with a hearty laugh.

"Listen, sir, I was just defending myself. You can ask anybody out here. That nigga came at me on some crazy shit. I tried to walk away, and next thing you know, he came at me, so I had no choice but to get him out of my face." With arms extended to the crowd around her and the man before her on the floor, Isis tried to maintain her composure as she explained the situation to the officer whose name tag read Langston.

"Listen, shit! I don't give a damn what you and RuPaul got going on. I just know that this ain't where the fuck it's going down at. Now, you and this pretty motherfucker right here better get your shit and get the fuck out of here before not only will I ban you two from future visits, but I'll make sure them boys on the other side don't see a judge for the next six months while they sit inside of the hole and get right with God." The other officer, who was quite taller than the first but with a wiry frame, spoke aggressively while the first officer was barely able to compose himself as he watched the injured man roll on his back like a turtle on its shell.

Taking the officers' warning into consideration, Isis took a firm grip on her bag and proceeded to exit the room through the crowd of onlookers, shaking her head at the unnecessary drama that she voluntarily walked into. A smile crept on her face as the thought of the man lying on the ground with the wig that she herself would wear crossed her mind. She couldn't wait to tell Blacka about what had happened as soon as the monitors had gone off. Knowing the smart-ass that he was, she knew that he would more than likely say that she provoked it and said something smart like, "That shit can only happen to you." As quick as that, her thoughts went back to her friend behind bars for what she believed was for him giving ungrateful people the opportunity to take care of their responsibilities. She thought that they should be able to accept consequences just like a man.

Exiting the building into the parking lot, Isis walked toward the cherry-red Mustang that sat toward the end of the row, going over her strategy in her head to make sure that Blacka would not have to spend much more time locked behind the steel-reinforced concrete walls of the jail. The first thing she had to do was contact Reef and his partner, as Blacka requested so that they could apply the necessary pressure on Dwight so that this situation could end. After listening to all of the things that Blacka did for this man, to know that he could betray him to a point where Blacka could lose everything, she felt that Dwight should lose everything around him slowly until he comes to reason. With her main focus being getting Blacka out of jail and freed of the charges that were pending against him, there was no time to play games. It was time for rash actions.

Deactivating the alarm to the car with a button on the keychain, Isis swung the door open and sat inside, reaching in the middle console for her cellular phone to make that call. Focused on her phone, she was shocked to see that she had numerous missed calls from the person she set out to call. Isis was unaware of the Dodge Charger parked directly next to her rental.

“Yo, my girl, if we woulda been two snakes, we woulda done bite your sexy rass by now,” said the voice from the passenger side of the vehicle as the windows slowly rolled down. That quickly caught Isis’s attention, not so much because of the words spoken but the familiarity of the voice. Pivoting her head slowly to the left, she couldn’t help but smile when she saw Reef talking.

“So, that’s what it takes for a bitch to get some attention. Blacka has to be in some kind of trouble, or the two of you don’t even think about little ol’ me,” she said, fighting the urge to jump out of her car to greet her friends. Isis smiled brightly while talking to the out-of-town visitors.

Reef continued. “You done know that me and the bwoy no stop love you, mi Empress. Just ’cause you no hear from we every day no mean seh we can forget 'bout the sexy redheaded goddess," Reef said, leaning back in the seat to remain inconspicuous from whatever surveillance that may have been in the parking lot, whether it be by video or just another motorist with a wandering eye.

"So, what we gonna do? Just sit here and make funny faces at each other, or will the two of you follow me so we can talk?" Isis said, adjusting the Prada shades on her face in the driver's-side window. Isis spoke loud enough for Reef to hear her without making it evident to anyone around. She loved the cloak-and-dagger style of the two Jamaican men who were definitely serious about their craft. It seemed that they were always on their guard and alert to their surroundings.

"Maybe next time we can link up an' talk about good times, but right now, we have fi pay a little visit to one of the bwoys that tink sey since the big man naw pon de street, him don't have fi pay the money that him owe. Just let we know who him want us fi deal with an' me an' my bwoy will take care of it," Reef said, explaining that he and his partner were rushing to collect an overdue debt from an insubordinate business associate. He requested that Isis inform them of any instructions Blacka may have.

Pausing in the mirror and looking around to ensure that there was no one within earshot, Isis thought back to the pain she saw in her friend's eyes as he explained how he was betrayed by the man he had done so much for. She thought back to the story of how he salvaged the house of Dwight's grandparents when they faced eviction and bought a car for some girl that the traitor was dealing with just so that she could transport her kids around. Blacka's instructions were to strip Dwight of everything while making sure that he remained unharmed so that he could somehow reverse his testimony. Isis felt there was only one way to bring equal justice to the situation.

"Leave Dwight in one piece so that he can tell them people the right story, but as far as everyone that he knows . . ." Using her hand as an imaginary gun, Isis pointed her index finger to her own temple and simulated the act of pulling a trigger.

"Wha' you mean by 'everyone else,' babes?" Reef questioned.

Looking over the top of her designer sunglasses, Isis slowly began to speak. "I mean *everyone*. The girlfriend, the brother. Even the fuckin' grandparents. Spare no one."

Reef couldn't help but smile as he watched the redheaded beauty snarl her lip and give the order for the kill. It was a thrill that both he and his partner enjoyed, and he was ready to play. Coincidentally, he and Dummy were en route to collect money from the same brother who was a part of the hit list that Isis just delivered. Happy to take the order, Reef used the back of his left hand and repeatedly delivered light slaps to Dummy's right arm, who sat in the driver's seat with the same smile.

"We ah get pon dat right away, mi Empress. Matter of fact, we was en route fi go collect from the brother now. It looks like it ah go be the poor bwoy's final payment an' disconnection notice rolled up in one. Truth is, mi never did like him anyway, so this will be business mixed with a whole lot of pleasure." Pleased to know that his already-planned visit to Dwight's brother would be more than just collecting some overdue money, Reef let Isis know they were on their way to deal with him immediately.

"All right then, babes. Just remember that Dwight has to be around to make it to the stand and make things right, so please don't touch him . . . at least not yet." Giving her final reminder to keep Dwight alive for the sake of Blacka, Isis started the ignition of the Mustang and proceeded out of the parking lot.

"Well, you hear that, my bwoy. It look like we ah go get fi have some fun after all. Since ah warpath, we ah go pon we have to make a little switch and change up the car. We need a beast that can chase down de rabbit in case him decide fi run." Reef realized they needed to switch vehicles for something more appropriate for the mission they were about to embark on. In his mind, he already knew that they could stop by Ox's house and swap cars. There was an old-school Cutlass in his backyard that Reef has had his eyes on since they met for the first time. With a hand motion, he signaled Dummy to start the car and get on the road to destruction.

Chapter 15

"Ay, man . . . ay, man!" With one hand gripping the passenger door and the other on the dashboard, Turk hollered while mashing his foot on the floor as though he had his own brake pedal. Why he let this nigga drive was still a mystery to him that, hopefully, he will live long enough time to solve.

"Yeah, I know, I know. Watch out for the cars, people, and other shit in the way. Right now, I got this. You just keep calling them niggas so they can be outside," Risky said, tightly gripping the wheel of the 2011 Infiniti M56S as he bent the corner at the housing project entrance. Once he made it out of the neighborhood and got on I-20, the outdated Oldsmobile Cutlass that pursued them had no chance of catching them on the open highway. Their escape should be simple if he could just get this nigga Turk to untuck his balls and deal with the situation like a soldier and not like a scared Girl Scout on a camping trip.

"Well, tighten up, cuz. I ain't buy this mothafucka for you to kill me in it, my nigga," he said, not really sure about what was more threatening to his life right now . . . the vehicle behind chasing him or the wild man driving the one he was in. Turk carelessly fumbled in his waist for the Glock 27 for some brief feeling of security as he looked in the side mirror and saw the black Cutlass fishtail violently out of the housing entrance in hot pursuit. The American-made engine roared like a lion, stating his territorial claim in a jungle as the Jamaican driver released the emergency brake, shifting the beast back into second gear. Even in the small mirror, Turk could see the car passenger in pursuit manipulating a large, black object out the window while aiming.

"You wanna drive, nigga? Shut the fuck up and let me handle this shit. Your chance at saving the day went out the window when you decided not to pay these niggas. How the fuck you drop sixty grand on this shit, and you can't pay these niggas a simple ten stacks? You niggas with y'all priorities fucked up are bound to get me fucked up!" The low-profile tires of the red sedan tore down the Southwest area of Atlanta in hopes of making it to the Hamilton E. Holmes entrance to the I-20.

"All I said is that them niggas had to wait. I ain't never said nothing about not paying a mothafucka. It ain't my fault them niggas can't understand what I'm saying." Truthfully, Turk dangerously underestimated the patience of Reef and his partner. He just assumed that all of the urban legends of them running up in schools to kill people's kids were just shit to boost their reputation. Now, he knew firsthand that these Jamaican boys were dead serious. Unfortunately, it was past the point of a mere apology.

"Understand? Yeah, those headhunting niggas understand that you got their money driving these little hoes back and forth to the nail shop while you tellin' them slick shit over the phone about when you gonna pay them. What the fuck did you expect? A fuckin' hug?" Risky looked down at the dashboard to see the speedometer rapidly increasing only blocks away from the entrance ramp to the expressway. Yet the Cutlass seemed to be catching up with remarkable speed. "I thought this shit is supposed to have a 400 horsepower engine."

Before Turk could respond, the back window of the sports sedan shattered from a burst from the Russian model AK-47 that was chomping on their heels. The 7.62 x 39 mm slugs lodged themselves into the dashboard, instantly dropping the value of the luxury car. The insurance deductible was not as much of a concern to him as his life was at this moment. Clutching the .45 caliber tightly in his hand, Turk took a deep breath to grasp an opportunity to return fire in hopes of slowing their pursuers. After a mental count of three that included two and a quarter, two and a half, two and three-quarters, Turk cowardly stuck his left hand over his shoulder and squeezed the trigger twice. To his surprise, as he fired his pistol, the rear passenger windows exploded glass into the car.

"What the fuck, cuz! You shooting right back into the car. Them niggas is *behind* us, *not* in the backseat! Shoot them or shoot yourself. Either way, use that shit to get them Zulu niggas to ease up," Risky said. His panic level increased when his so-called gangster homeboy just shot his own car because he didn't have the nerve to shoot straight. It takes a lot more than watching *New Jack City* to make a nigga into a gangster. Turk was now turning into a living testimony to that statement. He mashed down on the gas pedal, increasing acceleration as the engine screamed out like a wild panther . . . but the lion was still in the chase.

"You seen what them niggas did to Craig back at the house? That can't be me. Please, God, that can't be me," Risky pleaded.

Not ten minutes ago, they were pulling up to their spot in expectations to see business as usual. Since it was the third day of the month, it was natural to assume that the trap would be jumping with fiends looking to make a buy. To their surprise, the only thing they pulled up to see was one of their strongest team members, Craig, standing in the middle of the parking lot butt-naked with Dummy standing in front of him with a hand cannon pointed at his face. The black, eight-and-three-quarter-length barrel of the model 500 Smith &Wesson kissed Craig on his forehead as Dummy slowly guided the hammer back. At the same time, his partner, Reef, interrogated him about the whereabouts of $10,000 that Craig honestly had no idea about.

To make matters worse, Craig could not understand what he was saying because Reef was screaming at him in a patois dialect and slapping him across the back with the flat side of a long, rusty machete. By the look of Craig's busted eye and swollen lips, they must have been having this "conversation" for a while now. Before they could put the car in park, they heard Reef's raspy voice bark at Craig. Tears rolled down Craig's trembling lips as the cold steel barrel bored an impression on his forehead that corresponded perfectly to the .50-caliber nozzle. His life was lost, and he knew it.

"Since you come inna this world headfirst, we ah go make sure you leave here the same bloodclaat way." The words boomed from Reef's mouth like a pastor performing a sermon at a Southern Baptist church. Without hesitation, Dummy pulled the trigger and blew a chunk of Craig's skull onto the top of a car parked five feet behind him. Before the half-headless body could hit the ground, Reef turned and spotted Turk and Risky sitting in the incoming car with their mouths open in astonishment and shock.

There was no way he was gonna end up laid out on some parking lot with his head painting the hood of somebody's car because of this nigga Turk's bad decisions. All he could do was get to the entrance and use the traffic as a defense. Until then, he needed Turk to man up and help keep the heartless islanders at bay with the gun he had been walking around with as though he were

Billy the Kid. But instead of being helpful, he was balled up in the passenger seat with three pounds of shit in his drawers and a river of tears running from his eyes.

"Cuz, what you gonna do? Hit them mothafu—" Risky's words were interrupted by another burst from the pursuing vehicle. This time, eight shots entered the rear of the car, with two hitting the dash, three pierced straight through the windshield, shattering it, and the remaining three bullets entered the back of the driver's-side headrest . . . and exited Risky's face.

The shrill cry of an 8-year-old girl at a horror movie escaped from Turk's mouth as the car glass once again exploded around him. He was unaware he was the only one in the car to hear it. The only person Risky would be talking to from then on was God. It wasn't until he saw that they were drifting dangerously fast to the right that he looked over and saw particles of his partner's face spread across the wood grain steering wheel. At the speed he was going, there was no way to avoid the stone barrier only yards away.

Once again, the Jamaicans opened fire upon the vehicle, causing more panic. The imported luxury car smashed into the concrete wall at sixty-three miles an hour, immediately ejecting Turk's body out of the already-shattered windshield, launching him a distance of eighteen yards. His twisted body landed on the side of the road. With a combination of a lack of a seat belt and a delayed deployment of the passenger-side airbag, the chances of Turk surviving such a crash were a million to one. Had it been a grand prize lottery draw, Turk would have cashed in for the big check. But right now, his only reward was the excruciating pain that came from all areas of his body that only covered a fraction of what he feared to come.

The glare from the headlights of his predators' vehicle blinded him as they came to a screeching halt only a few feet away from Turk's mangled body. The sound of his heartbeat thundered in sync with the idling engine of the chrome-trimmed, black muscle car as he anticipated his demise.

Chapter 16

The roar of the modified engine was now at an idle purr dangerously close to Turk as he lay on the roadside awaiting his fate. Scared to even look at the approaching men, Turk tried his best to remain perfectly still with attempts to play possum. The sound of the car door opening and closing echoed in Turk's head as he attempted to keep still. Although his eyes were closed, he had a full visual of what was going on just by the sound pattern of the footsteps around him.

At first, he could hear the men approach the crashed Infiniti to see if anyone was alive there. Turk already knew the answer to that, but he wasn't sure if Risky's body was still in the car or if it had also been ejected from the vehicle. The muffled voice amongst the Jamaican thugs wasn't clear to Turk, but they were indeed getting closer and closer to him as he took a deep breath, intending to hold still and hope that they believed he did not survive the crash. It was a roll of the dice, but at this point, it was the only hope he had. A strong hope and a million mental promises to God raced through his mind as the footsteps finally stopped by his head.

"This one ah Dwight brother, right? Yeah, man, ah him dat," Reef said to his partner, looking at the apparently dead man they came to collect their money from.

With a grin and a nod, Dummy verified that the critically injured man laid out before them was indeed Turk. To add insult to injury, Dummy spat on the man like he were just a piece of the road. A smile of satisfaction engulfed the face of the sadistic hoodlum as he looked down at the allegedly dead man. Just like a cat with a dead mouse, he was pleased with his accomplishments. Yet, he still had an urge to play with the dead carcass some more. Ever since childhood, Dummy had an inner evil that was constantly being prayed over by his grandmother, who would testify that looking into the child's eyes, she saw no reflection of a soul. His sinister ways went much further than just throwing rocks at girls and torturing little animals. His taste for blood and thrill from human anguish fueled his engine.

His biological mother committed suicide in prison after receiving a life sentence for killing the man who attempted to kill her son, so his grandmother took on the responsibility of raising him. As a child, Dummy never cried for any reason. Whether he was hungry or had a dirty diaper, the infant would not cry, supporting the grandmother's theory that the child had no soul. At the age of 5 months, she put the child in his crib for bed at eight o'clock in the evening. During the night, the grandmother got up to check on the child because of the movement sounds in the boy's room. Unexpectedly, she found the child standing straight up in the middle of the crib. The fact that the child was standing for the first time ever without even attempting to use the crib railing for support did not astonish her more than when she looked at the child's face . . . and he snarled his lips. Doing so revealed eight full-grown teeth, four on the top and four on the bottom.

Terrified, the grandmother immediately grabbed the child, put him in a bathtub, and began filling it with water. She grabbed a bottle labeled "Seven Holy Herbs Bath" from the shelf and added it to the water. From memory, the grandmother recited Psalm 118 seven times as she held the reluctant boy down in the tub. For a mere infant, Dummy put up a struggle that became almost impossible for his grandmother to handle.

After taking the child out of the tub, she took the crib out of the child's room and placed it in the hallway of the small home. She stood next to the crib until sunrise the following day and continually repeated Psalm 145. She continued to pray over the child throughout the years as she watched him mature rapidly into a vessel of Satan himself. She was aware of his sadistic manner of playing with other children, like when Dummy was in class and set fire to the ponytail of the little girl who sat at the desk in front of him.

It was years later that the old woman finally died and left him alone with only a friend that was close enough to be a brother . . . Reef. During the funeral service, Dummy could hear the crowd of hypocritical attendants who really never cared for the old woman make negative remarks that they thought were unheard by him. The mention of his mother's name, how she shamed the family by going to prison for murder, and how the best thing that she could have done was kill herself were among some of the whispers. They spoke of how the old woman wasted her time on a dumb, mute child who was destined to be nothing but a problem just like the rest of his family, to the point where tears began to form in the young child's eyes.

The child slowly marched up to the open casket where his grandmother lay and leaned forward and kissed her on the forehead just before he and Reef walked out of the church that was filled with hypocritical mourners showing their last disrespects to the departed woman.

From the back of the old church, the boys retrieved two canisters of gasoline tucked away behind some bushes. Each boy doused either side of the church.

Returning to the front of the church, the young boys put a padlocked chain around the church doors before striking a match and setting it on fire. The death of the grandmother was the birth of the carnage that the two brothers had delivered to anyone that they felt necessary.

Now, seeing his enemy laid out before him in anguish and pain was a sight that was all too familiar to him . . . familiar enough to let him know that the man on the ground in front of him was not actually dead. Dummy leaned forward to get a closer look at the badly but not critically damaged body of Turk to follow up on his instinct. Like a wild animal stalking prey, the Jamaican man focused his senses to detect any signs of life.

Lying on his chest on the lonely road in the Georgia night air with his body contorted in an excruciating position, Turk could hear all movements around him with keen precision. He forced himself to regulate his breathing to appear completely motionless while keeping his eyes closed without any signs of strain. His left leg was broken at the knee and lay at a ninety-degree angle from his body. His left shoulder was perforated from Dummy's assault rifle, and his face was severely damaged from a combination of the windshield impact and the baseball slide that he did on his face once he was ejected from the car. Under his body was his right hand, miraculously still clutching the .45-caliber weapon that had proved useless up until this point.

He fought the urge to tense his body as he could feel his predators get closer. Fear and anxiety were surging through his brain as he prayed for God to come and take him out of harm's way. Unfortunately, unless God was a pair of Haitian sociopaths, Turk's prayer was not going to be answered, at least not as he expected. His body was cold, and he was losing feeling fast. The only thing that he could feel was fear and the weight of the gun in his hand.

The sudden touch on his side by the tip of Dummy's construction boots startled Turk, causing him to gasp for air, alerting his attackers that he was still alive. Turk's mind raced and focused on one thing . . . his survival. To do that, he had to use his balls for more than just producing bastard children. With as swift a motion as his body would allow, Turk turned over, using the remainder of his energy, and fired two quick shots with his Glock 27. If he was going to die, at least he knew that he would not be the only one being zipped up in a black bag. One of the two men would join him on his eternal rest.

Surprisingly enough, his aim was much better than his earlier attempts, which caused the back window to shatter. This time, the slugs went straight at the face of Dummy, who was taken entirely by surprise. Turk could see the dreads on Dummy's head quickly separate as the bullets made their impact. He felt he could accept whatever came next from the other brother as long as his body wasn't the only one left on the ground. The only problem was Dummy's body never hit the ground to join him. Only Turk remained alone on the ground . . . to die alone. It turned out the only thing he shot was the hair of the Jamaican. Otherwise, he completely missed Dummy's head. The only thing that made an impact was the construction boot that stomped down, pinning his hand with the gun to the ground.

"Look like my bwoy still ah have a little fight left in him. Glad fi see that you still here wit' us so we can talk fi ah little bit. You have sumthin' that belong to mi boss, an' him want it. But most importantly, since you have a brother who don't know how fi keep him mouth shut, we have fi make an example starting with you," Reef said as he leaned down to formally greet Turk. In a way, he was glad to be able to speak to him face-to-face, at least while he could respond. His dark, charred lips curled into a sinister grin as he stared into Turk's eyes as his wrist was being fractured by the mustard-yellow Tims of his silent but deadly friend.

"Y'all niggas are trippin' . . . Your money is always good on my side, man. I just had to get it to you," Turk expressed with an exhausted voice of agony. However, his words were barely audible.

"It too late fi all ah that right now 'cause you already had a whole heap ah time fi pay de bill. You ah ride up and down in dat pretty car dat you done crash up inna de wall over there, so that could have paid the man three times an' would ah still have change left over," Reef spoke directly to Turk's face in a calm and rational tone as he traced the side of his head with the nozzle of the Smith & Wesson hand cannon.

"Six grand. I got six grand cash on me right now, and the rest is at my crib. I can get it to you today, man, I swear." Turk's lips trembled with fear as he used his cash as a bargaining tool for his life. Right now, he was reaching for any chance that he was given to live another day. "It's right in my pocket . . . six grand . . . The rest is at my crib . . . real talk."

Without showing any compassion toward Turk's pain and suffering, Reef callously rolled his body completely over so that Turk was now lying on his back. With one leg still perpendicular to the other, a sharp snap along with the projection of bloody spit caused by a scream of anguish indicated that Turk's leg was only being held together by a few ligaments and torn tendons. The bone was completely broken and piercing through his flesh. The sound of the dying man's scream went into deaf ears as Reef dug through his pockets and pulled everything out, including a rubber band-secured roll of twenty-dollar bills. With his experience of dealing with money, Reef could tell just by the weight and thickness of the knot of money in his hand that it was just about the six grand that Turk claimed it to be. There will be time to count it later once he concludes his face-to-face encounter with Turk.

"Look at what this had to come to over a little amount of money. This could have been a night of celebration, but now look where we are. Laid out on the street is no place for businessmen. Let me get you some help so we can get you cleaned up. Hold on, my friend." Reef tossed the money roll over to his partner, who was itching to repeatedly kick Turk in the head until whatever was on his mind was spilled out onto the asphalt road.

Getting help for the man who had just come millimeters away from blowing his head off was definitely not on the silent man's agenda, and he had no plans to change it. Dummy raised the AK-47 and aimed at the skull of Turk with only a distance of two inches between the nozzle and his head.

With a calm motion, Reef's hand redirected the gun away from Turk's face to prevent his impatient partner from splattering his brains on the ground. "I'm sure our friend here has learned his lesson from his past mistakes. With the loss of his buddy who smashed up into the steering wheel over there, let's say that we can start all over again. Besides, money isn't everything. Isn't that right, my friend?"

Acknowledging that Reef was basically about to spare his life, Turk attempted to nod in agreement with him, but his body would not cooperate. The only thing he could muster up the strength to do was to let out a series of bloody gargles that sounded similar to the words, "Yeah . . . It . . . Ain't . . . Everything . . . I'm . . . Sorry." In frustration, Dummy kissed his teeth, returned to the Cutlass, and got in on the passenger side. He couldn't understand all of the Tom and Jerry games that Reef wanted to play with this punk, call the $4,000 a loss, and let his family bury him with it. Tossing the assault rifle in the backseat of the muscle car, he sat back in the passenger seat, waiting for his partner to return to the car as he kept his eyes on the road. The area was clear of all traffic and any eyes that may serve as witnesses for what transpired out there. But it would probably be helpful if someone did come by so that his brother would hurry up and get them out of there. After what seemed like forever of watching Reef fumble through Turk's pockets and saying things that Dummy could only assume were more worthless babble, the driver's-side door opened with Reef's arrival.

"You ready fi go already? We come all this way, an' you always wanna rush an' do things inna haste." A short burst of laughter followed Reef's words of sarcasm as he looked over at Dummy's pouting mouth, which was similar to a child being denied the privilege of watching television.

"Our friend has been so kind to give we the keys to him apartment and the key to him safe so that we can get the rest of our money. See, sometimes it pays to be nice to people. You owe that man an apology for your bad manners over there." Reef continued to chastise his frustrated partner as he put the Cutlass into gear and proceeded slowly. "Don't look at me like I'm joking, either. You're gonna apologize to that man even if I got to sit here all night an' wait."

At a slow creep, Reef pulled the classic car over to where Turk lay, awaiting his assistance getting to a hospital. Dummy remained, trying to register whether Reef had lost his mind or was joking about him telling this little punk he was sorry. This just might turn out to be a fight between the two friends. Carefully maneuvering the vehicle toward Turk, Reef brought the car to a stop right on a slight bump on the road before turning back toward the passenger seat of the Cutlass.

"You in such of a rush to get out of here, so hurry up and open the door, shake that man's hand, tell him that you are sorry and what a pleasure it has been doing business with him." Reef's commanding voice contradicted his grin as he reached across Dummy's lap to open the door. "Go ahead, now. Apologize."

Dummy's look of anger and confusion immediately transformed into a wide-mouthed grin as he looked out on the ground outside the car. He decided to do as his friend asked. He stepped out of the car, reached down, and took Turk's hand in a handshake.

Turk did not respond to Dummy's gesture of apology at all. No moans of anguish or spitting blood came from the man. At this point, nothing was hurting anymore . . . not his broken leg, his wrist that was stomped to a fracture, or the three bullets in his left side. There wasn't anything at all that he could say because he had a lot on his mind at the moment, which was mainly the extra-wide high-performance tire of the Cutlass that parked on his skull, crushing it into the sidewalk. The pressure from the vehicle caused his eyes to pop out of their sockets and the back of his skull to burst open, exposing his brains.

"Now, that's rude. Would you believe that after that sincere apology, he could have at least said that he accepts it and appreciates that you ah try fi mature as a person," Reef said while shaking his head as Dummy climbed back into the vehicle. "That's why I hate expressing myself to others."

After two quick bumps, the brothers continued to drive down the road and entered I-20 en route to Turk's apartment to collect their debt. The night turned out to be fulfilling to both their pockets and their thirst to kill. Unknown to Turk and many others, the brothers worked for a much more sadistic man with plans to spread his vengeance on all Dwight even remotely cared about. Without results come consequences, which was the motto of their employer, and these Jamaicans always went beyond the call of duty to ensure they got the job done to his satisfaction.

Once they left Turk's apartment and dumped the car, their next stop was scheduled to be Hartsfield Airport for the next departing flight to New York.

Chapter 17

"Do you know your name and why you are here?" The voice, accompanied by a bright light directed at his retina, alerted him to his surroundings.

"Yeah . . . It's Dwight . . . and where is here?" Bewildered by his surroundings, Dwight found himself lying on his back with an oxygen mask strapped across his face, looking up at a stranger wearing a light blue shirt holding a mini flashlight to his eye, rocking back and forth in what appeared to be a moving vehicle.

"You have been shot, and you are in an ambulance on your way to King's County Hospital's emergency room. You've lost a lot of blood, which rendered you unconscious. Luckily, the injury doesn't seem to be more than just a superficial wound. The bullet passed straight through your upper arm, but it's hard to determine whether it shattered a bone." The paramedic steadied himself, kneeling over Dwight as the emergency vehicle raced down Clarkson Avenue, moments away from the hospital's entrance.

Not knowing when and how he got into the ambulance, Dwight tried to recollect the recent events. He remembered being shot in the arm, running out of the bedroom window, Reef yelling across the street, and the police pulling up, but everything else up to this point was a complete blur. As the ambulance abruptly halted at the entrance, the pain in Dwight's arm rekindled. In a natural reflex to grab it, he found that his movements were being restricted by a set of handcuffs on both wrists, attaching him to the steel rails of the stretcher. Another face emerged from over his head as he struggled to get his arm free. It was the face of a New York City police officer who served as an escort for him to get to the hospital.

"Calm your ass down, and sit fuckin' still, dickhead, before I light you up with this healthy helping of shut the fuck up!" With the 50,000-volt police-issued X26 eagerly retracted from his utility belt, the hostile officer screamed in Dwight's face. The five-foot-seven African American officer was already irritated that he was appointed to babysit him to the hospital. He knew he was an informant for Stephens and Braxton, which made him look at Dwight as though he were the lowest form of life.

"Just calm down, sir. The police have you in custody for the time being due to the nature of the scene. We don't want to irritate your wound any further, so please keep still," the paramedic interjected, trying to de-escalate the tension from the officer. "We'll have you fixed up in just a minute, and then Officer Creighton will escort you down to the precinct."

Swinging through the emergency doors, the paramedic escorted Dwight to the triage area, where he was placed in a wheelchair. Officer Creighton secured ankle shackles on Dwight to ensure that he didn't attempt to escape from his custody. He had been given specific instructions to ensure he gets delivered to Braxton's desk. His hatred for Dwight for being an informant made him regret that he didn't have the opportunity to add some more injuries to his doctors' to-do list. In a moment, he just might get that chance once they place Dwight in a solitary area since he couldn't be placed among the other patients while in police custody.

The paramedic rolled Dwight through the congested emergency room, where he entered a small room at the far left corner. It had walls made of glass windows, and the interior was concealed with dark grey curtains. The room was empty except for the old hospital examining table with a long strip of disposable examining paper. Dwight struggled to make the transition from the wheelchair to the bed, shackled by his feet and without the use of his right arm.

"Hello, I'm Dr. Matovu, and you, my friend, are here because of a . . . gunshot wound to the upper arm, minor abrasions on your head with a loss of consciousness . . . Besides that, how are you doing today, sir?" The sarcastic physician entered the room, reading a chart that contained the notations taken by the paramedics who transported him to the hospital.

"Can I get something for the pain? This shit is killing me. It feels like my arm is on fire," Dwight said in a low moan. He pleaded for some form of anesthetic to comfort him.

"Well, we must see if you are allergic to anything we may be giving you. It says here that the paramedics were unable to provide any of that information on the scene because you fainted. Do you remember what happened to you before you fainted?" Looking closer at the bump on the back of Dwight's head, the doctor pulled a pen from his pocket to get the information needed before he could properly treat Dwight.

"Yeah, I got shot, that's what happened . . . That bitch shot me and was trying to kill me," he spoke through gritted teeth in agony.

"What bitch, sir? You know who did this to you?" The doctor further inquired in a Middle Eastern accent.

"Yeah, I know that bitch . . . It was my girl until this shit," he said, using his foot to adjust the uncomfortable ankle shackles that were resting on his bone. Dwight grunted through the excruciating pain that he seemed to be suffering from all over.

"What happened . . . You don't eat the pussy, right? That's what's wrong with you young guys. You don't want to put in quality time in licking the coochie. My wife has been with me for twenty-eight years, and every day, I eat that pussy from eight o'clock to nine o'clock. With the amount of times I have rocked the little man in the boat with my tongue, she would never shoot at me. I bet you if you were doing it right, you wouldn't be sitting in this bed right now with a peephole in your arm," the doctor jokingly spoke to Dwight as he continued to add notes to his chart, causing Officer Creighton to burst into laughter.

"Just hurry up and give me something for my arm. This ain't no goddamn joke . . . I've been fuckin' shot, and you crackin' jokes and gigglin' an' shit!" He no longer cared about what mistreatment Creighton may pose to him while he was in his custody because the infernal burning from Dwight's arm felt as though it were traveling throughout his body.

"You better watch your fuckin' tone before you don't get shit, and you can watch that shit turn gangrene for all I give a fuck!" Not appreciating Dwight's tone with the elderly doctor, who was just trying to make a joke, Creighton stepped across the room toward the examining table.

"It's all right, my friend. I have something for you in just one second. Everything is going to be okay. We are going to administer a local anesthetic while we prep you for X-rays to see exactly how badly the bullet damaged your arm," the doctor said, pacifying Dwight while rubbing alcohol on his hand. Dr. Matovu prepared to inject an intravenous needle into the back of the anguishing patient's left hand.

After a series of X-rays, Dwight lay on the bed in the same room with Creighton waiting outside the door. He was tired from the eventful day that had just occurred and felt a slight comfort knowing that his diabolical predators wouldn't take the high risk of trying to do him harm within the confines of the hospital. Now that the painkillers had taken full effect and his mind was a little more focused, he wondered what happened to Sandra, whether she was in police custody, and if she was indeed being detained, who was taking care of her children. The question of why he was being handcuffed to the bed had still gone without answer. After all, he was the victim in this situation, so he should be catered to as such and not as though he were the one caught with the smoking gun in his hand. His patience began to deteriorate while waiting for the results of his X-rays. He sat up straight and maneuvered his body to the only comfortable position his bonded arm allowed, looking toward the door, hoping for someone to walk in.

"Well, my friend, it looks as though you weren't as lucky as we all hoped. The little rascal did a number on the inside of your arm," Dr. Matovu said, walking toward the illuminated boxes on the side of the room wall. He held up Dwight's X-ray as he again examined the images of the damaged limb. He placed the pictures of Dwight's injured arm on the outdated display monitor and prepared to explain the severity of the damage to his arm.

"When am I going to get some more painkillers, doc? I damn sure don't want to be waiting for y'all to do whatever it's gonna take to get me out of here, and I don't want that pain to kick back in. Just give me a couple more shots of that shit and let's wrap this shit up," Dwight said, now feeling anxious to get out of the confined area and find out what was going on with Sandra.

"Unfortunately, it's going to take just the opposite of that to help you, sir. Apparently, your girlfriend was a better shot than we all hoped for. As you can see here on the X-ray, the bullet tore through your brachialis muscle, causing extreme inflammation to the biceps brachii. It also shattered your humerus bone as it exited on the opposing side of your arm. It's hard to determine whether you have sustained any nerve damage from this by looking at the X-ray, so we will have to perform a few advanced reflex exercises. For us to do so, your arm has to be completely alert to what we are doing so we can see if the wound affects your involuntary muscle reactions." Pointing to the images, the doctor broke the news to Dwight that he would have to endure the pain without the assistance of the pain medication until they determined whether his arm would ever be the same.

"What kind of shit is that? How the fuck do y'all expect me to deal with a fuckin' hole in my arm with no kind of nothing to kill the pain? Somebody better fix this shit and let me the hell up out of here before—"

In a state of frustration, Dwight's outburst alerted Creighton, who stood in the corridor, bored and mentally begging for a legitimate reason to administer 50,000 volts of electricity through the insubordinate patient's body.

"Only thing somebody better do is to give you solid advice to shut your fuckin' mouth. You must think I'm made out of fuckin' candy, and I won't do something to your bitch ass up in here. Let me hear your ass say anything else loud to the doctor or anybody up in here, and I promise, you gonna be one Brooklyn fried nigga up in this mothafucka." With the taser once again drawn on Dwight, Creighton delivered the harsh warning while biting on his bottom lip in anticipation of being able to follow through.

"It seems as though I'm your only friend, Mr. Dwight. Let's play nice, and I promise I won't call your girlfriend to come back to shoot you in the other arm. The quicker we get the tests done, the faster we can provide you with more medication, and I'm sure that in about ten minutes, you will want something for the pain that is sure to resurface." The doctor made a one-sided bargain with Dwight so that he could proceed with his treatment. He was amused with Officer Creighton's threatening tactics. Not fully understanding the tension between Creighton and Dwight, the physician felt it would be in his best interest to hurry up, treat the patient, and get away from any feud these two were obviously having.

Chapter 18

"Hey, there, sunshine . . . How are you doing? I heard that you got into a little catfight with the wife, and she kicked your tender little ass." The new voice that entered the room unexpectedly belonged to Investigator Braxton, who decided he didn't want to wait any longer at the station for Dwight to arrive, so he went to see him first.

The investigator stood in the doorway, leaning on the doorknob as he smirked at the wounded Dwight with a fraudulent look of concern. The forty-two, long, navy Ralph Lauren suit accented with microstripes complimented the broad shoulders of the six-foot-one Black man. He tapped the left sole of the brown Oxford Stacy Adams shoe that crossed over the front of his right leg against the loose vinyl tiles of the hospital floor. Braxton looked like the cover model for the NYPD edition of *Ebony* magazine. Using his right hand to remove the Armani Exchange frames from his face dramatically, Braxton used a simple head nod as a gesture toward the officer and the doctor to leave the room. Initially, Matovu was hesitant just to walk away from the patient while treating him. Still, when he was presented with the badge and stern look on the face of the bald investigator, he once again thought of what would be in his own best interest and exited the room as requested.

The fifteen-year veteran slowly paced toward the bed where Dwight sat speechless, wondering why this man had come to chastise him. The thought of anyone seeing him and Braxton holding a conversation always gave him an uneasy feeling that showed all over his face as he looked around the room as though other people might be watching.

"With all of the ways to cry wolf, you two fuckin' idiots decide that you taking a bullet in the arm is going to get you some special attention. Let me tell you, from now, I don't care if your ass gets mauled by a grizzly bear while taking a piss in Prospect Park. I want you to deliver that information that we agreed upon, and I'm getting fuckin' tired of waiting." Using a handkerchief from his inside jacket pocket to clean the lens of his glasses, Braxton spoke in a low, intimidating tone.

Dwight replied, "You think we did this shit on purpose? That bitch tried to kill me when she found out that I was working for you guys, and you gonna come in here and act like I set this shit up? Get the fuck out of here with that bullshit." Dwight's usually timid voice boomed louder than the investigator expected. He was finally fed up with dealing with everything that was going on around him for the day and was no longer going to tolerate any more verbal abuse from anyone. "So before you come in here with some demands about what you need, you better do something about everybody that's trying to kill me just because I'm fuckin' with you!"

"Listen to the big man . . . That bullet must have been lined with courage or something. Let's get this straight once and for all. *I* am in charge, and *I* will tell you when you can do anything. As a matter of fact, I don't remember giving you permission to get shot in the first place. As far as that woman of yours trying to kill you because you were fucking with me is a bunch of bullshit. She punctured your ass because you lied to her up until the last minute. As far as I'm concerned, you should have just kept your mouth shut, and maybe your boys would get lucky enough to get her before I get them."

With a cocky tone, Braxton stood directly in front of Dwight with his hand resting on his hip, exposing the black plastic handle of the chrome Smith &Wesson 5946 that was holstered on his waist. Knowing that he had the upper hand on Dwight from the moment that he was initially brought into the station, he smelled weakness in Dwight. He was going to use that weakness to mold him into a valuable pawn to get a conclusion to the murder case that had the whole department baffled.

"All right then, Detective, since you in charge, tell me what the fuck I'm supposed to do now . . . Do you think I am *really* going to be able to get anything for you now? Them dudes already know what the deal is and are looking to kill me, so if you think that I'm going to just walk up to them and ask them about what the fuck happened to some dead nigga that all I did was sell weed to, you must be out of your fuckin' mind." Dwight was no longer intimidated by the investigator, but his tone remained semihostile while he explained why the agreement could no longer be fulfilled.

"I don't care if you have to dress up like Santa Claus, sit 'em on your fuckin' lap, and ask them if they were naughty or nice. The clock is still fuckin' ticking. Unless you want me to run your girlfriend in for attempted murder and assault with an illegal firearm along with charging you with the murder of Troy, I suggest that you come up with a new strategy and make it fast." Recognizing that no matter what protest Dwight may have, Braxton was still in the position of power. He spoke with confidence that he would be getting full cooperation from Dwight. If not, Braxton was ready to commit to his promise and charge Dwight with the unsolved homicide of Troy. It made no difference to him who took the charge. As long as the case was closed, he would be satisfied.

Dwight was quickly getting tired of hearing threats of being sent to jail. At this point, concrete walls reinforced with iron bars seemed more like protection rather than punishment for him. He pondered that if hc did just accept the charges of murder and go to prison for whatever period of time, he would be free of having to look over his shoulder in fear of his enemies. With all things considered, he may even regain the respect of the people who now see him as a low-class snitch. Most of all, his deadly adversaries would have to consider it as him doing them a favor to get the police off of their trail. Yet, the thought of spending numerous years isolated from the free world hindered him from telling the investigator that he would accept those charges by confessing to the murder.

"I already know that you don't give a shit whether I live or fuckin' die, but you ain't got to throw me in front of a bullet just because y'all are too lazy to do your job yourself. The shit I gave y'all already, you say, is worth nothing, and I'm trying to tell you that they ain't gonna speak on it no more, especially to me. It's like you're either deaf or you truly don't give a fuck, but either way, the shit just ain't possible. So if you talking about taking me to jail for some shit that you know I didn't do, go right ahead." Dwight's voice went from the tone of aggression straight to the sound of a defeated man. Realizing that his next words were going to determine what he would be doing for the next twenty-five years to life, he felt himself about to break down in tears.

"It's fuckin' sad to see that your tail is so tucked between your legs that you're willing to take the fall for these guys. But it's up to you either be the bitch coward and take the fall for something that you claim you had nothing to do with, or you can find a pair of balls in your pants and get the information that we both need to make this all a thing of the past." Braxton knew that he had Dwight on the verge of his breaking point and that it wouldn't be long before he had him on the witness stand or at the defendant's table. The only thing wrong was that there was evidence that there was more than one person involved in the killing. There was no way that Dwight could have done it himself, and without proper proof, he could very well walk away from the charges, leaving the burden of continuing the investigation on his shoulders. He would have to persuade Dwight to continue trying to get him something concrete enough to get a conviction. The truth was that without Dwight's participation, the department would be clueless about who was involved with the crime.

"Man, I should have just said no . . . I should have just said no, and I wouldn't be in this shit. Y'all ain't have shit to show that I had anything to do with this shit besides I came to drop off some weed. Y'all should have just charged me with that shit and let me go about my business and not get me involved in this shit." The lack of a painkiller was causing Dwight to break out in a cold sweat as he once again dealt with the pulsing pain in his arm while expressing how he wished he had done things differently up to this point.

"Look, man, we both want this thing behind us, and I know that this is not what you bargained for when you signed the deal with us, but the truth is that it's out of my hands. If my superiors don't get some kind of satisfaction that you have proved to be cooperative with this investigation, you will likely end up in prison. Just remember, we have a video of you leaving the scene hours before the body was discovered in the house. You've got a lot to lose here, and it's time to decide who is more important . . . you or them." Trying a more tender approach, Braxton continued to try to manipulate the distraught man. He couldn't let him give up before he could at least get testimony on the man he had in custody, but it seemed like the two men Dwight spoke of obviously put the fear of God into his informant.

Feeling the vibration of his cellular phone on his waist, Braxton pulled the device from its case and depressed the icon, instructing the phone to forward the call to voicemail until he could conclude his visit with Dwight. Then he brought his attention back to the injured man. Braxton returned his phone to the leather holster, only to feel it ring again.

"Investigator Braxton speaking . . ." He decided to take a moment to answer the apparently urgent call, so he held up his hand in a gesture to Dwight to wait as though he had any choice in the matter. Braxton's facial expression immediately transformed as he listened to what the caller on the other end was saying.

"Are you sure this shit is legit? What time did this happen? Hell yeah, I want to talk to him. Have him leave a number so that he can . . . This way, I can make sure that I get in touch with him and not just sit around waiting for his call . . . Why the hell didn't anyone tell me this when it first happened? You mean to tell me that this guy just walked in there saying he wanted to give it all up? Shit, keep him isolated until I get a chance to speak to him. I'm on my way down there right now, so make sure Verona keeps his ass there so I can speak to him first."

Ending the call, Braxton looked at the phone, lost in thought. If what he just heard was true, they would no longer need Dwight and his crybaby tactics. The call he had received from the station informed him that someone had just come forward and volunteered to provide all the necessary evidence to guarantee a conviction against Richard Nelson. Excited and curious at the same time, Braxton turned and prepared to leave the room and head down to the station to find out precisely what this new informant had to say and what he wanted in return. Unfortunately, by the time the detective arrived back at the station, the anonymous person had disappeared.

"So, what gonna happen once they fix my arm? I'm going to jail just because I can't do what you want? Whatever it is, just get that doctor in here so he can do what he got to do so I can get on with this shit. I'm through playing cops and robber with you guys." Dwight's words fell on deaf ears as Braxton walked toward the door to call Creighton back into the room. Upon entrance into the room, the investigator instructed the officer to unlock the restraints on Dwight's wrist because he was free to leave after he was through with his treatment for his arm.

"Think of this as your lucky day. It looks like you ain't got to worry about your buddies doing anything to you or that trigger-happy girlfriend of yours. It seems like somebody out there has balls enough to help me get these punks off the street, which may end up saving your pathetic life. If this goes as good as it sounds, we won't even need you to get on the stand and say anything." Braxton's words shocked Dwight, causing his head to spin toward the door where the investigator stood. If this were true, it would definitely be a blessing in disguise.

"Are you serious? You guys got somebody at the station right now ready to talk? Who the fuck could be that stupid . . . and what do they want in return?" The questions came out of Dwight's mouth rapidly without giving Braxton enough time to answer, even if he was willing to do so. Unfortunately for Dwight, Braxton wasn't interested in answering the curious man. He was more interested in getting down to the station to meet the brave informant and find out how helpful he would be.

"Don't worry your little head anymore. The big bad wolf isn't going to get you now. We may have both of them in our grips as early as tomorrow morning. You just get better, and don't pick up and go anywhere too far in case I need you for any reason. Until then, try to stay out of trouble and not get shot again." With those words, Braxton exited the room en route to the precinct to follow up with the latest developments, leaving Dwight alone to think.

The one thing that made Dwight uneasy was that Braxton claimed he had someone who had facts willing to talk in the station since eight o'clock this morning—knowing that the only people who knew any concrete facts about anything that took place in that house that day were a part of Blacka's close circle. It baffled him about who would make such a daring move. The only people present were the two Jamaicans he knew wouldn't be at the precinct for any reason. Blacka was in jail, and his brother-in-law, Malachi, was a part of the operations. Reaching to scratch the back of his head as his mind raced, Dwight was reminded of the hole in his arm as a jolt of pain surged through his body, crashing into his brain.

Chapter 19

"You act like your hands dem make out ah' cotton. Knock pon de door like you want the people dem fi hear you nuh, man." Ridiculing his partner, Reef glanced up and down the dark block as he and Dummy stood at the front door of the Brooklyn residence. Waiting for the occupants to answer the knock at the door was making him wary that someone would pass by and see them at the scene of a future crime.

Bracing his hands on the frame of the door, Dummy used the steel toe of his special work boots and kicked the base of the door with enough force that whosoever was inside was guaranteed to hear it before placing his ear to the door to try to hear if there was any movement inside the house. Hearing the sounds of the old steps inside of the home creaking, he was aware that someone was approaching from upstairs of the two-level home and used a hand motion to let Reef know that someone was about to answer the door to let them in. The fact that they were waiting for these people to open the door wasn't even rational to him. But Reef and Isis liked the idea of playing games with Dwight and not just getting rid of him. The one thing Dummy carried as a creed was that a dead witness is the best witness, and not even a dead man can talk with his tongue cut out of his mouth.

"Is about time them people come and answer the bumboclot door. Them must tink sey man wanna stand out here all like sey me nuh have nuttin' better fi do." Talking under his breath, Reef approached the front door in time to hear an elderly woman's voice.

"Who is it?" the woman inquired.

"It's Thomas, ma'am. We are friends of your grandson, Dwight, and we wanted to know if he can help us with a flat tire that we got down the block." Reef answered the woman while masking his Jamaican accent. He made his face visible in the peephole to appear nonconfrontational.

"I'm sorry, sweetheart, but Dwight doesn't live here anymore. He stays with his girlfriend in Flatbush. The only one here with me is my husband, and I don't think an old man can be too much help for you." The short, elderly woman opened the door and stood in her housecoat and slippers. A nylon scarf concealed her thinning grey hair. Knowing that they were acquaintances of her grandson, she felt comfortable opening the door and offering whatever help she could.

"Is there any way you can call Dwight and ask him if he has a jack so we can get the car up to put on the spare? I kept telling myself to buy one, but since I'm always running back and forth to work, I never found the time." Still speaking as though he was born and raised in the United States, Reef realized that he had captured the trust of Dwight's grandmother and would soon be able to execute his plan without any complications.

"Of course, my dear. Come inside and let me go and get the phone and call him so you can speak to him. I bet he's with that girl right now. I don't know why he doesn't find a nice woman and not some girl who just goes around having kids with any man who can pronounce her name properly," she said, leading the men inside the house. Dwight's grandmother spoke her opinion of her grandson's recent choice of women.

"Annie, who was that beatin' down the damn front door like they ain't got no goddamn sense?" the raspy voice of an old man barked from upstairs.

"It's Dwight's friend, Thomas. His car got a flat, and he needs a jack to change the tire," she replied, waving her hands in the direction of her husband's voice while continuing to walk the two men toward the kitchen so that she could offer them something to drink while she called her grandson.

"I wouldn't give a damn if it was Barack Obama and the wing just fell off of Air Force One. Don't bang on my goddamn door!" Now standing at the top of the landing of the staircase, the short, bald man stood looking down at the top of the unexpected visitors' heads. "You mean to tell me with the money that these nappy-headed niggas save on haircuts, they can't pay a few bucks to have a jack in their own car?"

"Sam, that's enough. You can't just talk to people any kind of way. These boys haven't done anything wrong for you to talk to them like that. You're just a big bully, that's all," she said, turning around and winking at the men who followed behind her. Mrs. Anderson playfully yelled at her husband.

"It's all right, ma'am. Everybody has a right fi say wha' dem wan' say. It naw go change who I am, and what I can do," Reef said in his native dialect. He spoke to Mrs. Anderson loud enough so her husband could hear from the top of the stairway.

"Hell, I'm just saying what them white people be wanting to say when they see these kids with their hair sticking every which way like a dirty mop." Sam continued to chastise the visitors until the one who followed in the rear of his wife brushed his hair from the front of his face to reveal a penetrating stare accompanied by a sinister grin. Not comfortable with the looks of the men his wife so carelessly allowed into their home, Sam backpedaled toward the bedroom to retrieve the pistol he kept for protection.

"Don't worry about him, my dear. He's just an old dog with a lot more bark than bite. Just have a seat and let an old woman get you something to drink," Annie said, pointing toward the chairs around the shaky wooden table in the kitchen corner while walking toward the refrigerator on the far side of the room.

"It's all right, ma'am. We aren't thirsty at all. If you could just call Dwight and let him know that we're here," Reef said, reluctantly taking a seat at the table. He turned down the woman's offer in hopes that she would hurry up and call her grandson so that they could get to the actual point behind their visit to the Anderson residence.

"We have lemonade, sweet tea, Kool-Aid, and ice water. I would offer you a beer, but I don't want Sam to come down and raise hell over a beer that has been sitting in this fridge since New Year's Eve," she said. Mrs. Anderson addressed Reef's silent partner. She stood in the open door of the refrigerator, informing the man of what she had to offer, only to receive a side-to-side head motion with no words spoken.

"He's all right, ma'am. We just don't want to put you out of the way more than we already have. Besides, I'm sure you have better things to do than spending your evening catering to two strangers." Once again, camouflaging his West Indian accent, Reef noticed the shadow of someone approaching from the same path that he had just come from. The sound of creaking floorboards alerted Dummy, who immediately stood up out of the chair and put his back against the wall next to the kitchen entrance.

"Sweetheart, it's no trouble at all. Look, I even have some cans of soda down here," Annie said, oblivious to what was transpiring behind her. The elderly woman stood bent over in the refrigerator, still insisting that her guests accept her offer of a cold beverage.

"I think you better just get that boy on the phone so that these fellas can get on their way," Mr. Anderson said. "This ain't Dwight's house, so we really shouldn't be entertaining his guests, especially this time of night." Mr. Anderson wore his old army jacket zipped up halfway, grey sweatpants, and house slippers. He entered the room mildly insisting that the two men hurry up and leave the house. His suspicions told him the men had an alternative motive that would not be in his or his wife's best interest. Tucked in the waist of the grey sweatpants, Sam concealed a .38-caliber, long-nosed, blue steel Special that he usually kept in his nightstand.

Watching as he entered the room, Dummy stood motionless against the wall as the old man remained unaware of his presence. With the fingers on his hands extended like the talons of an eagle ready to strike its prey, Dummy had his eyes focused on the frail neck of the elderly man with the deadly intention of violently twisting it until it snapped. The whole idea of playing this cat-and-mouse charade that his partner insisted on playing proved unnecessary to him. He was ready to handle the business that he was sent to do. Had it been left up to the sinister man's discretion, the old woman would have had her throat slit from the moment she opened the door. The old man would have had his skull fragments imbedded within his own brain from the impact of the blunt end of a hammer before being given a chance to get up from his seat in front of the television. Taking a slow step toward the unsuspecting Sam, his partner's voice stopped him in his tracks.

"Like I said, Pop, we really don't want to put Mama out of her way with the drinks and tings like dat. All we really need is fi get a hold of Dwight to get the car fixed. If we did know that you would get all upset, we never would have bothered you, trust me. Me an' my friend can wait outside if you like," Reef said while making direct eye contact with Dummy. Reef continued playing his role as an innocent, stranded motorist looking for assistance from a local friend. Knowing Dummy, Reef could tell that he was about to make a detrimental move that didn't correspond with his plans to get Dwight's undivided attention, and at this point of the game, he couldn't afford that to happen.

"Sam, I don't know why you're acting like this. These boys have not done anything for you to behave like you are. At your age, you should be more concerned with receiving your blessing from our Lord for loving thy neighbor than following your selfish, devilish ways of turning your back and putting these boys out on the street. Need I remind you that not too long ago, we were on our knees praying that the Lord would make a way so that we could keep this very house? Now, you want to turn your back on the first person to knock on the door we have been blessed with. Shame on you," Annie said, placing the three Heineken beers she pulled out of the refrigerator on the counter next to the sink. She spoke sternly, commanding the attention of all in the room.

Dwight's grandmother made it clear that she was the voice of authority in the house as she brought her husband's argument to a complete halt. She reminded Reef of his own mother, and was amused at how she handled her husband with mere words that led him to cower near a chair at the table. Using eye contact and a simple head gesture, Reef motioned for his partner to sit back down and relax.

"Now, one of you open these bottles while I go get my phone. When I get back, you boys better be drinking and getting along, or else Grandma is going to have to get out her belt and start spanking some bottoms," she warned, walking out of the kitchen. The old woman playfully slapped Dummy on his behind as he made his way to the chair.

The unexpected slap caused the silent man to jump forward because he was surprised by the woman's boldness. With his mouth hung open, he turned around and looked at the woman as she continued to strut out of the room, looking back at him, winking her eye.

The look on his partner's face as he stood there with the palm of his hand covering his right butt cheek, gazing at the woman in shock, caused Reef to erupt in laughter. In the years he ran with Dummy, he has never seen that look of confusion plastered across his face. It was times such as this when he wished that the man could speak so that he could hear the shriek of surprise that went with the face he was making.

"You better hurry up an' sit down before Grandma get her belt and draw down your pants an' finish whup that backside," Reef managed to say while laughing at his friend, who stood there in the doorway with his mouth still hanging open in shock.

"I already know that she is a hell-raiser. That's why I sat my ass down and didn't say shit else when she started talking. Once that woman gets started, there ain't shit built on this earth that can stop her, and if there is, I need to buy a dozen of them with a lifetime warrantee on each," Sam said. He looked down the hallway to make sure that no one outside of the room heard his words. Sam spoke while discreetly adjusting the pistol he had concealed on his waist. No matter what his wife had to say about it, his gut feeling told him that these men had ill intentions. He was sure to be prepared for any potential problems, whether toward them or his grandson.

Grabbing the three beers off the counter, Reef reached into his pocket, pulled out a lighter, and used the bottom end to remove the tops from the bottles before handing them out to the others in the room. Observing the old man fidgeting with his waistband but thinking nothing of it, Reef pulled up a chair beside him and took a long sip of the beer he knew Mr. Anderson didn't want to share. An awkward silence filled the air in the room as Sam stared at the men he didn't want in his home drinking his beers. They stared right back at him for what seemed like forever. Finally, the sound of his wife's voice talking on the telephone while approaching the kitchen broke the silence. She explained that she had company at the house. They all assumed it was Dwight.

"Yes, baby, they are right here in the kitchen . . . a young man whose name is Thomas and another quiet fella with the same dreadlock hairstyle . . . Yes, baby, I believe that's what he said his name was . . . Here, you can speak to him. He's right here in the kitchen," she said, approaching Reef at the table. Grandma Anderson spoke on her cellular phone with a bewildered look, as though whoever she was talking to had no idea who Thomas was.

"Tell him it's Reef. That's a nickname that all of my friends call me," Reef said, tipping the beer from his mouth. He knew her grandson would recognize *that* name much quicker.

"He said his nickname is Riff or something like that. He's right here, so you can talk to him and come and help him with his car." She handed the phone over to Reef. Then she walked toward the refrigerator to satisfy her urge to finish the fruit she was reminded of while searching for something to drink for her guests.

"What I don't understand is how somebody can have a friend and not even know his real name. I thought when you become somebody's friend, you start off by telling each other your names," Sam said under his breath as he placed the beer bottle back on the table after taking a drink. Looking up as he wiped the foam from his top lip, he noticed the stern glare of his wife was once again trained on him. "If you don't want somebody to know your real name, you should stay the hell away from them. That's all I'm saying."

Glaring at the bitter old man from across the table, Dummy sat in anticipation for the chance to silence Sam's remarks permanently, unaware that the frail old man had his right hand adjusting the pistol in his waist. While his partner seemed to enjoy the shenanigans of the elderly couple, he was not there to get comfortable and drink beers. The only thirst that he felt the need to quench was the mentally dehydrating thirst that he had adopted since an early childhood murder—the thirst for a kill. Since the whole thing was to be planned to look like an accident, he had already predetermined that he could simply crack the back of the man's skull and snap his neck, blaming it on an accidental fall down the stairs. The pleasure of hoisting the slick-mouthed old man down the stairs to stage the scene of the accident correctly brought a grin to his face that he could not mask. Keying in on Reef's conversation, Dummy sat back, took the first drink from the beer before him, and waited for his time to handle his business.

"So, why haven't we heard a word from you since you got here? You at least going to tell us your name or even a thank-you for that beer you're drinking?" Sam asked, confident that his pistol was more than enough to handle any problems these men may cause. He attempted to lock eyes with the silent visitor's penetrating stare . . . only to find himself cowardly looking away, bringing his attention to Reef as he spoke on the phone to his grandson.

"W'happen, bredren? You act like you don' know who me is. It come in like me and you ah no friends again," Reef said, using his strong native accent. He knew the person on the other end must have been terrified at the thought of him being there with his grandparents. He leaned back in the kitchen chair on its two back legs, a grin crept across his face, knowing that the element of surprise must have made Dwight's heart drop in his chest as he heard the slow gasp of terror escape from his mouth as he spoke.

"What the hell are y'all doing at my people's house when I'm not there? Matter of fact, what are y'all doing there, period? They ain't nothing to do with what me and Blacka got going on, and y'all know it." Trying his best to mask his already fully exposed fear of the monsters of the Caribbean, Dwight attempted to put on a deep, threatening voice that didn't even have himself convinced. The thought of what carnage the diabolical duo was capable of doing to his grandparents made him break out in a cold sweat. With a combination of fear and instinct, Dwight reached for the lead pipe that he kept on the side of his bed since Sandra took his gun, forgetting about the fresh bullet wound in his arm. The jolt of pain that shot through his shoulder made him redirect his hand toward the prescription bottle of oxycodone on the nightstand.

"Look here, mi friend. You already know that we have a situation that only you can fix, so it's up to you whether anything have to happen to Big Mama and Pops over here," Reef stated. Realizing that he had the full attention of Dwight's grandfather, who practically tipped the chair over on its side in an attempt to lean closer to hear his conversation, Reef inconspicuously used his foot and kicked the legs out from under the chair, causing the old man to fall to the ground.

Finding himself sprawled out on the floor, Sam didn't have time to let out a cry of anguish as his bad hip collided with the ground before the hard rubber sole of Reef's boot was pressed against the side of his face, pinning it to the ground. Dwight heard the ear-piercing shrill cry that immediately filled the air from across the room, accompanied by the sound of a Pyrex dish crashing on the ground as Mrs. Anderson witnessed the assault on her husband. Reef held the phone toward the old man on the floor so that he could capture his moans.

"Oh my Jesus, Sam . . . Sam!" were the only words that could escape Annie's mouth before Dummy, who was ready for action, stood from his chair and bounded across the room and restrained the woman's mouth with the palm of his hand. Her attempts to struggle with the mute man's animal-like strength proved to be useless as she watched her beloved husband struggle under the weight of the foot that belonged to one of the men that she trusted enough to invite into her home.

Hearing the chaos erupting over the phone, Dwight scrambled to his feet and struggled to put on the pair of shoes within reach. The sounds of his grandparents screaming under whatever sadistic methods of madness that he knew Reef and Dummy were capable of instantly maddened him to the point that fear was no longer an issue. With or without the pistol that he felt was his only form of protection against the demonic duo, he was not going to let his grandparents just fall victim to them without putting up some sort of fight. In his rush to get to his grandparents and play the role of a handicapped hero, he suddenly remembered that he no longer had transportation since Sandra didn't want anything to do with him and took her car. A feeling of complete helplessness sank into his soul as he placed the receiver back to his ear to hear his adversary's sinister laughter, proving there was no line they would not cross to get their point across.

Chapter 20

"Yo, bredren, you still on de phone? Me can't hear a word from you at all. You act like you no want talk to me." With his foot firmly planted on the side of Dwight's grandfather's face, Reef casually spoke into the phone. Holding the phone close to his ear, he wanted to make sure that he could hear the faint breathing of despair that unconsciously escaped from Dwight's mouth as he helplessly listened to a loved one suffer the consequences of his actions. Reef looked across the room at his counterpart manhandling the old woman up against the counter to restrain her. His only regret was that Dwight wasn't there to witness the demise of his grandparents.

"Annie . . . Annie . . . Get your motherfuckin' hands off of my wife, you nappy-headed piece of shit. Let me up from here, and I swear to God that if you don't die under my hand, I'll eat my own fuckin' tongue!" Struggling to remove the heavy foot from grinding in his temple, Sam threatened Dummy to release his wife from his brutal grip. His only refuge was tucked in his waist, but his hands were occupied, trying to push away some of the pressure that Reef was applying to his skull.

"Let them go . . . This shit is about me, so come and get me and get the fuck away from my family!" Bellowing in despair, Dwight felt his eyes swelling in tears as he heard the useless heroic threats made by his grandfather, along with the muffled grunts of his grandmother. If there was anything that he was willing to trade his life for, it was his grandparents who raised him since his mother was found unfit to take care of him by the courts due to her issues of substance abuse.

"Oh, there you go. Me did start fi think that you did hang up de phone pon me, mi friend. So you say you don't wan' we fi hurt you people dem, right? Well, that really is out of my hands right now. You see because you don't fully understand that sometimes it is better to keep your mouth shut, we have to send you a message that even a blind man can read." Using his left hand, Reef reached into his inner jacket pocket and pulled out the three-star ratchet knife that he had been carrying since he confiscated it from someone who pulled it out on him and didn't have a chance to carry out their plan of executing him. He flicked it open with a swift motion of his wrist.

"Wha . . . What? I don't understand what you're talking about. Whatever it is that we need to work out, consider it done. Just let them go—please," Dwight begged in a weak, defeated voice.

"Truth is, mi friend, me really like Mama and me no really want fi have to do anything fi hurt her, and even though the old man love fi run him mouth like him ah gangsta, me can respect him. But like me said, this thing is out of my hands and in the same hands that used to feed you, and you had the nerve go and bite them. Long story short, *you* ah go decide which one of them ah go bury the next." Reef used the back of the sharp razor to scratch the side of his face as he prepared to give Dwight the proposal for the game he was preparing to play with his mind.

"Reef . . . Please, I don't understand what it is that y'all want from me right now. If you want me to tell the police that I was lying, I will do it—whatever it takes, I will do it. Just don't hurt them, please," he repeatedly begged for mercy on behalf of his grandparents. Dwight found himself on his knees in the middle of the floor with a face full of tears.

"Ay, bwoy, stop you' bloodclaat crying an' hear wha' me have fi say before me just dust off the two of them and go 'bout me business." Holding the phone away from his face, Reef scolded Dwight and commanded his attention so that he could move forward with his intentions. Watching his partner grow impatient, waiting to bring harm to the couple, he knew that it was just a matter of time before Dummy took action into his own hands and spoiled his fun. Biting down on the right corner of his bottom lip with a sadistic scowl, he reached down and ran the razor's sharp edge of the blade across Sam's face from his ear to his chin to increase the already heightened tension in the air by hearing him scream in agony.

"Aauugh . . . aaugh . . . fuckin' shit. Jesus, help me, help us, merciful Father God . . . Goddamn it, get this demon the fuck out of my house," Sam yelled, mixing prayers for help and blasphemy. He screamed in anguish as the burning sensation of his skin being split, followed by the warm blood running down his face, made him see that it was far past time to do something to retaliate against his attackers before they did something that would seriously harm his wife.

"All right, all right, I'm listening. Just don't hurt them, man, please. Whatever I got to do, just say it, and it's done ASAP." Stuck on his knees in the middle of the floor, Dwight was totally engulfed in a helpless feeling as he continued to beg for the lives of his beloved grandparents.

"Good, me see that me have your attention now. Since you wanna play the role of police, we ah go give you a promotion and let you be the judge for the next five minutes . . ." Knowing that his statement had to baffle

Dwight's mind, Reef took a dramatic pause waiting to hear the man's reaction.

"I . . . I . . . I don't understand what you mean by that. I ain't trying to be the police, and I don't know what kind of judge you're talking about," Dwight said, confused as his antagonizers expected. He responded exactly as expected, as though he were reading from a script written by Reef himself.

"Well, tonight, you ah go be the judge, and we ah go be the executioner on duty. Now, as your first case, you have to decide which one of these nice people will be around to see what the weather ah go be like tomorrow mawnin'." Finally delivering Dwight the ultimatum to decide which one of his grandparents would die at his hands and that of his partner, Reef looked down and took notice of Sam, whose hand was fidgeting with the waistband of his pants as though he was in dire need to use the bathroom. Annoyed by the man's antsy behavior, Reef delivered a swift kick to the arm of the old man on the ground that triggered the sound of an unexpected gunshot.

The loud boom that echoed throughout the room startled all the room's occupants. The origin of the sound was a mystery to all but one. In his desperate attempt to retrieve the .38-caliber pistol from his waist, Sam's nervous state of mind, coupled with the kick to the shoulder, caused him to prematurely pull back on the trigger, discharging a round . . . into his own leg. The intense pain struck the elderly man as the full metal jacket bullet ripped through the top of his thigh and exited behind his knee before lodging into his calf.

Dummy, in a natural defensive motion, used his left forearm and pinned Dwight's grandmother to the kitchen counter while using his right hand to reveal the chrome 9-mm Ruger concealed behind his back. Using the nozzle of the pistol to scan the area, he slowly panned from right to left before training the sight on the old man who lay bleeding on the floor. Not quite sure about what just happened, his first reaction was to place the nozzle on the handheld automatic pistol to the base of Mrs. Anderson's skull as she lay helpless on the counter. Looking over at his partner, Dummy couldn't understand what the hell Reef could be finding so funny as he sat there looking down at the wounded man, laughing hysterically.

With his wife being in immediate danger, Sam tried his best to focus on the situation at hand and make sure that both of the intruders felt the same pain that he was feeling, but in a much more critical condition. Pulling his hand up from out of the waistband of his pants, Sam looked up to see that his captor was so consumed with laughter that his hands were busy wiping tears from his eyes. Grasping the moment, Sam attempted to block the pain and used a trembling hand to raise the pistol upward at Reef's head before firing a single shot . . . only to miss. With arthritis already playing a significant part in his everyday life on top of the excruciating pain that came from his self-inflicted gunshot wound, maneuvering the trigger proved to be difficult for Sam as he attempted to discharge another round with a shot that he was sure would put a hole straight through Reef's forehead. However, Sam's attempt was in vain as Reef grabbed the barrel end of the pistol and disarmed the old man.

"Yo, old man, gimme this rassclot before you shot off you next foot. You must think you name Yosemite Sam or some shit." After taking the gun out of the old man's hand, Reef spun it around and pressed the hot nozzle of the gun firmly against Sam's right eye socket. Knowing that Dwight was still on the line without a clue about what was taking place at his grandparents' house, Reef decided to use the commotion as a playing piece for his scare tactic to taunt Dwight.

"Hey, bwoy, you still deh pon de phone listenin' to wha' gwan over here, or you run gon' left you granny fi fight against de devil?"

"I heard shots, man, I heard shots. Please, oh God, please, don't tell me. Please, God, no!" In shock, Dwight spoke almost incoherently into the phone, confused about what happened there. Breaking into a cold sweat, he felt the bottom of his stomach churning to a point where his mouth filled with the taste of fresh bile that was moments from surfacing. Rushing his words, he continued to ramble. "You said I had to decide before you did anything, and I told you I was ready, and you did it anyway."

The joy Reef received from hearing the grown man cry on the phone like a little baby would cry for a bottle was expressed by the grin plastered on his face that exposed his surprisingly white teeth. He pressed the barrel of the gun harder into the old man's face and cocked back the hammer while making sure that Dwight could hear the sound of the barrel rotating to align the bullet with the firing pin of the hammer over the phone.

"All right, since you say dat you ready fi make decision, make one now. Which one of dem ah go bury the next? Daddy or Mama?" With a sadistically calm tone, Reef delivered his ultimatum to have Dwight decide which grandparent would suffer the consequences of his actions.

Happily following suit, Dummy used his right thumb to guide back the hammer of the Ruger that he had firmly planted in the base of the helpless woman's skull. Without putting up any kind of struggle, Mrs. Anderson lay facedown on the counter with her eyes closed. Her lips moved soundlessly as she prayed for the mercy of God to intervene with the bad intentions of the evildoers who had invaded her home. Tears rolled down from her face to the counter as she was under the impression that it was Reef who shot her husband because of something that he may have said in protest of their presence. The sounds that she heard from across the room convinced her that it was only a matter of seconds before she would become widowed at the hands of her grandson's alleged friends. By the tone of Reef's voice, she was no longer reminded of the kind young man who knocked on her door earlier in need of assistance from her grandson. Listening to the chaotic demands that Reef was giving Dwight over the phone, she became painfully aware that her life was merely a part of some cat-and-mouse game that somehow she and her husband were participating in.

"Listen, man, I can't make no call like that. That shit is crazy—this whole thing is crazy. Just let them go, and we can straighten this shit out without involving them." With hands gripping at the flesh of his own face, Dwight pleaded with tears flooding his eyes. Regrets of spending all of his time trying to protect Sandra and her children while leaving his own family vulnerable to the attack of his enemies crowded Dwight's mind, making it impossible to form a rational thought.

"Listen . . . You want me fi listen? No, my bwoy, *you* listen to what me have fi say, and you better talk quick before we make we own judgment and kill the two of them," Reef stated. He repeated his demand for the final time. Then he slipped his finger into the trigger guard of the pistol and prepared to send Sam to his final resting place. Dwight heard the incoherent cries that escaped from Sam's mouth because Reef made sure to hold the phone close to the old man's face just to add to the mental anguish that had Dwight dangling on the edge of insanity.

A sudden feeling of calm took over Dwight as he stood in the middle of the room and wiped the tears from his face using the back of his hand. Gazing forward at the empty wall in front of him, the pressure of the torment that he was enduring from the whole situation finally seemed to collapse on his brain. At this point, he was well aware that the chances of his grandparents escaping the grips of his predators were beyond possible, no matter how much begging he did. Embarrassment engulfed him as he thought of the power he gave the two men by showing them fear. At that moment, he decided that he would no longer sit back and play the role of anybody's puppet. He was a man pushed too far over the edge, exposing a personality that was a stranger to even himself. Looking at the phone that still amplified the cries of pain from his grandfather, Dwight decided that he would learn to live with his decision. He stared expressionlessly and began to speak.

"I'll play your game, bruh, but I want to make sure that you put me on speaker so that everyone can hear and understand my decision." With a surprisingly calm yet commanding tone, Dwight made his request, confident that his voice was being taken seriously.

Noticing the change in Dwight's tone, Reef immediately became intrigued about what he would say that he wanted everyone to hear. Using his thumb, Reef depressed the icon on the phone, transferring the call from the earpiece to the speakerphone. He held it up so that everyone in the room could hear.

"All right, mi friend, mi have you pon the speaker, an' everybody can hear wha' you have fi say. Just remember it ah go be the last words that one of them ah go hear, so you better make it good." With a slick grin, Reef reminded Dwight that his finger was on the trigger, ready for action.

Ignoring Reef's smug remarks, Dwight began to speak. "Grandma, Daddy, you both know that I love you more than words could ever describe. I cherish the sacrifices that you have made for me throughout my life when my own mom chose to run the streets and do drugs rather than take care of me. For that, I will ever be grateful. I could sit here and tell you how much I owe you my life and how much I regret that you are involved in this, but we don't have that kind of time on our hands. I just pray that when you look down on me from heaven, you won't be ashamed of the monster that I have become and understand that I never meant you any harm."

"Yo, my yout', me no really have time fi sit here and listen to some long testimony about how much you love them and what you owe them. Them tings you should ah tink 'bout before you run off your mouth to the police an' fuck up the operations." Finding himself getting more bored than interested at this point, Reef insisted that Dwight hurry up and decide so that he could carry out the execution. He turned to his partner, who had the grandmother still pinned down on the counter with the barrel of the gun in his hand, to tell him to bring her over to where the old man lay bleeding from his leg. "Yo, bring Mama. Come so that they can say goodbye to each other."

Grabbing the old woman by her neck with his hands, Dummy snatched her off the counter and shoved her toward the floor in the direction of her wounded husband. Scrambling on the ground into her husband's arms, Mrs. Anderson placed her hands on Sam's cheeks, rested her forehead against his, and gently kissed his lips. Not sure what her fate was, she was confident of one thing. Whether it be her or Sam who dies, life will no longer be worth living for either of the two.

"Since you are in such a rush, I will make this easy for everybody involved. Tell Blacka that there is a whole world out there with a lot of shit going on in it, and the last thing that he should spend his time worrying about is whether I testify against him," Dwight said. Paying no attention to Reef's haste, Dwight continued to speak in the same tone and said what was on his mind, which began to irritate Reef even more.

"Since you wan' play like you no want to make the decision, we ah go leave it up to Dummy an' make it fair. Me ah go take out all of de bullets an' leave one inna de barrel. With that one bullet, him ah go choose who ah go live an' who ah go die," Reef stated. Taking the remaining bullets out of Sam's revolver, Reef placed one of the full metal jacket .38 long bullets back into the pistol and handed it to Dummy, who stood confused about why they were still playing this game.

Tucking his Ruger back in his waist, Dummy took the pistol from his partner, unsure of his next move. In his mind, he debated whether he was going to continue to participate in Reef's silly games or was he just going to use his own judgment and kill the grandparents?

Looking down at the couple who sat embraced face-to-face with teary eyes, he cocked back the hammer of the revolver and pondered about who would get the single bullet from the high-powered handgun. The thought of leaving behind any one of the two to serve as a witness didn't bother him as much as missing the opportunity to end the life of someone else, for this was his passion in life. In many aspects, he considered himself a craftsman dedicated to his art—and his art was war. Although he respected his partner's strategic choices, most of the time, he wanted so much to take his own route. Walking around to position himself behind Sam, he pressed the barrel to the back of his skull, forcing the old man's head forward into his wife's, who sat crying with her eyes fixed on Dummy's arm as he extended the gun.

"Well, my friend, it look like it time fi get out the old man good suit 'cause him half fi look good inna him a casket, at least from the neck down." Reef snickered into the silent receiver as he narrated to Dwight that his grandfather was about to be killed.

Pointing down at the devastated facial expression on Mrs. Anderson's face, he continued to heckle. "No worry yourself about nothing, mi dear. Think of it dis way. At least him did stick around til death did uno apart."

Helplessly watching the knuckles in Dummy's hand tense up around the rubber grip handle of the same gun that she has begged her husband over the years to get rid of, Mrs. Anderson leaned forward to kiss her beloved husband a final goodbye. Seizing the moment to satisfy his urge to kill the old man, Dummy fired off a single round, penetrating Sam's skull through the rear, pitching his body violently forward.

"Judgment!" hollered Reef as Sam's body limped forward on his wife, who also lay motionless with her head leaned back. Grabbing the phone off the ground, Reef spoke directly to Dwight, only to discover the call was disconnected.

"Hello, hello . . . Kiss mi rass. The bwoy mus' ah hang up de phone to bumboclot. How him fi do that an' never say goodbye. Him no have no manners to rassclot," Reef said, looking at Dummy. Reef joked, imagining what Dwight's mind must be going through at this very moment. To be forced to listen to the execution of his grandfather on the phone was guaranteed to let him know that they were not here to play any games.

To add salt to the wound, Reef grabbed the same cellphone and initiated the camera feature so that he could take a picture and send it to Dwight's phone. Standing above the couple, trying to angle the camera so that he could get a clear view of Sam's dead body slumped over on his wife's chest, whom he thought merely passed out,

Reef realized that the woman was more than just unconscious. She was dead. Along with Sam's brain matter that covered her face, blood slowly poured from the dime-size hole in the dead center of Mrs. Anderson's forehead from the high-powered bullet that exited from her husband's head and entered hers.

"Mi give you ah inch, an' you wan' take a whole bloodclaat yard. Mi tell you fi kill jus' one ah dem, and look wha' you do. Me don't know wha' fi do wit' you sometimes. You too hardheaded, man," Reef said, snapping the picture of the couple on the floor. He playfully chastised his partner, who didn't so much as crack a smile as he tucked the murder weapon in his waistband before turning to exit the room.

With his phone shattered up against the room wall, Dwight stood perfectly still while his insides seemed to be trembling rapidly. This situation went past the point of no return. No matter the costs, someone would have to pay retribution for his losses. He owed that much to his grandparents, if nobody else.

Chapter 21

"Did he call yet? What the hell is his problem anyway? It has been over three weeks. You would think he would at least call and let me know what's going on with the case. How selfish can one person be?" Kanisha spoke out loud as she entered the room. She had been confined to a wheelchair for going on three years. She maneuvered the motorized chair through the wide doorway of the Brooklyn home that she shared with her husband.

"No, baby, he hasn't called or anything. You have got to stop worrying yourself about him. Your brother is a big boy; you know he's a survivor. Besides, it's not like they're torturing him up in there. As long as we keep money on his books, he'll be all right until he gets out of there, which shouldn't be too long from now." Malachi spoke as he continued gathering a few items of clothing in preparation for a quick out-of-town business trip. It became a routine that his wife would roll through the house speaking about her concerns for her younger brother, who was in the middle of his trial in Florida.

"I just don't get it. He just stopped calling and sending letters. I want to know what's going on. I knew we should have gone down to Florida regardless of what the hell he has to say about it. I hate feeling so helpless being way up here and unable to do anything about it. That lawyer better be doing his damn job to get him out of there." Kanisha was overly concerned with her brother's well-being, as though she had given birth to him herself. Since their parents died in an elevator accident, she adopted the role of mom for the man, who was in his early thirties.

"You know he didn't want you traveling down there, especially when your doctors have advised against it. You can't risk taking that kind of trip with your dialysis treatment. Just try to relax. I'm sure he'll call as soon as he can. Right now, he has to have a lot of shit on his mind because he's facing a lot of time." Malachi continued to pacify his worried wife nonchalantly as he continued to pack. Truthfully, he grew tired of hearing the same thing every night at about the same time. He wished that she would finally face the fact that her brother may not be coming home any decade soon.

"And where are you off to this time, Malachi? What's the bag for anyway?" Taking time to notice her surroundings, Kanisha asked her husband where he was packing to go at such a last-minute rush.

"Well, instead of listening to you complain about him not calling, I'm going to go down there and see for myself exactly what's going on so that my beautiful wife won't sit here and worry herself sick. I was just about to tell you, but you came into the room, saving me the trip to the other side of the house. I'll be back in two days, so you won't be alone for too long." He kissed Kanisha's forehead, then knelt in front of her chair and took her hand into his own. He knew that she also wanted to go, but her failed kidneys due to diabetes prohibited her from making that trip on such short notice.

Shocked that Malachi was willing to make such a trip to bring her a sense of security, she always considered herself blessed to have a husband who always made her the number one priority in his life.

"So, when were you going to tell me, Mr. Stewart? You see me around here going crazy, waiting for the phone to ring. I swear, between you and that hardheaded boy,

I don't know who will drive me crazy first." Dramatically throwing her arms in the air, Kanisha sarcastically vented.

"I got to wait for you to stop talking before I can tell you my plans. You know, once you start talking, it takes a minute before you take a breath, and I damn sure ain't dumb enough to interrupt you while you're talking," Malachi joked with his wife.

"You better stop playing with me all the time. You act like all I do is talk nonstop around here like some little old lady." Putting on a fake pout, Kanisha responded to her husband, who was playfully being a smart-ass.

"I figure to go down there and sit through his trial so you can know everything firsthand. Besides, I'm sure that no matter what he says, he would like to have a familiar face in the courtroom for some moral support. It's the least I can do for him. When he was out here doing his thing, he always made sure that we were straight, so it's our turn to be that support that he needs. I know you wish you would be there if you could, so I will be your eyes and ears." Malachi zipped up the travel bag and moved back across to Kanisha, who looked like she was about to burst into tears.

Sure enough, Kanisha's watery eyes released a stream of tears that ran down her cheeks. The tears she shed were of joy to know that she had such a supportive husband in her corner. Sometimes, she felt as though she was a burden on him because of her illness. She would often cry to herself, thinking that he would be better off without the hassle of having to take care of a sick wife. It was only a year after they got married that she was diagnosed with the illness that hindered many plans that the newly wedded couple had planned. Never would she be able to provide him with children because her body could not sustain the pressure of childbirth, and that alone made her feel less than a woman.

"I have to run downtown to pick up a few things before I get on the plane tonight, but I can't leave here with you crying, baby girl. Everything is going to be fine. I tell you what. We can go to the Negril restaurant and get some of that Escovitch fish you love so much." Seeing the tears stream down her face, Malachi comforted his emotional wife with promises of her favorite meal from her favorite West Indian restaurant. It was one of the few entrees that she could still enjoy since the doctor recommended that she change her diet for the sake of her health.

"That's your solution for everything, huh? Just shove food in my mouth and shut me up. I like your style, Mr. Stewart," Kanisha said, wiping the tears off her face with the back of her hands. She cracked a smile at Malachi's proposal of food. She knew that he was pacifying her like a child, and she loved it.

"You know I got to keep my baby happy, at least I better, or who knows what your crazy-ass brother will do to me once he gets home," Malachi teasingly spoke, knowing that he had hit a sweet spot with Kanisha.

"What do you think is going to happen to him, anyway? His lawyer says that without a witness testimony, all the state has is circumstantial evidence, giving them a very slim chance of conviction." Switching the topic back to her brother, Kanisha asked Malachi for his opinion for what he swore was the thousandth time.

"With all the money that he's paying that lawyer, I hope he's doing much more than just 'hoping' that nobody will show up," Malachi answered. Knowing that all of the witnesses the state hoped would testify against Richard would not cooperate because of the messages he relayed to his associates, who had Richard's best interest in mind. Malachi took responsibility for just about all of Blacka's underworld business ventures in his brother-in-law's absence. The idea of being the top boss gave him a surge of power that he enjoyed. It was easy to see why Blacka refused just to walk away from a life where money, power, and respect played a significant role in everyday living. Suddenly, the sound of the doorbell interrupted the couple's conversation. Malachi looked at his watch, seeing that his expected visitors were promptly on time.

"You must be expecting company, baby. I guess that was another thing you were getting ready to tell me when I finally shut my mouth. You just don't care who sees me looking a hot mess," Kanisha complained, using her fingertips to adjust her hair while watching her husband walk toward the door, looking at his watch. "Who is that anyway?"

"Actually, a couple of your brother's drivers wanted to stop by to check on how he's doing. The same Jamaican guys that you sometimes see around," he said, pausing in the hall. Malachi told Kanisha just enough without having to lie to her. She would have a heart attack if she knew what "services" they provided for her brother.

"They need to stand before that judge and speak on his behalf. That's the kind of help he needs right now," she said.

Low laughter greeted Kanisha's suggestion. The thought of these two men standing before a judge voluntarily made her husband chuckle. "I'll ask what they think about that. I'll be right outside talking to them. Get dressed, and we can get that lunch I promised," he said, exiting the front door. Malachi politely dismissed himself to greet his visitors.

Chapter 22

"Mawnin', sir. You ready fi hit de road, or you still ah get inna de airplane?" Standing near the door, Reef greeted Malachi. He and Dummy were driving and wondered if Malachi had changed his plans and would be going with them.

"No, sir. I have seen Dummy drive, and I really can't be cramped in a car for damn near twenty hours when I can get there in two hours by plane," Malachi replied. Knowing that the rented Dodge Charger that the two men were driving was more than likely loaded with all types of arsenal, not to mention the chronic marijuana smoking that would be taking place en route, Malachi decided the safest way to go was to fly.

"We ah go reach down way before twenty hours. You see that bloodclaat hemi ready fi tear down de rassclot road. You nuh have to be scared of Dummy driving. Him never get a ticket yet, or at least him never stop fi one yet," Reef joked without cracking a smile.

"There is really no need for you guys to take the trip down there. It's not like y'all are gonna go inside of the courtroom. I'm just going to make sure that lawyer is doing his fuckin' job and not sitting back and watching them fuck over Blacka," Malachi replied, voicing his concern about his brother-in-law's trial. Malachi turned his head back toward the door as Kanisha opened it, trying to be nosy and see who was there.

"Just making sure that you ain't slip off without telling me," she said, looking up to see the two dreadlocked men. Kanisha's face immediately expressed disapproval. There was something about Reef and Dummy that she didn't like at all. Just looking at the silent men made her feel as though she were staring into the eyes of demons.

"No worry yourself, Lady K. We naw let him run away from you, mi dear. We have him under close observation. If him even step foot off ah dat step, we ah go tie him up so you can beat him for misbehaving," Reef said, exposing a surprisingly bright smile. He opened up the conversation with Kanisha by making a joke. She responded with a frown.

Looking at the two men she knew as drivers for her brother's business, Kanisha got an eerie feeling that she may have walked into a conversation that wasn't meant for her to hear. Everything about the two men on her porch was suspicious to her, especially the quiet one they called Dummy. She could never recall him ever saying anything, whether in the form of a note or even sign language. Yet, the man he always accompanied invariably seemed to know what he had on his mind. Her instincts told her that if her brother had any wrongdoings going on, these two men somehow must be tied to it.

"I hope I don't have to wait all day just to get one piece of fish because if that's the case, I can just make myself something to eat, and I'm sure that plane ain't gonna just sit there waiting for you to finish playing with your friends," she stated. Not justifying Reef's joke with a response, Kanisha pointed out that Malachi had more things to do than standing around having an idle conversation. She was more disturbed with whom he was talking to than anything else. As far as she was concerned, these were the people who deserved to be sitting in a jail cell instead of her brother. She believed he was just somehow influenced by their bad ways.

"Baby, we'll leave as soon as you get dressed, and I sure ain't gonna miss the plane. It doesn't leave until eight thirty, and I don't have any bags to check since I'm just bringing that one carry-on. I was just letting them know that I'm going down to check on Blacka—" Before Malachi could finish explaining, he was interrupted.

"I don't know why y'all keep calling that boy Blacka. His name is Richard or Junior. This 'King Blacka' shit has got to stop. That's why his ass is locked up now, not being satisfied with what he already has. Let me go inside and get dressed before I *really* get started," Kanisha said, making a dramatic exit. She maneuvered her powered wheelchair back into the home while expressing her feelings about her brother being addressed by his street name rather than his real name.

"Look like you have one angry woman pon your hands, bredren. Better we just leave and link up with you when we reach down ah Florida inna de mawnin'. We ah go jump pon de road now, so if anything, just call we an' let we know ah wha' gwan wit' King Blacka. But right now, you betta' get your rass inside dat house before my girl get out her whip an' skin your backside," Reef said, extending his fist to give Malachi a pound while making fun of the attitude that he was receiving from his wife. Following behind his partner, Dummy nodded toward Malachi as the two men left the stairs and approached the car that awaited them.

"Don't worry about her. She is more bark than bite. Besides, I'm the man of this house . . . as long as she's not around," Malachi joked as the two men exited his front steps. He knew his wife acted the way she did because she didn't like Reef and Dummy, unknowingly for all the right reasons. Although she was naïve to the operations of her brother's trucking business, she knew nothing about these two men resembled truck drivers.

"My bwoy really feel like him ah de top dawg around here now ah try fi give we orders pon de side. You hear him awhile ago 'bout we nuh have fi take de trip down there. Him ah go make sure the lawyer sort things out and all ah dat fuckery," Reef said, sitting on the passenger side of the Charger. He looked over and spoke to Dummy, who nodded in agreement. "Me can see dat since Blacka get bite by the police, the bwoy ah move like ah him ah de boss over we. Him betta watch him place before man make a place fi him somewhere him naw go like."

Truthfully, neither Reef nor his partner was fond of the idea that Blacka had left his brother-in-law in charge of things he really didn't have too much of an idea about. Sure, he knew how the business worked, but he was never willing to get his own hands dirty. They respected Blacka because he did more than just point fingers and expected to get results. Like Emperor Haile Selassie I, he was a general willing to get on the battlefield with his soldiers.

"If him really think we ah go let him go down there and keep watch over the case and we sit down up here and naw do nothin', him is sadly mistaken. Me naw put my trust inna no man, especially that one there. Anyway, me ah go call one of the bwoys so we can get some of that high-grade thing we did ah burn the other day. That was a wicked draw of weed, and me need something fi did long ride ahead of we," Reef said.

Turning the key in the ignition, bringing the powerful Hemi engine alive, Dummy pulled from in front of the Flatbush home. He drove to the East New York section of Brooklyn, where he and his partner could purchase some marijuana for their own consumption during the trip to Florida.

"What did they want?" Kanisha asked Malachi with a frown. She was sitting on the other side of the door with her arms folded across her chest when he entered the house.

"They were just checking up on your brother to see if there was any new word with his case." Again, Malachi managed to answer his inquisitive wife without telling her a lie. He was only going to tell her exactly what she needed to know while managing to keep his brother's secrets.

"You didn't tell me those two hooligans were going down there too. If they care so much, they should go and speak up for him instead of just going to look in his face," she said.

"Believe me, baby, if it was that easy, I'm sure they would be glad to help him out, but the chances of their words meaning anything in those white people's courtroom is slim to none. The only thing that matters right now is how hard his lawyer fights for him, and I'm going down there to make sure that he does just that." Malachi did indeed have every intention of making an impactful appearance at the trial . . . so impactful that he was sure that his words would make a substantial contribution to the jury's final decision. Besides, with the plans that he had in mind, he didn't want Reef or Dummy in the courtroom with him at all.

The last seventeen months proved to be a trying time for both Malachi and Blacka. With Blacka locked up out of town and not being there to manage operations, all of the responsibilities had fallen on Malachi's shoulders. He had to deal with those who thought that since King Blacka was no longer in the free world, they were no longer obligated to pay their outstanding debts to him. This didn't prove difficult, with Reef and Dummy exercising their interpretation of "customer relations" that their clients were willing to do everything to avoid. If things went according to his plans, his days of lying to cover for her brother would be past. The conclusion of Blacka's trial would prove to be redemption for the whole family.

Despite what her husband and her brother tried to tell her, Kanisha felt that there was more to what was going on than what everyone was telling her. She was aware of the trucking business he started by investing money they received after their parents' death. Over the years, he had made her proud of how well the business expanded to where he employed so few but profited so much. In her eyes, her baby brother was an owner and operator of a small trucking company who happened to be a victim of mistaken identity, and she was waiting for his high-paid lawyer to prove it.

"Tell me something, Malachi . . ." Knowing that his wife only addressed him by his first name when she was upset or very serious about something, Malachi mentally braced himself for whatever was about to come out her mouth.

"What is it, my love?" he simply replied.

"Those guys are drivers for the company, right?"

"Yes, baby. You already know that. They have been working with your brother since he started his out-of-state shipping." Confident in the answer that he delivered to his wife, Malachi felt that that was the end of her questioning and proceeded to prepare for their lunch date.

"Then why have I never seen them in a truck or any of their names on any of the Department of Transportation log books that I was looking through in Richard's office when I went down there? If there is something more to those two men I should know about, I expect that you should tell me, as my husband." Staring in her husband's face, searching for the truth, Kanisha revealed that she had snooped through her brother's paperwork in his home office.

"He pays them off the books, babe. Those guys don't have legal papers to be in this country, but he trusts them to do the work. All he does is change the records by putting the names that are listed on the driver's licenses that they have." Shocked that his disabled wife took the time to travel to Blacka's home to search through his things, Malachi quickly made up a lie to satisfy Kanisha's curiosity. He could only hope she believed the story and would stop asking further questions. Right now, he was more focused on his trip to Florida and what the next few days would result in.

"Listen, darlin', I know that you are worried about your little brother, but truth be told, he is a grown man, and you have to realize that he can make decisions without you having to look over his shoulder to make sure he ties his shoelaces. What do you think he would say if he knew you were out here putting that kind of strain on yourself because you are worrying about him?"

"I don't care what he would say. If he were here, it wouldn't make a damn difference at all. What you two need to realize is that since Mommy and Daddy died, you guys are the only family I got in this world, so I won't sit back and cry about being sick when I know I could be doing something to help. I just think that there is something extra going on, and somebody needs to tell me something before I find out on my own and really show my ass." Accepting Malachi's alibi regarding the roles the two men played in her brother's business, Kanisha made it clear to her husband that she wanted to be aware of what was happening.

Chapter 23

"Sir, you have a caller on line two who says he needs to speak with you about some information on the Troy Mandel murder. I asked his name, but he said he would like to remain nameless until he speaks directly with you." Lightly tapping on the door that was slightly open to get his attention, Braxton's secretary spoke in a low voice. She knew he was already on another line with his girlfriend, and they tended to argue daily.

"Listen . . . listen . . . I will talk to you later . . . yes . . . 'cause I got shit to do, that's why. Whatever . . . I'll call you back when I can . . . Don't answer the goddamn phone then!" Holding the index finger of his left hand up in the air, he gestured for his secretary to hold on for a second while he ended his conversation.

Shaking her head slowly while slightly pursing her lips, his secretary remained in the doorway as instructed, wondering what kind of sick relationship Braxton was involved in. It baffled her how two people who do nothing but point out each other's faults and argue during just about every conversation they have can even claim that they are attracted to each other enough to sleep together. She couldn't count how many times she had overheard arguments that, in her opinion, didn't hold any substance. Yet, the two would go at it until they yelled at the top of their lungs.

"Fuck . . . I have got to let that woman go before I end up going to her daddy's house and shooting him in the dick for even making such an evil bitch. I swear to God that she's starting to make me love my wife more and more every day," Braxton grumbled as he leaned back in his chair with the palms of his hands pressed against his temples once he disconnected the call.

"Well, Cassanova, don't forget that you have a call on line two that just may be the break in the case you're working on. The caller claims that he has information on the Troy Mandel murder, but he only wants to speak to you," the secretary reminded him of his anonymous caller.

"Yeah, well, what kind of info does this guy have, and what is he trying to get for this information?" Braxton questioned, knowing that when someone volunteers to do "the right thing," they usually do it for personal gain.

"All I can tell you is that he doesn't want to speak to anyone else but you. Every time I tried to ask him anything, he kept saying that he would only speak to whoever was in charge of the investigation, so I patched him through," his secretary replied, shrugging her shoulders.

"So he didn't ask for me by name?" Braxton asked

"No. As I said, he asked to speak to the head of the investigation, and according to the sign on the door, that would be you, so he's on line two," his secretary said as she turned her back and grabbed hold of the doorknob to pull the door closed as she exited.

Looking down to see the LED light on the phone slowly blink, indicating that someone was indeed on the other line, Braxton sucked his teeth, hoping that this was not going to be a waste of his time. Frustrated that his secretary didn't properly screen the call before forwarding it to his desk, Braxton snatched the receiver off the phone's base and pressed the flashing button.

"This is Braxton. How may I help you?" Expressing his frustration through the tone of his voice, the investigator spoke into the phone to give the caller the impression that he was not in the mood for games.

"Yeah, is this the head of investigations for the Troy Mandel case?" the caller asked in a low voice, further provoking Braxton's frustration.

"This is Lead Investigator Terrence Braxton speaking, and what, may I ask, do you know about the Troy Mandel case?" Braxton asked, getting right to the point.

"Well . . . I have some information, but I need to make sure that my end is covered before I speak more about it. I just want to make sure that you guys don't try to bring me down for this shit too," the caller spoke with a cracked voice as though Braxton's tone had stolen away his confidence.

"Before anybody can make any kind of promises, I have to know the details of your involvement. But what I can tell you is that any cooperation in the apprehension of whosoever is responsible for this murder will be greatly smiled upon." By analyzing the unknown caller's previous statement, Braxton felt the person on the phone was more than just a possible witness. He was somehow possibly tied to the crime himself.

"Let's just say that although I had absolutely nothing to do with it, I can tell you step-by-step what happened and who did it," the caller said before pausing. "But y'all got to understand that we were forced to be there and watch that shit. We all tried to talk him out of it, but there was no stopping him."

"Did you say 'we'? So, are you telling me that there are others involved? You know what? Just come on down to my office, and we can sit down and talk. This way, I can get a clearer understanding of what it is that you are trying to tell me." Suggesting that his mystery caller come down to the office, Braxton leaned forward in his chair, hoping the caller would cooperate.

"Listen, me coming down there would be like me sending out invitations to my own funeral. If anybody was to see me voluntarily going to the police, I'd be the next body that you find strapped to a table lookin' like leftover pasta." The caller turned down the invitation to the investigator's office.

Getting up from his desk, Braxton walked over to his office window and lightly tapped on the glass to get his secretary's attention. Once she looked at him, he used his left hand to cover the phone's mouthpiece and loudly whispered to her to trace the call's origin on his line. To his liking, his secretary winked her eye and let him know that she had already started the trace from when the call first came in.

"So, what do you want me to do if you can't come down here? I can't just lock somebody up for murder because I got a call from a guy who is too scared to speak to me face-to-face," Braxton said, removing his hand from over the mouthpiece.

"Ain't nobody said anything about being scared to speak to you face-to-face. I'm actually looking forward to it. I'm just telling you that it ain't gonna be at your office. We're going to have to meet somewhere that I feel more comfortable. Now, if you are willing to do that, I will be free for the rest of the day," the caller said, using a much more confident tone of voice.

Grabbing a pen out of a cup at the edge of his desk, Braxton decided to find out how authentic this guy was and said, "OK, what's the address?"

Braxton hung up the phone, and a smile crept across his face as he tore off the sticky note that he had written down the address the anonymous caller gave him. The meeting was set to be in two hours in the Red Hook section of Brooklyn near the Ikea store that was recently built. But before Braxton got there, he had to do a little research on who he was about to be dealing with. Luckily, he had the advantage of government equipment that could track any phone location, regardless of whether the caller thought they were smart enough to block the call.

"Ranaisha, please tell me that we got a positive fix on that call that just came in," Braxton screamed out of his office door.

"It's coming up from downstairs now. It was a cellphone used in the Troy Mandel area of Brooklyn. A name and billing address should pop up when the records get up here." Holding her hand over the receiver with the phone still at her ear, Braxton's secretary spoke from her desk, letting him know that the trace came back with positive results so he could locate the mystery caller.

"This asshole wants to bargain straight out of the gate, talkin' about he wants to make sure that he doesn't get in trouble too. If he turns out to be another spineless piece of shit like that punk Dwight, I might just lock both of their asses up along with this King Blackass," Braxton said. He turned around and walked back toward his desk, beginning to get irritated with the fact that these guys must really believe that there isn't any space in prison for them or that Braxton and his squad couldn't bring this case to a close.

"The best thing to do is to bait him in by letting him tell you what you need to hear and then bring him in as an accomplice to the crime along with Dwight. Once they all get locked up, let them try to build whatever empire they think they have inside a federal prison. Besides, there hasn't been a case that has crossed your desk that you did not close. These clowns don't know who exactly they're up against. I wouldn't be surprised if this thing gets resolved tonight after you meet the informant. That's why you're lead investigator," Ranaisha said, stroking the investigator's ego by reassuring him that a positive outcome would soon arise.

"That shit sounds good, but for some reason, this shit is getting more and more complicated. One says this, and one says that. This guy wants me to believe that our boy Blacka committed the whole act while the others stood there because they were too scared to stop him. Yet, Dwight claims that there are two other guys from Jamaica or some shit that did it on Blacka's command," Braxton said, recapping the different versions of the story that he has heard thus far. He reached down into his desk drawer and retrieved the pocket recorder he had used to record statements made by different informants over the years. He was going to make sure that he had some kind of documentation of this meeting. It was rare that someone would be willing to offer any law enforcement a helping hand, especially if that person had any involvement. So Braxton was going to take all precautions when approaching what could be a Trojan horse.

Chapter 24

"Now, who was that on the phone this time?" Kanisha asked as she entered the room, curious about who her husband was talking to on his cellphone. The smirk on his face was as though he had something intense on his mind.

"Huh . . ." Malachi responded, startled to hear his wife's voice. For a woman in a wheelchair, Kanisha always seemed to move quietly through the house.

"On the phone, babe . . . Who got you smiling like you just hit the lottery or something?" Kanisha repeated.

"Oh, that was just a friend who could help out in your brother's case. We were talking about his charges and the evidence against him. By what he says, there may be a chance that Richard can beat this, but he is not sure. I'm supposed to go and meet up with him in about an hour and a half so we can talk more about it," Malachi said, quickly coming up with a lie. He returned his phone to the leather carrying case attached to his belt.

"I hope he can do something to get him out of this mess that he put himself in 'cause it doesn't seem like anybody else gives a damn about what happens to him but me. I've been trying to get in touch with Angela for the last couple of days, and she still hasn't answered or returned any of my calls. I've left her messages on her voicemail and sent her about a million text messages, and this bitch doesn't even take two seconds to text me back and at least say, 'Fuck you.' This nigga sitting in jail waiting on this trifling whore to get him a lawyer that's gonna get him out of this shit, and now, this bitch ain't nowhere to be found. I shouldn't even care and let his stupid ass learn about trusting these money-chasin' bitches out here," Kanisha said while holding her phone in her hand as proof of her countless attempts to get in touch with her brother's alleged girlfriend. She felt relief that her husband was initiating some form of help for her brother's current situation.

"I doubt that Angie is just ignoring you, babe. Maybe something's wrong with her phone, or maybe she lost it. You know that she ain't the type just to haul ass and don't say anything to someone, especially when she knows that Blac—I mean Richard needs her." Glad to see that his wife was not as focused on his phone call as she was initially, Malachi tried to rationalize why Angela could not be contacted.

"Whatever the fuck she and her phone got going on is not helping none of this shit, and that's the bottom line. How the fuck is the man you suppose to love so much sitting in jail, and you out shopping and shit? I ain't heard about no lawyer, no bail—nothing. Hell, she ain't even ask if that nigga has soap to wash his ass, but yet, this nigga wants me to sit back and trust that she gonna get this shit straightened out all by herself?" Kanisha continued to complain about Angela's absence.

"She's probably looking around for the right kind of lawyer to handle this type of case. You don't want some old run-of-the-mill ambulance chaser going in there wearing a polyester suit and a bow tie representing him. They might never let him come home," Malachi responded, continuing to make excuses for Angela while focused on his meeting with the investigator.

"You and I both know that the only way that girl gonna find a good lawyer is if Macy's starts selling them in the designer clothes section. That girl's only concern is what a man can do for her. Now that Richard can't even do shit for himself, she's probably off to find the next dumbass to take care of her, and y'all two are just too blind to see that," Kanisha yelled, frustrated with the excuses that her husband was making up for Angela.

"Well, don't even sweat it any longer, babe. We can take care of everything ourselves, so we don't have to worry about Angela doing what she said she would. If anything, Richard will have two lawyers up in there fighting for him." He kneeled down to kiss his wife on the forehead. Malachi realized he needed to stay with the home team and spoke with false sincerity.

"I just don't understand why Richard is so blind to other people's bullshit all the time. You would think that this situation alone would be an eye-opener on who you can and cannot trust, but no, he wanna run around acting like he ain't got no damn sense." Kanisha continued shaking her head in frustration, then lowered her head into her palms and fought back tears.

Watching his wife go through emotional turmoil has become a familiar scene ever since she was diagnosed with her illness a few years ago. Since then, it seems things only got worse as the days passed. There was a time when her tears would instantly make him feel as though he was failing her as a husband, so he would do whatever it took to make sure that he was all the support that she needed. But now, he was becoming numb to the things she allowed to trouble her mind. He concentrated on the meeting he set up with the investigator in less than two hours. If everything went according to his plan, Blacka's case would soon be brought to a close one way or the other, leading to better days for everyone—especially himself. All he had to do was manipulate the truth to build the perfect lie so that he didn't end up in a jail cell as well.

"This friend of yours that you'll speak to, is he a lawyer or something?" Kanisha's voice broke through, interrupting Malachi's thoughts.

"Lawyer . . . huh?" Malachi snapped back to reality, only catching the end of his wife's question.

"The person that you just finished talking to on the phone that you said you were going to meet . . . Is he a lawyer?" Emphasizing her words so that her husband could better understand what she was saying, Kanisha repeated the question.

"Oh . . . Naw, he ain't a lawyer, but he's even better than that. He's a detective that works with cases like this all the time. He just got a couple of things that he feels that we should know about how they can use certain evidence against him," Malachi said, making up the lie as he went along. He looked down at his watch and turned away to avoid eye contact with his wife.

"What evidence do they have on him anyway? I don't understand how they could hold him there without giving him a bond just because somebody else said that he did it just so that they stay out of jail." Kanisha raised her voice again due to frustration and confusion running through her mind. She spoke as she lifted her face from her palms.

"I know it doesn't sound fair, baby, but sometimes, that's all it takes to put somebody in jail," Malachi said, attempting to make his wife accept that her brother may indeed be going to prison.

"I don't need to hear what it takes to put someone in jail. Right now, the only thing I'm interested in finding out is what it's gonna take to get my baby brother *out* of jail," she snapped defensively.

"I know it's hard, but you need to relax before you end up getting sick. I don't want to have your brother screaming at me because I wasn't taking care of you properly. Baby, I ain't trying to hear that shit. When I get back from my meeting, we can sit down and find Black—I mean Richard, a good lawyer, even if we got to go and dig up Johnny Cochran to pull off one of those O. J. Simpson miracles." Malachi gently rubbed his wife's cheek, hoping to bring a smile to her face by adding a little humor to the situation. His comfort to her also helped him balance out his conscience for what he was about to do. With the information he was about to give the investigator and what he knew about running the operations, it wouldn't be long before he could take control of everything without worrying about Blacka's barbaric interference.

Oblivious to her husband's menacing, traitorous thoughts, Kanisha slightly smiled at the fact that Malachi treated the situation with her brother as a top priority while others seemed not to care. For as long as she can remember, whenever she felt like she was in her darkest hour, she could remember that Malachi was always there to wipe the tears from her eyes before they could reach her cheek. He was and will forever be her rock.

"Thank you, baby, and I really mean that. Without you, I probably would have completely gone crazy by now. I swear I don't deserve you, but yet, every morning, I wake up, and there you are, right next to me, ready to deal with my bullshit better than I can. I tell you what. When you return from meeting your friend, I'm gonna give my baby boy a treat for being so good to mama." She provocatively licked her lips with her eyes focused on her husband's penis. Kanisha expressed her gratitude for his continual support.

"Awww, shit . . . I need to do whatever it is that I am more often. How about giving me a sneak peek at the comin' attraction?" Malachi said with a grin on his face as his hands manipulated his belt buckle so that he could pull down his pants. Truthfully, his physical attraction toward his wife has diminished ever since she had been restricted to her wheelchair, but he cared too much for her to let her think that he looked at her any differently. Looking back at his watch, he continued the charade and said, "It only takes about an hour to get on his side of town, so that gives us plenty of time to make some magic, mama."

"Yeah, right. Next thing you know, you'll be curled up in the corner of the bed, sleeping with your thumb in your mouth," said Kanisha as she playfully slapped her husband's hands away from his belt buckle. The thought that she was still able to get him sexually aroused even though she had been through so many physical transitions for the worse pleased her.

"All right now, when I get back, I don't wanna hear that you were just kidding or that you're too tired when I come running in the house butt naked, screamin' like Tarzan. You're lucky anyway 'cause I got to stop off at your brother's warehouse to make sure that the other drivers are dispatching like they are supposed to," he said, using a lie as an excuse to exit. Malachi leaned forward and kissed his wife on her lips with a false sense of passion. "I'll call you on my way home to see if you need me to bring anything you need. Love ya, baby. I'll see you when I get back."

"Love you more, papa. I'll be here when you get back," Kanisha responded as she gazed at the man she loved as he exited the room.

Grabbing his car keys off the counter and preparing to walk out of the house, Malachi gathered his thoughts to deliver his story with conviction. Planning to keep everyone else's name clear from blame, Malachi intended to inform the investigator of Blacka's dealings with Troy, how there was a misunderstanding about some money, and that Blacka took things too far just to teach everyone a lesson. Not willing to risk losing two of the best henchmen he has ever seen, Malachi decided he would not involve their names in the killing. This way, he could still employ them once he made sure that Blacka would not be getting out of prison. As long as he insists that his testimony remains anonymous, Malachi would not have to worry about anyone knowing that he helped lead to his brother-in-law's conviction. This way, the police would believe that since Blacka was locked away, all his operations would halt, taking their eyes off what he would be doing. It was the perfect plan that was ready to be executed.

Chapter 25

"Me done tell you already that bwoy can't be trusted. Ah wha' de bumboclot him ah go way out here fi go sit down an' talk with that white bwoy about? Me nuh care wha' nobody say. That bwoy ah' work with the police on sumthin', an' him ah try fi hide it," Reef said to his silent partner as they sat inside the dark-tinted Mercury parked inconspicuously in the parking lot of the housing complex that sat across from the coffee shop in Red Hook where he and his partner followed Malachi.

It has been about half an hour since he and Dummy followed Malachi without his knowledge after he left his house. The two men both suspected that Malachi was up to something that could prove harmful to Blacka's situation, and they intended to find out what it was. Since Blacka got arrested, Malachi had been masquerading around as though he were the headman in charge. But the truth was, he was just another weak link in an operation that they witnessed Blacka build. In Reef's opinion, before a man could be considered an army general, he must first be a soldier. And in his opinion, Malachi was nowhere close to being a soldier, so he was not worthy of wearing any stripes on his shoulders.

After witnessing Malachi walk inside the coffee shop across the street and sit down at a table with a white man resembling one of the officers that pulled over Dwight's car when they were inside, Reef knew that his suspicions were on point. Still, he just needed to understand what Malachi's intentions were. Without hearing what the men were talking about, he would remain clueless about what was happening until it was too late.

"Me wanna know what them two in there ah talk about fi so long. Me know that bwoy is up to no bloodclaat good. Me soon walk go in there an' stand up in front of him an' watch him turn white an' start fi stutter," Reef stated as he continued staring across the street at the coffee shop. Then he saw a young man walking a bicycle in front of their parked car. Without letting Dummy know his intentions, Reef rolled down the window and lightly tapped the horn to get the pedestrian's attention.

Hearing the horn of the car that sat idly running, the young man turned to see if whoever was in the vehicle was someone he knew. Squinting to see through the dark windshield, the man heard an unfamiliar voice with a Caribbean accent calling out to him.

"My yout', come here a minute. Me a beg a favor, and you can make a little change fi put inna yer pocket," he said, sticking his arm out of the passenger window. Reef signaled the pedestrian to come toward his voice while proposing for him to make some quick money.

"Wassup, bruh? What you need?" the young man said as he cautiously approached the black car. The opportunity to make money enticed him and made him curious about what he had to do.

"You see that shop across the street? Me have a friend in there who ah talk to somebody an' me wanna know what them ah talk about. You get wha' me ah say?" Reef leaned forward in the seat and spoke to the man while holding a fifty-dollar bill. "When you come back an' tell me wha' them ah talk about, me have anotha' one of these ah wait pon you."

"The coffee shop right there on the corner? Shit, what your friend look like? I'll sit so close to that nigga's mouth that I'll be able to tell you what he ate for breakfast by the food that stuck between his teeth," he said, extending his hand toward the crisp fifty-dollar bill. He was excited to earn one hundred dollars for such an easy task that he didn't care to ask why they wouldn't do it themselves.

"Just make sure you have sumthin' good fi tell me by time you come back out here to me," Reef said as he glared into the teenager's eyes while handing him the money. It amused him how eager the boy was to earn the money that he didn't take his eyes off of it like a hungry vulture that spotted an injured coyote out in the desert.

"I got you, man. I'll stay in there as long as they do so that I can hear as much as possible. I probably am gonna have to buy something to eat so they don't rush me out of the store. Y'all got five dollars so I can get something to drink and a sandwich while I'm up in there playing spy?" the young man boldly asked, causing Dummy to instantly grin at the thought of him trying to hustle up a few more dollars.

"You ah try fi take all of the little bit of money that me have, my yout', band you nuh even walk across the street yet? Bwoy, me ah tell you it hard pon the street nowadays," Reef replied, looking back and forth between Dummy and the young man who had his hand extended for some more cash. Reef couldn't help but laugh as he pulled a ten-dollar bill from his pocket and handed it to the young man. "The bwoy ah charge we fi him business expense to bumboclot. My yout' is a born hustler fi real."

"I'm gonna leave my bike over here so I don't have to worry about somebody trying to run off with it 'cause I ain't got no chain to lock it up. So make sure y'all keep an eye on it for me while I'm over there," he said, resting the old, beat-up mountain bike on its side between Reef's car and the car parked next to it. Then the young man folded the two bills and jogged the street toward the coffee shop.

Entering the shop, it wasn't hard to tell who the man in the car wanted to get the information on by the limited number of people seated inside the small restaurant. In a booth near the restroom, two men sat. They were talking with only two coffee cups at the table that they ignored. To the young man's luck, an empty table was available behind the man who seemed to be doing most of the talking. He couldn't help but notice the stern look on the face of the man sitting across from the man talking. Reading the two men's body language, he could tell that the man listening wasn't quite convinced of whatever the other man was trying to tell him.

Sitting down in the booth with his back turned to the two men that he was sent in to surveil, the young man reached into his back pocket, pulled out his phone, and quickly searched through the applications for the audio recorder he had downloaded not too long ago. Initiating the recording process with a touch of a finger, the young man inconspicuously held the phone as close to the partition as possible so that he could record the remainder of the conversation between the men.

". . . It was like the devil was inside of him or something. All we could do was sit back, watch, and pray that he didn't try to do some of that crazy shit to any of us. The way that he cut that boy's stomach open made me so sick that I threw up all over myself and the floor," he overheard one of the men saying as a waitress approached with a notepad in her hand, prepared to take his order.

"What will you have, baby?" the older woman asked as she wiped the table with a dirty cloth.

"Let me get a cheeseburger deluxe with no onions, some fries, and a large fruit punch," the young man ordered after a glance at the menu.

"Will that be all, sweetheart?" the waitress asked.

"Yeah, that will be it. Can I get that as soon as possible? I'm in kind of a rush to get out of here." Wanting the waitress to hurry up and leave, the young man quickly ordered his food so the recorder wouldn't pick up too much of his conversation while the man on the other side of the chair continued speaking. At this point, he was also interested in the context of the conversation. There must have been something good by the cloak-and-dagger routine that the Jamaican man in the car had him going through. He made a mental note to tell the waitress to make his order to go just in case the men concluded their conversation before he had a chance to finish eating his food. Over his shoulder, he could hear the man's voice sitting furthest away from him, getting louder and more aggressive.

"You must think I don't have a fuckin' television in my house or something. Do you really think I'm gonna sit here and believe this bullshit that you are trying to tell me? You must think that I ain't got nothing better to do than run across town to sit inside some rat hole restaurant to listen to some asshole tell me a fuckin' fairy tale," the white man with the bald head barked from across the table.

"That shit may sound crazy, but that's what happened that day, I swear. Ain't none of us wanted to be there at all. What he did to that kid was totally unnecessary. Before he gets it in his head that I deserve some shit like that, I would rather y'all lock his ass up for good," Malachi nervously spoke, hoping that the investigator would believe the story that he was telling. He figured that as long as he stuck with the same story no matter what Braxton said, everything should be in his favor. It wasn't like anyone else involved would contest the fact that they had no involvement with the murder.

"Then tell me what you plan on gaining by coming forth with this information. I doubt if you expect to receive some crime stopper reward or a key to the city, but there has got to be something," Braxton stated, sitting back in the chair while staring Malachi directly in his eyes.

"As I said, all I wanna do is make sure that this nigga don't try no shit like that on me just because he feels like playing God or something," Malachi said while taking a sip from the tepid cup of coffee in front of him in an attempt to break eye contact with Braxton.

"You must think I am one of these dumbass local cops out here chasin' little motherfuckers smokin' weed in the project staircases. I'm gonna give it to you as real as it mothafuckin' gets right now. I've got your boy about to be extradited up here so that I can make sure that his ass answers to the Troy Mandel murder, and from what you're telling me right now, you just may end up jacking his dick in a prison cell with your shirt tied around your waist, wearing fuckin' makeup. So, if I were you, I would decide right now if you wanna tell me the *real* reason why you got me sitting here listening to this bullshit," Braxton said as he leaned forward in the chair and reached behind his back, pulling out a set of handcuffs that he calmly placed on the table.

Malachi paused momentarily with the coffee cup only an inch away from his mouth, staring at the handcuffs on the table before him. He wasn't sure what kind of answer Braxton wanted to his question. Like a child without explanation for a bad report card, Malachi continued to sit there looking at the handcuffs.

"Let me make this easy for you 'cause I can see right now that you ain't the smartest mothafucka that tried to run game on me," Braxton began as he leaned back and draped his arm across the back of his seat. "You wanna be the head nigga in charge, don't you?"

"I . . . I don't know what you mean. I told you all I—" Malachi started before being interrupted.

"All you wanna do is make sure that this Blacka guy is not around so that you can continue the legacy, making your pockets fatter while he rots in jail. I mean, when he's gone, you ain't go and repent your sins and work in Wendy's. You gotta do something to keep the money rolling in. Don't make sense to fight a losing battle for your boss when you can jump on the winning team and work for yourself, right? C'mon, if you're gonna bullshit me, at least be real about it," Braxton said without breaking his stare with Malachi.

Placing the cup back on the table, Malachi considered that maybe Braxton was trying to get on the same accord as he was and just wanted to see if he would completely confide in him.

"You seem to have all the answers already, so what you think? Of course, I wanna run shit, but admitting that will only give you a reason to send your boys to come and fuck with me and shut me down," Malachi braved up the nerve to say, not sure what Braxton's angle was.

"What you dumb mothafuckas don't seem to understand is that there ain't no reason for me to fuck with y'all unless y'all start leavin' dead bodies all over the place like this is some kind of third world country or something. Keep bodies out of my morgues and pay your taxes, and you ain't got shit to worry about," Braxton said, using his finger to rim the coffee cup. His tone got lower as he spoke.

"Taxes . . . What you mean 'taxes'?" Malachi asked while raising an eyebrow in surprise.

Reaching into his pocket, pulling out six dollar bills and placing them on the table, Braxton smiled and said, "That cup of coffee you're drinking will be the last thing you get from me for free, my friend. From here on out, everything is gonna cost you big."

"What you mean by 'cost'?" Malachi said, looking from the money on the table to Braxton.

"You really carry this acting dumb thing to its limits, don't you? 'Cause I refuse to believe that someone who doesn't seem to have a clue about shit wants to be the head of a drug operation. Them little young niggas around gonna take everything that you got before we even get a chance to even fuck with your ass if you don't tighten up your game, son." Braxton continued to clown the confused Malachi.

"Man, I ain't dumb, but I just wanna make sure that we're talking about the same thing. The last thing I wanna do is end up getting fucked up for trying to bribe the police," Malachi said as he took a quick glance at the handcuffs still on the table. He refused to make any insinuations no matter how many blatant hints Braxton was dropping just in case there was a slight possibility that he was wrong. Still, he was 99.9 percent sure that Braxton wanted him to pay for immunity to continue running Blacka's operation while he was gone.

"C'mere . . ." Braxton said, using his index finger to summon Malachi to lean forward toward the table as he did the same. "Let me give it to you like this. If you plan on selling anything without having to worry about me coming back to snatch you up for narcotic possession along with accessory to murder, you're gonna do two things for me. The first is you're gonna pay me handsomely so I can make sure that a blind eye will be turned toward your operation as long as no more dead bodies are found all over the place."

Chapter 26

"How much are we talking about, and how am I sure that you don't just take the money and come and fuck with us anyway? It's not like you gonna give me a receipt and a warranty just in case I get ran up on by your local boys," Malachi spoke while his nose suffered from the smell of coffee mixed with the stench of old Marlboro cigarettes that projected over the table from Braxton's mouth as he spoke.

"Twenty-five thousand, and you won't have to see my face until our sixth month anniversary, where I collect my next twenty-five thousand. Of course, you can't forget the one-year security deposit since you have yet to establish any credit with me," Braxton said, exposing a yellow-stained-tooth smile.

"That's a hundred grand off rip, and you ain't did shit yet. You jokin', right? There's no way that you can expect me to pay that shit right off the bat. Shit, we ain't been seeing no money since y'all snatched up Blacka anyway, so where do you expect for me to get this money from?" Malachi responded with a surprised look on his face. There was no way that he was willing to turn over that amount of money to this man just because without a guarantee that he was going to live up to his end of the bargain.

"I need you to pay attention and keep up, son. That's seventy-five thousand now and another twenty-five six months from now unless you wanna pay for the whole year at once. That's completely up to you, big baller. As far as where you gonna get the money from, I suggest that you get on your fuckin' job and get that shit together 'cause you have twenty-four hours to have it in my hands." Braxton's grin immediately transformed into a stern look as he delivered his ultimatum. He was aware of the moves that Malachi and his associates were making, and with the estimation of the money they were bringing in, he figured that a third of the profit should go to him.

"Personally, I would rather you be a free man so that we can build a beautiful business relationship where everyone gets what they want, but if you don't wanna share my happy vision by not paying your taxes, then I'm gonna feel obligated to perform my official duties and take you off the street. Hell, I'll even offer you the platinum package at a reduced price and make sure that every dealer and junkie on the East Coast will be crashing into each other on the highway to get some of your product after I lock everyone else down. But honestly, I don't think you could afford that."

"It doesn't look like I got much of a choice since you put it like that. I've got no choice but to trust that you'll keep up your part of the bargain. Just let me know the time and place, and I'll have your cash," Malachi said in a defeated tone.

"Think of it as a positive investment in your future success as a poison-pushing piece of shit, something that you could look in the mirror and be proud of. Now that we got that out of the way, let me tell you what the second thing is that you are gonna do. You're gonna supply a recorded and written statement of the events that took place so I can use it as evidence in your boy's trial. Once we get you on the stand and convince that jury with a polished-up version of that same bullshit story that you tried to get me to stomach, a conviction will be guaranteed."

Braxton dropped the second part of his demands for Malachi while casually waving for the waitress to come and collect the money for their coffee.

"Are you fuckin' crazy? There is no way in hell you can expect me to get on that stand and come out alive. You got to come up with a better plan than that," Malachi said, protesting against Braxton's demand.

"What I don't understand is if you claim that all of y'all are innocent lambs working for the big bad wolf, who have you got to fear if he's locked away? Unless there is something that you *didn't* tell me, and I know that you *wouldn't* want to keep any secrets from your new friend, right?" Braxton said as he cocked his eyebrow, questioning Malachi's hesitation to get on the stand.

"I just don't want nobody going around calling me a snitch or no shit like that," Malachi said, once again trying to break eye contact with the investigator.

"I hate to be the one to tell you this, but maybe I should since I know firsthand. The moment that you picked up the phone and called my office, you became a snitch, so you might as well accept who the fuck you are, homeboy," Braxton said, once again smiling. "Don't worry. You ain't the first so-called 'Real Nigga' that crossed my path that would sell out his own mother if the reward was great for himself."

Malachi stopped for a moment and pondered over the words that came out of Braxton's mouth. He knew deep down that he was right. He was a snitch, but for what he believed was a better cause. Mainly 'cause he wanted a better life for himself. Now, he realized you truly do have to pay the cost to be the boss.

"Well, I would love to sit here all day and continue to give you life lessons, but I got a case to go and work on. Plus, I got to stop at the store, pick up some flowers for my wife, and break up with my girlfriend. Just do us both a favor. Make sure that you call me tomorrow before I even get a chance to think about calling you," the detective said, getting up from the table and preparing to exit. Braxton looked down at Malachi, grinning, knowing he had him exactly where he wanted him.

"So, you're telling me that I don't have any choice in this shit at all. I came here to help y'all out, and now I'm caught up in a trap," Malachi said, looking up at Braxton standing over him.

"I'm not saying that you don't have a choice. All I'm saying is that it would be in your best interest to choose carefully. Don't think I don't appreciate the help, but the truth is that you trapped yourself when you decided that working at a regular job wasn't good enough for you. Makes you think about the choices that we make in life, don't it? Had I chosen to be a bus driver like my father, and had you decided to teach Sunday school, we probably would have never met. Tomorrow, your best bet is to make sure that I'm glad I ain't driving the fuckin' bus. Holla at ya later, boss," Braxton said, throwing up his right hand with his index finger and middle finger extended, representing a peace sign. He turned away to exit while taunting Malachi by singing a portion of T-Pain's hook, ". . . *It's just another day in the life of the goddamn boss.*"

Left sitting at the table, holding his head in his hand and engulfed in a mixed feeling of accomplishment and bitterness, Malachi watched as the investigator exited the restaurant. The money that Braxton requested was not bothering him nearly as much as the fact that he had to get on the stand and testify against Blacka for his plan for domination to take full effect. He didn't mind the fact that he had to give a statement as long as he remained anonymous, as he stated before meeting with the investigator. Now, the tables had turned against him.

Although he still gets what he wants, he is being extorted to pay a price he was not excited about paying. The sound of someone trying to stifle a laugh brought him out of his thoughts, cueing him to get up and exit the restaurant.

"Here you go, baby: cheeseburger, fries, and a fruit punch. Can I get you anything else, sweetie?" the waitress asked as she returned, placing the young spy's food on the table before him.

So wrapped up in the drama that was taking place in the booth behind him, the young man was startled to hear the woman's voice, although she stood directly in front of him. Right behind the waitress, he witnessed the man he was sent to spy on walking toward the front door to exit.

"Yeah, if you could just wrap this up for me real quick so that I can leave, that would be great," the young man said in a haste to get outside so that he could collect the rest of his money from the two men in the car that was parked across the street. Pressing the playback button on his phone to hear the recording he just made, he was amazed to hear that it picked up everything the two men said in such high quality.

"Here comes the little yout' right now. The li'l fucka buy a plate food for real. Mi hope that him have sumthin good fi tell we," Reef said as he spotted his young recruit jogging across the street with a Styrofoam container in one hand and a big cup in the other.

"Hey, man, I thought them dudes were gonna be in there forever by the way they were talkin'. One nigga look like he was about to slap the shit out of the other one at one point. One thing that I can tell y'all is that your man in there is a real bitch-made nigga if he do what he was talkin' about doin'. Even the cop told him that in not so many words," the young man said as he approached the open car window.

"So, you hear wha' them was talkin' about or what?" Reef leaned forward in the passenger seat and asked.

"Hell, yeah. I heard every word, at least every word once I got there. That nigga was talkin' about giving a statement, takin' over, and payin' seventy-five stacks. Man, that nigga was in there talkin' about all types of shit. I recorded that shit on my phone just so that you could hear that shit." He was waving his hands in excitement that he had captured the conversation that he overheard.

"Play the 'ting and make me hear it then. Me wan' know wha' him have fi say to them Babylon boy," Reef said, interested in what Malachi told the police. He wanted to hear it for himself.

Taking the phone from the boy and holding it with his left hand so that Dummy would be able to hear the recording, Reef sat back and listened to the audio between his associate and what appeared to be the same cop who stood at the side of Dwight's car when he and his partner were in it. After less than three minutes of listening to the contents of the recording, Reef looked over at Dummy, who sat there, slowly nodding his head as though they had the exact same thoughts.

"My yout', you di good, so instead of the fifty dolla' that me did promise you, me ah go give you this instead, and we ah go keep this phone." Reaching into his pocket, Reef pulled out a knot of money, peeled off ten worn-out bills, and then extended his hand out the car window toward the young man. Looking the young hustler up and down, Reef admired that the young man thoroughly took on his task and stood strong like a soldier without showing fear to ask for what he wanted in return.

Reaching back in his billfold, Reef counted out seven more bills and handed them to the boy standing outside the car. "Use this fi make sure next time me see you pon the road, you ah ride sumthin' better than that ol' worthless bicycle. Look how the rain ah start fi fall, and you 'affe push that piece ah junk 'cause it naw work."

"Man, ain't nothing wrong with my bike but a bent rim and a flat tire. I can fix that in no time, and my baby will be as good as new. Besides, ain't nothing wrong with walking in the rain every now and then. If I had been riding my bike, there would have been no way for you to stop me to go to the diner. As far as the phone, y'all can go ahead and keep that shit. Don't nobody call me on that shit anyway." Suddenly, he realized that all the bills the man in the car handed him were hundred-dollar denominations. Looking closer at one of the bills, the young man slowly bent down to pick up his bike and said, "Yo, why this money look like it got bloodstains on it?"

"My bwoy, you have fi know by now that in America, all the money have blood pon it whether or not you can see it," Reef calmly said as he rolled up the window to the car while Dummy slowly pulled off down the rainy Brooklyn street.

With Dwight already working with the police and Malachi's willingness to testify against Blacka, the walls of the organization that were supposed to have been built on loyalty were crumbling down around them. Looking down at the phone that he just paid handsomely for, Reef decided that before he and Dummy took any actions against Malachi, they would do a little bit of snitching themselves. The only difference was that neither he nor his partner planned on involving the police in their plan.

Chapter 27

Dwight stood outside in the rain, contemplating his next move for the third day. His mind was far past the cold rain that drenched his clothes as he stood on the rooftop of the Brooklyn apartment building. With his eyes trained on a single house across the street below, thoughts of his grandparents and brother no longer brought tears to his eyes as they did only a few days ago. Now, when he thinks of how they were brutally murdered at the orders of Blacka, his mind deliberates on only one thing, and that is vengeance. He couldn't believe that Blacka allowed things to go this far before they got a chance to negotiate a solution where he would not have to be haunted by the sound of his grandparents begging for their lives moments before getting a hole blown through both of their heads. It was time to retaliate to make the playing ground a little closer to even by taking away something that he knew that Blacka loved as much as he loved his money . . . his daughter, Crystal, who had just turned 16 years old.

Just yesterday, he sat on the same roof and watched as young Crystal and her friends gathered together to celebrate the young lady's coming of age. The sight of Blacka's daughter enjoying life as a young, innocent girl while his brother and grandparents were beginning to rot away in a cemetery didn't seem close to being fair at all. The Jamaicans who were immediately responsible for the death of his loved ones were also on his short list of revenge, but he knew that going up against them may not turn out to be in his best interest. Putting that into the equation, Dwight decided that it was in his best interest for him to make his first attack on Blacka. Since Blacka claimed that he wanted to take things back to the ways of the Old Testament, Dwight felt it was only right to include Exodus 11. Since Blacka was portraying the role of the Pharaoh, who wouldn't let the innocent leave the land, Dwight would eliminate the firstborn of his tormentor.

Besides the get-together that was held at the house, everything was routine. Crystal would go to school while the mother stayed home and entertained her company, who usually would show up around noon, always with what appeared to be lunch in hand.

Today, another visitor pulled up to the front of the house in a cherry-red Mustang convertible that Dwight can't remember ever seeing. Yet, the driver, whose hair was only a shade darker than the car, looked familiar just by how she walked. Taking a moment to wipe the rain running down his exposed forehead to his eyes, Dwight leaned forward, squinting to see if that was indeed who he thought it might be. As he suspected, there was no doubt that was the same woman he met five years ago at a Pilot Truck Stop in North Carolina. The distinctive walk first lured him into the web that he found himself tangled in today.

Upon seeing the redheaded woman whose beauty could be compared to the mythical image of the Greek goddess Aphrodite, he immediately found himself lost in a trance as he looked into her spiritually hypnotic eyes. He was shocked that such a beautiful woman would even look in the direction of an average blue-collar worker, much less a truck driver like himself. He built up the courage to approach her and introduce himself, and she seemed fascinated with every aspect of his career choice. It monopolized every conversation they had for the following few weeks, and they stayed in contact via telephone until she invited him to lunch. To his surprise, the lunch was more than his opportunity to share a meal with this enchanting woman. She brought a friend who needed a driver with a valid commercial license willing to make a little extra money on the side.

Now, five years later, that same friend of hers just ordered the death of his loved ones from behind the bars of a jail cell that was states away. In a way, he could hold the beautiful Lady Isis at fault for the catastrophe that his life turned into. He thought of adding her to his short list of people that he needed to avenge the death of his family members. No matter what he decided, he would not divert his first priority of getting Blacka's daughter. Everything else would have to wait until after he got what he felt his enemy treasured the most. So until the time was right, he would remain in the distance and stalk the young girl's every movement as he contemplated his first strike at revenge.

Ringing the doorbell and knocking on the front door simultaneously, Isis placed her hand over the small glass window that served as a peephole to deliberately block the view of whoever would answer the door. It had been over three years since Isis was back in Brooklyn to visit since she moved down south ten years ago, and she was excited to see the young girl she considered her niece. She knew Crystal would be surprised to see her after such a long time. Just yesterday, Crystal turned 16, and Isis wanted to take her shopping so that she could get most of the things that her father would have if not for his absence.

"Who is that? You better move your hand, or you can stay out there in the rain all day," the female voice from behind the door stated loudly.

"Girl, open this door with your scary ass." Moving her hand and sticking her face dramatically close to the window, Isis replied, recognizing the voice behind the door as her niece's mother, Theresa.

"Isis?" Theresa exclaimed as she swung the door open to embrace her friend with a hug. "Bitch, I knew that your ass would be showing up soon. I told Crystal that I knew there was no way her birthday would pass and she don't hear from you."

"I was gonna call her and tell her happy birthday yesterday, but I decided just to drive up and take my girl shopping for the day or something," Isis said as she stepped forward and hugged Theresa. "You standing behind the door barkin' like a little Chihuahua actin' like you gonna hurt somebody. Let me get in here before my hair get soakin' wet. I swear I can't stand this New York weather. That's the only thing keeping me from comin' up to the mothafucka."

"It's supposed to be raining for the rest of the week, so you better get used to this shit. Had you come yesterday when it was nice out here, you could have been at Crystal's surprise party that her boyfriend planned for her," Theresa said as she walked inside, welcoming Isis into her home.

"Hold on a minute. Whose boyfriend did *what* now? I know you ain't said what I know you said. Since when Li'l Miss Thang got herself a boyfriend, and what else have I missed?" Isis questioned, shocked to hear that her baby niece had grown into the stage of having a boyfriend. She was even more shocked that Theresa sounded like she approved of it.

"Shit, ain't nothing little about Miss Thang anymore, girl. I scared to send recent pictures to her father 'cause I'm scared that nigga would have some crazy niggas armed to the teeth following her everywhere so that *nobody* will talk to her," Theresa joked as she walked Isis into the living room where she was watching the news on television. "Speaking of being all grown up, where's my little husband, Genesis? Why he ain't with you?"

"Shit, right now, Genesis is on a cruise to the Cayman Islands with his grandmother. I would have been here yesterday, but I wanted to see him when he got on the boat. His li'l ass called me last night, talkin' about I better not come up here without him so he could see his baby, Theresa. I told him that it was Crystal's birthday and that I had to come up and see her, and he had the nerve to tell me that I better not be coming up here to see nobody else. Told me that I better go and come back and don't do nothing without him." Isis smiled as she spoke of her 6-year-old son. "I swear that boy thinks he's my daddy sometimes."

"I know he's down there driving them little girls wild with his charmin' self," Theresa said, adjusting the volume on the television.

"He ain't paying them little girls no mind. It's the big women that he be chasing down all the time. Let me tell you, we were standing in line at the supermarket, and a woman was behind us with a tight black dress wrapped around a body that had every man and woman turning their heads. While I'm giving the girl at the register my card, I hear this li'l pimp behind me saying to the chick, 'Hi, my name is Genesis. That means the beginning . . . the beginning of *your* happiness.' I tell you, that boy is just too damn much, and I love him to death," Isis said while chuckling until tears ran from her eyes.

"I'm telling you that boy is gonna be the King of Hearts by the time he turns 16. Tell him if I catch him cheating on me, I'm gonna divorce him," Theresa said while laughing along with Isis.

"Where is Miss Thang anyway? I wanna find out about this boyfriend that you are talkin' about. He better be treating her right, and his ass better not be some bum nigga that's just trying to put his li'l thang inside of my little princess. We don't need no babies running around here, at least not until probably next year when I visit," Isis grinned while rubbing her stomach slowly in a circular motion, insinuating that she was pregnant.

"No . . . you . . . having a . . . what . . . shut up . . . who . . . stop . . . You having another baby?" Happy to hear the news of her friend's expected baby, Theresa found herself at a loss for words, although she had a million questions bouncing around in her head. "And you talkin' about you wanna find out about Crystal and her business. Bitch, what you been up to, or better yet, what's been up in you? You know I got to meet him and find out how he got past Genesis's security check."

"Believe me, that shit was not easy at all for his ass. The first time he approached me, he asked me if I had a man, and I said no, but I got a king that ain't willing to share his throne with just anybody. Genesis did everything but fingerprint that man. It took him about a month before Daddy G allowed us to be alone for more than five minutes. As far as meeting him, you better book your flight ahead of time 'cause if you wait two months and buy it at the last minute, you'll be spending money that you could have spent on my wedding gift," Isis said as she slowly draped her left hand across her chin exposing the one and a half carat Chanel-set diamond engagement ring.

"Shut the fuck up. I can't believe this shit; somebody done came along and made you fall in love. Look at you over there glowin'. You makin' me wanna pack my shit and come down south so I could look at that happy girl," Theresa said, expressing her sincere happiness for Isis. "Wait until Crystal hears this. She is goin' to be so excited when she sees you and find out that her auntie is getting married and having a baby. How far along are you now 'cause you damn sure ain't showing?"

"I'm only six weeks, but I damn sure gonna try not to let this baby stretch me all out of shape. Genesis tried when I carried his ass, but I bounced right back. Now that I got me a husband, I got to make sure that none of them skinny bitches try to give me a reason to snatch they eyes right out of their heads," Isis said as she ran her hand across her stomach.

"I just spoke to Blacka on the phone yesterday, and he even told me that you went to go visit him, but he damn sure ain't mention nothing about you having a baby or getting married. He probably asked you a million questions about this guy like he did when Kanisha got married to Malachi. I remember the hell that he put that poor man through just to get to his sister," Theresa said, knowing that Isis was her baby father's best friend who was as close to him as any woman could be. Occasionally, she would look at Isis and wonder why she and Blacka never became an item since they had such a tight bond between them.

"I haven't told him yet. We spoke about everything else besides what's going on with me. With all the shit that he's going through right now with this case that they trying to hang him with, I just wanted to find out what he needed me to do to help him out. Besides, he already know that if anybody can get past Genesis, they must be on they shit," Isis said, masking the fact that she was uncomfortable discussing her intimacy with another man with Blacka. "Did they make any moves on his case yet, or do they still got him sittin' there in limbo waiting for nothing?"

"Yeah, he just went to some kind of hearing yesterday morning, and the judge said that they are supposed to be extraditing him up here so that they can prepare for trial sometime soon. Only thing is that he don't have an exact day that they will be transporting him, so it could be any time from today to next year. He won't know until they wake him up one morning and tell him to pack his shit and go," Theresa explained, looking toward the front door as though she was afraid that someone would overhear what she was saying.

"I hope they move him soon so that he can at least be closer to getting this shit over with. I know that he is probably losing his mind inside, thinkin' about how that nigga Dwight put his neck on the chopping block. I just hope that he keeps a cool head and doesn't get into any trouble while he's in jail, giving them crackas a reason to fuck with him. You already know how them rednecks feel about them big city boys," Isis said, shaking her head, thinking about the ordeal that her friend was going through.

"I hope that things work out soon enough, but whatever happens, I feel sorry for Dwight when Blacka finally gets out. On the phone, he says he will wait and let the truth come out and prove his innocence, but we both know better. There is no way that Blacka is gonna just turn the other cheek and let Dwight get away with taking away his freedom, especially when it made him miss Crystal's birthday," Theresa continued.

"Of course, that's what he's gonna say on the phone 'cause he knows they listen to all the calls. Let's just say that if I were Dwight, I would do everything I could to straighten that shit out and still pack up and fuckin' disappear. Right now, the thing burnin' Blacka the most is that he looked out for Dwight and his family like he knew that nigga for years just on the strength he wanted to let him know that he had his back when he needed him. And the first time the heat gets turned up a little bit, Dwight just turned on him without hesitation," Isis said, interpreting Blacka's emotions when she visited him in jail.

"I mean, let's get real now. Having someone's back and taking a murder case for somebody is two different things. There is no way that a nigga would take a murder case for his mama, much less take one from some nigga that he knows off the street, 'cause at the end of the day, that's all that Blacka is to him or any other nigga that smiles in his face and swears that they got his back. I've been trying to tell his ass that since day one, but he always think that he know every goddamn thing, so you can't tell him shit until he feel that shit biting him in the ass." Crossing her arms and expressing her true feelings, Theresa gave her justification for Dwight's actions.

"Not taking the blame is one thing, but putting the blame on someone else because you are jammed up is a bitch move if you ask me. Mothafuckas need to learn to let the police do their jobs and stop trying to earn points with them by snitchin' on people. He should have kept his mouth shut, and they would have let him go, still scratchin' their heads trying to figure out what the fuck was going on," Isis retorted with a slight attitude.

"Oh, I agree that the nigga should have kept his mouth shut, but at the same time, Blacka needs to know the people he has around him, especially if he gonna live the life of a boss. I love the nigga and all, but he needs to realize that at the end of the day, he can't blame anyone but himself for the mess that he's in now," Theresa said, sticking to her argument that Dwight was not to be completely blamed for the situation that the father of her child was in. "Sometimes, you need to take responsibility for your own actions."

The sound of the front door of the house opening brought the ladies' conversation to a pause, knowing that Crystal had arrived. Not wanting to hear more of Theresa's opinion, Isis was relieved that the interruption came before the urge to tell Theresa exactly how she felt about what she was saying came to surface. Hearing the sound of her niece approaching from the door, Isis cleared the negative thoughts from her mind and began to smile in anticipation of seeing Crystal.

Chapter 28

"Mama, everybody is trying to go to the pool hall tomorr . . . Auntie?" Entering the room, ready to ask her mother a question, Crystal stopped midstride when she saw her aunt Isis sitting there. The shock of seeing her aunt after such a long time made the teenage girl run toward Isis with her arms wide open so she could embrace her with a hug.

Just as shocked as Crystal, Isis watched as the little girl who was no longer a little girl came running toward her in the chair she sat in. The thin little girl that she remembered was now a fully developed woman. She could see why Theresa was reluctant to send Blacka any recent pictures.

"Look at my baby all grown up. Girl, I would have walked right past you on the street and would have never known that was you. I can't believe this. Look at how grown your ass is now," Isis said as she stood up out of her chair to greet her enthusiastic niece.

"I didn't know you were coming. When did you get here?" Crystal exclaimed, hugging Isis tightly as they both rocked back and forth in excitement.

"I know I'm late, but I had to come and say happy birthday to my baby with her grown an' sexy-looking ass. Look at you, girl. Last time I was here, you were my little skinny mini wearing baggy clothes, and now you got on two-inch heels with bigger titties than your mama," Isis said as she stepped back and examined the teenage girl.

"I told you that Li'l Miss Thang ain't that little no more. I don't know what the hell happened, but it seemed like one morning, I looked up, and I seen a grown-ass woman walkin' out of the bathroom with my baby's pajamas on. She damn near got shot up in here that night," Theresa said from across the room, commenting on the growth spurt in her child.

"You should have come yesterday when I had my party. It was off the chain for real, Auntie. Almost everybody I knew told me happy birthday on my Facebook page, which Mommy finally allowed me to get two months ago. She be all up on there, jumpin' in conversations between me and my friends like she ain't got friends of her own to talk to," Crystal said to Isis while giving a sarcastic smirk toward her mother.

"You lucky that I let you even have that shit at all with all the shit them little boys be saying on your pictures. All that 'hey, sexy' and 'love your lips' stuff that those boys be posting is *not* cute. They need to find something better to do with their time," Theresa responded to her daughter's slick remarks with complaints about her activities on the social network.

"Please, Mom, that's just one boy, and he already has a girlfriend. Plus, he knows that Tashawn is my boyfriend," Crystal said, defending the intentions of the young man her mother referred to.

"It sounds to me like Tashawn and whatever that boy's name is girlfriend need to go and beat his ass for blatant disrespect. I wish I would catch my man telling some other woman that her lips are so sexy and all that other slick shit, especially in public. I might just shoot that nigga on the spot and call it a crime of passion," Theresa said as she dramatically pointed her finger as though it were a gun.

"Listen to me, girl," Isis said, addressing Crystal. "You are a young, beautiful woman with your whole future ahead of you, so don't get caught up in the bullshit and what these boys out here promise you. Treat yourself with respect, and any man can sense your strength from the moment you enter a room. Trust me, once a man knows you are not dependent and willing to do for yourself, he will break his neck to make sure that your attention doesn't go anywhere else. But if you show that you will tolerate the bullshit you let them feed you, they will see you as a whore before they see you as their wife."

"I understand that, Auntie, and I love you for taking the time to make sure that I have my head on my shoulders. Anybody can tell you that I am not running the streets like most of these stupid girls out here. Tashawn can tell you how many times he sat there begging me to give him a little more than a kiss, and all I do is laugh in his face. I ain't trying to end up pregnant with no babies, especially when I ain't even finish high school yet, so y'all ain't got to worry about me. If anything, feel sorry that I don't have the shoes that I saw in the mall the other day that go perfectly with the dress and bag that I wouldn't mind as a belated birthday gift from my favorite aunt," Crystal said while looking up at Isis and batting her eyes in the fashion of an innocent little girl.

"This little heifer must think that she's cute to me or something. Baby girl, you outgrew that shit since you were able to sit on the potty by yourself," Isis said, looking down at Crystal with a plastic frown on her face. She wanted to give her a hard time, although, in the end, she planned on taking her shopping anyway. "Besides, I'm sure you got a closet full of clothes upstairs. What you need a new outfit for? Where you going anyway?"

"I was about to ask Mommy when I came in, but then I saw you, and I almost forgot," Crystal said as she turned to her mother in preparation to ask her a question. "Mom, I wanted to know if I could go to East New York with Tiffany, Sasha, and Kajsa tomorrow. We all want to go to the pool hall and hang out with some kids at my party yesterday."

"If you want me to believe that you wanna buy a brand-new outfit with shoes and a bag to match to hang out with a bunch of girls, you must think that I was born this morning. Now, tell me straight up before you end up staying at home . . . Who else is going to the pool hall with y'all, and what do y'all plan on doing after playing pool?" Theresa questioned with an accusing tone.

"Yeah, there are gonna be some guys there, but that doesn't mean I'm gonna be doin' sumthin' with any of them. We just playing pool and probably get something to eat and then return home. I just wanna make sure that I look good 'cause I know Kajsa is always takin' pics and posting them on her Facebook page. I don't wanna get caught wearin' something that she already got a picture of me in." Crystal's explanation of why a new outfit was necessary came with a side-eyed look toward her mother as though the answer to her question should be obvious.

"I can't believe that the same little girl that used to throw her dolls on the floor so she could play outside in the dirt has grown up to be a diva. I drove up here thinking that I was gonna have to strap her down to the chair and force her ass to get her nails done and come to find out that she done turned into Kimora Lee, rockin' French manicures an' shit," Isis said with a smile on her face. Then she grabbed Crystal's hand, examining her freshly painted nails.

"Well, Mom, can I go?" Crystal said, addressing Theresa as she playfully snatched her hand from her aunt's grip.

"I'm gonna let you go, but don't think that you gonna be out on the streets all damn night. I want you back in this house by ten o'clock, and I don't care if you got to hijack a plane to make it here on time. Let that clock say ten o'one, and you ain't in this house, and I'm gonna get in that ass and keep you locked up in this house for the rest of the summer. So try me if you want to," Theresa said with her fight fist pressed against her left palm. She thoroughly explained the consequences if Crystal should break her ten o'clock curfew.

"All right then, let's go and see this outfit that Miss Lady is trying to break my pockets with," said Isis with a grin.

"Thank you, Auntie, thank you, thank you, thank you . . ." Excited to get the Dolce & Gabbana outfit that she had had her eyes on for a while, Crystal grabbed Isis with a tight hug and expressed her gratitude while rocking back and forth.

"You better wait until I see how much this is gonna cost me before you start with all that thank-you shit, and you better stop rockin' me so hard before you make my baby retarded," Isis said, revealing the news of her expected baby to Crystal.

After briefly pausing to register what Isis had just said, Crystal leaned back from her aunt, her eyes wide open in shock. Looking back and forth from her aunt's grin to her stomach, Crystal slowly guided her hand toward Isis's stomach and held it there while her mind filled with questions faster than her mouth could produce them.

"When . . . who . . . you're . . . you don't look . . . how . . .?" Confused about what to say, Crystal stumbled over her words without taking her hand off of Isis's stomach.

"You just like your mama, girl, except she didn't start stuttering until I showed her this," Isis said as she extended her left hand to Crystal's face to bring her attention to her engagement ring.

"Ohhh . . . is that? It better not be a . . . You're jokin', right?" Crystal continued to stammer on.

"I swear I should have recorded this shit so the two of you could look back and laugh at yourselves 'cause y'all both had the exact same dumb look on your faces," Isis said as she laughed at the similarity between the mother and daughter's reactions to her pregnancy and engagement. Instead of standing there to give Crystal all of the details that she knew that she wanted to know, Isis decided that she could let her know all about the wedding and baby while they went to Manhattan to do some shopping.

"Now, you can stand there with your mouth wide open, or we can go look at this outfit and get something to eat so I can tell you everything. I wanna go out to Herald Square to pick up some things from Macy's for Mom while I'm up here anyway."

"Okay, let me go change real quick before we go, and I wanna know *everything* 'cause this is so crazy," Crystal said while starting a slow walk backward to go upstairs to get ready to go shopping.

Forty-five minutes later, the women walked out the front door and hurried toward the rented Mustang, trying to avoid getting excessively wet from the still-falling rain. The car was parked at the curb directly in front of the house. So caught up in the excitement of spending time together after such a long time, neither one of them noticed the lone image that looked down on them from the roof of the building directly across the street.

Drenched from the rain, Dwight stood there watching as Blacka's daughter and Isis raced toward the car to avoid the same rain he had been standing in for hours. The sight of Blacka's daughter happily running toward the vehicle while he mourned the loss of his loved ones enraged him to the point where he felt his own heartbeat in his throat. It was time Blacka felt the sorrow that had turned him into a walking zombie. It was time that he lay at night haunted by the images of his family's last moments alive. With that thought, Dwight decided that his time of surveillance was complete. He would no longer lurk from above like a vulture waiting for something to die in the desert. The next time Crystal left the house alone would be the last time she would be seen alive.

Chapter 29

"Baaaby . . . baby . . . oh shit . . . fuck . . . stop, stop . . . oh shit . . . I'm comin' . . . I'm comin'!" Digging her acrylic nails into the back of Anthony's skull, Theresa's back arched off the bed, thrusting her pussy in his face while her legs violently trembled on his shoulders.

Refusing to yield to her cries of passion, Anthony continued to pleasure her. The power of being able to bring her body to this euphoric state excited him more than anything else. Moving his head from side to side, he resembled a hungry dog tearing the meat off a bone as he lifted Theresa's lower body off the bed by bracing her thighs between his forearms and biceps. Balancing her with the back of her head and one shoulder on the sweaty cotton sheets, he stood up in the bed and continued to use his lips to pull on her clitoris as though he were drinking a milkshake with a coffee stirrer. Bringing her to her fourth orgasm within the last fifteen minutes, he reached with his right hand to use his fingers to separate the lips of her sexually saturated pussy while he rapidly flickered the tip of his tongue to lash against her pulsing clit.

Sticking his index and middle fingers inside her creaming pink hole, he could feel her inner walls contract against his knuckles as her cum leaked onto his hand. This was just the beginning of what he had planned for his sexy partner. Thrusting her back down on the mattress, Anthony took a moment to enjoy watching her body react to his oral performance. Her firm size thirty-eight D breasts heaved up and down as her stomach visibly contracted with her mouth wide open, gasping for air. Reaching down and reinserting the same two fingers inside of her, his dick swelled when he heard her moan for pleasure while slowly raising her chin and bringing her shoulders up toward her ears.

Stroking her G-spot with the tip of his fingers on his right hand while firmly gripping the shaft of his dick, he gazed at her face as it expressed the joy her body was feeling. Not yet ready to penetrate Theresa, he lunged his head back down toward her throbbing pussy to continue to pleasure her orally. He spread her legs wide so that her lips parted and spat down into her contracting hole.

"Fuck me, baby . . . Fuck this pussy, daddy . . . I want it . . . Give it to me . . ." No longer being able to take the anticipation of her new lover finally getting inside of her, Theresa squirmed on the bed, begging for Anthony to penetrate her. The pressure of the years that she had spent without sharing her body with anyone brought an intense sensation that she felt on the inner walls of her vagina that made her willing to do things that she never anticipated upon meeting the Midwestern man three months ago.

"I'll tell you when you want it and when you will get it . . . That ass is mine to do what I want with, and right now, I wanna hear you scream my name just for making me wait so long," he said, slapping away Theresa's hand as she grabbed for his thigh to pull him closer. Anthony once again hoisted her legs off the bed with his head buried in her crotch.

Extremely turned on by his dominating manner, Theresa's decision to finally give in to the Minnesota man's desperate pleas to get her attention seemed to be paying off. She was shocked that the timid sandwich artist from Subway had the best head game she had ever experienced. Usually, she couldn't see herself so much as sharing a conversation with a guy like him. He was shorter than she was, skinnier than any guy she had ever been with, and didn't have a car to call his own. In short, he was the exact opposite of what she sought in a guy. The day she met him while waiting for her girlfriend to pick her up from the Kings Plaza shopping mall, she only took his number in her phone so that she would not appear rude, causing him to possibly further harass her for being conceited. Never did she think that this man, whom her friend described as a hood version of Jiminy the Cricket, would be in her bed.

Since her last boyfriend's indictment, she has lived a life of celibacy, focusing on her well-being and her child's. She did not make time for any social activities, especially since now men only seemed to want the privileges of fucking without taking on the responsibilities of providing for that woman. It was only because she accidentally called his number while her phone jostled around that he was able to acquire a way of contacting her. What started as harmless small talk led to him coming over to bring some food for her to eat while her daughter spent the day with some friends in the East New York section of Brooklyn. And somehow, she ended up with her legs around his neck while his tongue probed her pussy.

"Let me suck it, baby . . . Put that dick in my mouth, and then I want you to fuck me until I can't take no more . . . please, baby," she begged, surprised at her own behavior. Theresa squirmed out of Anthony's clutches. She was horny beyond control, and she could no longer tolerate being teased by his tongue. She made it clear that she was ready to be fucked, and she was about to take action to make sure that it happened sooner than later.

Rolling over on her stomach, she slithered across the bed and was ready to claim her prize. Grabbing the waistline of the Fruit of the Loom boxer briefs that Anthony wore, she pulled him toward her, licking her lips in preparation for sucking his dick until he felt as weak as she did. His resistance by pulling away from her as she attempted to pull his underwear down to gain access to his penis made her only try harder. Although out of practice, she was sure that she could deepthroat her playmate into submission.

"Hold on, baby . . . It ain't ready for you yet . . . Just wait a minute. I'ma get in that ass for real. Ain't no need to rush this shit, girl, 'cause when I start, it's gonna be hours before I climb out of that pussy, so be careful what you ask for," he said, silently struggling to get out of Theresa's grip. Anthony monologued his stall tactics while checking the texture of his penis to see if the over-the-counter male enhancement pills that he had purchased before arriving at Theresa's house had taken effect yet. According to the packaging, within thirty minutes after taking the blue pill, his penis should be noticeably bigger with a much-better performance. It had been almost forty-five minutes since he popped the pill into his mouth, and yet, he felt no difference in size. It seemed like he has been trying to get to this girl forever, and he was not about to let a genetic disadvantage put him out of the game. He figured he could keep her warmed up by eating her pussy until his investment paid off.

"What's wrong with you? We've been doing this for damn near an hour. What you mean it ain't ready for me yet? Is there something wrong with me, something I need to do? I told you that I haven't been with anyone since my husband went to prison four years ago, so it's been awhile for me, but I am ready to—"

Finally maneuvering Anthony's drawers past his penis, Theresa paused in the middle of the queen-size bed with her mouth gaped open. Not knowing what to say, she slowly took her hand from the band of his underwear and covered her mouth before the wrong words spilled out. Unfortunately for Anthony, her hand was much too slow.

"Hold on, baby. I want to taste you some more. I know you like the way I eat that pussy. I got you creamin' all over the place. Lie your ass back down, and let me make that ass squirm some more," he said, quickly pulling up his underwear and trying to divert Theresa's attention away from the obvious. The pills that he took proved to be worthless. He was still at his originally embarrassing size.

"Are you serious right now? That can't be what . . . Let me see that shit again. Is it hard?" Disappointed and amused at the same time, Theresa couldn't help but chuckle as she sat up on the bed and pointed her finger at Anthony's small package. She couldn't believe the nerve of this man to walk into her bedroom with a dick that looked like it should be wrapped in a Huggies diaper. There was no way she could even waste her time by having this man breathing in her face and lying on top of her with a three-inch penis.

"I told you it's not ready yet. I just want to wait a little while. That's all. Give me a few minutes, and I got you, baby girl," Anthony said, embarrassed about the situation. He was at a loss for words as he stood at the end of the bed, being ridiculed for the shameful inheritance from his father.

"Baby boy, it's gonna take more than just a few minutes for you to be ready, and neither of us has that kind of time. But if you think eating this pussy is gonna make you grow, I'm gonna let you get all you can eat. I'm going to let you do something else for me. Reach under the bed and grab that blue shoe box," Theresa said. Deciding to let him at least provide her with the joy of oral pleasure, she instructed Anthony to retrieve one of her toys from under the bed. The way she figured it, since he was there, he might as well satisfy her one way or the other. Since he seemed good with this tongue, she might as well ride it for the whole nine yards.

Embarrassed yet still happy to be able to stay, Anthony bent under the bed, retrieved the blue box, and handed it to Teresa, who sat there shaking her head, grinning. His moments of control were now over. She was about to entertain herself at his expense in more ways than one. She knew that Anthony wanted her much more than she wanted him, and she would make him prove it. Theresa popped open the box, revealing an assortment of toys that all outsized the pathetic package that Anthony had to offer.

"We gonna work around those little problems you got with this right here. All you gonna do is follow my lead, and mama gonna make both of us happy. I want to introduce you to Stanley," she said, pulling out her favorite toy and putting the box to the side. On many lonely nights, she had brought herself to satisfaction with the pink, eight-inch rubber dildo. She was gonna combine Anthony's tongue performance with the deep vibrating penetration of her toy that she named Stanley. Using her index finger, she gestured to Anthony to resume his position with his head between her legs, and she handed Stanley to him.

Without hesitation, Anthony grabbed the toy and used it to circle the outside of her pussy, turning the knob at the base to make the apparatus start vibrating as though he was already familiar with the toy. He was more satisfied that Theresa didn't laugh him right out of her bedroom. He hoped he would be able to arouse her to the point where she might even be willing to do something to satisfy him. So, whatever assignment she was about to instruct him to do, he was damn sure going to put forth all effort to make sure she was satisfied.

Her moans of pleasure returned as he used the tip of his tongue to lick her clit while penetrating her with the rubber substitution lover, only this time, she was definitely being much more forceful by pressing the back of his head into her pelvis, giving him barely enough room to breathe.

"Baby . . . ooooh, baby . . . get that shit . . . That's right, get that shit . . . right there . . . right there . . . fuuuck!" Grinding her pussy in Anthony's face almost faster than he could keep up with it, Theresa felt herself once again about to climax all over his face. Her enjoyment was bringing discomfort to Anthony as the top speed of the vibrating toy was rubbing against his chin as Theresa continually thrust her pelvis forward.

"Come and sit on my face, baby girl, and let me get up in that properly. Just flip over and let me lie on my back," he said, feeling like he was losing all control over the situation. He lifted his head for a moment to catch his breath. His suggestion was in hopes of getting Theresa in a closer position to put his dick in her mouth.

Tracing her right hand across the base of her stomach as her left hand clutched her breast, Theresa bit down on her lip and nodded in agreement. She cupped the dildo inside of her and maneuvered on the bed, allowing Anthony to lie under her. With his arms wrapped under her legs, while gripping her ass, Anthony pulled Theresa down toward his face to gently bite down on her clitoris and once again began to satisfy her orally in hopes of getting her head to sway downward with her mouth open.

The walls of Theresa's pussy contracted with pleasure from the euphoric sensation that the combination of

Stanley and Anthony's tongue were providing. Then just like Anthony hoped, she reached her hand under the band of his underwear and began massaging his dick so close to her mouth that he could feel her breath against the head of it. The anticipation of her putting his penis, which resembled a king-size Tootsie Roll, in her mouth had him excited to the point where he felt a strong pulse begin to surge through the vein that ran on the back of his shaft.

Trying hard to focus on pleasing Theresa so that he wouldn't ejaculate prematurely, the Minnesota man used his lips to pull harder on her swelling clit. The joy of the blood rushing down to her happy spot once again contracted her pussy, causing the dildo to pop out and land on Anthony's nose, executing a quiet sound. The long, pink plastic rumbled down to the side of his face and continued to hum against his earlobe.

Suddenly, the sound of the doorbell immediately took Theresa's attention away from his penis toward the front door. Whoever was at the door must have known that someone was home because they rang it nonstop, which got on Theresa's nerves.

"Who the hell is that banging on my damn door like they pay rent up in this house? Crystal, you better have your key, or else you can go right back to where you were hanging out and find it!" Irritated at the disturbance from the quality time she was spending with her lover, Theresa stomped toward the door, yelling while pulling Anthony's shirt over her head.

Moving aside the curtain from the glass window on the door, Theresa looked outside to see that it was indeed Crystal with a man who appeared too old to be standing so close to her daughter. Her moments of euphoria crashed to a halt when she witnessed what she thought was her innocent daughter with her arms wrapped around this grown man's neck and her head buried in his chest as he embraced her waist. Upset that not only was Crystal late, but she had the nerve to show up ringing the doorbell while hugging up with some strange man, she swung open the door and prepared to raise hell.

"Ma'am, I think that your daughter may need your help. She's not looking too well right about now." Before Theresa could speak her mind, the stranger spoke as he balanced the disoriented young girl while briefly explaining what was going on. "I don't know if her keys are inside her pockets, but I was trying to make sure she didn't end up lying on the ground out here."

"Oh my God, oh my God . . . Crystal!" Taking a closer look, Theresa could see that her daughter was using this man as a crutch because she could not stand alone. The young girl's legs were obviously too limp to maintain her weight. Her head bobbed back and forth as the Samaritan struggled to keep the child from falling. A black leather jacket that she could only assume belonged to the unidentified stranger blanketed the child, exposing only her legs and top of her head. With the shock of her daughter standing in the doorway totally incoherent, Theresa didn't take the time to notice the thin line of blood that leaked slowly from the young girl's mouth.

Tossing and turning all night with a strong feeling of uneasiness, Blacka sat up on the steel bed and placed his bare feet on the cold floor of the two-man cell that only he occupied. From the edge of the bed, he looked through the narrow, steel-reinforced window that led to the facility's recreation yard and focused on what seemed to be the only star in the dark southern sky. Suddenly, the image of his daughter as a baby vividly flashed before his eyes while the sound of her first words rang loudly in his ear. "*Daa-ddy.*" He heard the sound so clearly that he spun his head quickly toward his right shoulder to see if it was more than just his imagination.

Staggering toward the sink that sat above the toilet, intending to splash the cold water on his face, Blacka attributed his thoughts of his daughter to the fact that he was not present for her sixteenth birthday celebration and the thought that he may miss many more to come. It was just two days ago that he spoke to her on the phone, and yet, he had the strong urge to talk to her again just to tell her that he loved her more than she could ever know. Bending his head down toward the sink with his right hand cupped over the faucet to catch the running water, Blacka repeatedly splashed water on his face, trying to shake the feeling that mysteriously troubled his soul.

To be continued . . .

High Risks II

Risky Business